RICHARD D ROSS

The Cobweb Enigma

A James Macrae Thriller Book 3

First published by Steel Door Publishing 2023

Copyright © 2023 by Richard D Ross

All rights reserved. No part of this publication may be reproduced, stored or transmitted in any form or by any means, electronic, mechanical, photocopying, recording, scanning, or otherwise without written permission from the publisher. It is illegal to copy this book, post it to a website, or distribute it by any other means without permission.

This novel is entirely a work of fiction. The names, characters and incidents portrayed in it are the work of the author's imagination. Any resemblance to actual persons, living or dead, events or localities is entirely coincidental.

Richard D Ross asserts the moral right to be identified as the author of this work.

Richard D Ross has no responsibility for the persistence or accuracy of URLs for external or third-party Internet Websites referred to in this publication and does not guarantee that any content on such Websites is, or will remain, accurate or appropriate.

Real-world characters are used only in a purely fictional context.

All rights reserved.

Copyright © 2023 by Richard D Ross

First edition

ISBN: 978-1-7778601-4-1

*This book was professionally typeset on Reedsy.
Find out more at reedsy.com*

'Observe calmly; secure our position; cope with affairs calmly; hide our capacities and bide our time; be good at maintaining a low profile; and never claim leadership.'

-Deng Xiaoping

Contents

Preface   iii
1 Chapter 1   1
2 Chapter 2   7
3 Chapter 3   17
4 Chapter 4   21
5 Chapter 5   28
6 Chapter 6   37
7 Chapter 7   41
8 Chapter 8   47
9 Chapter 9   54
10 Chapter 10   61
11 Chapter 11   66
12 Chapter 12   72
13 Chapter 13   82
14 Chapter 14   91
15 Chapter 15   99
16 Chapter 16   110
17 Chapter 17   125
18 Chapter 18   140
19 Chapter 19   151
20 Chapter 20   165
21 Chapter 21   178
22 Chapter 22   184
23 Chapter 23   190

24	Chapter 24	199
25	Chapter 25	207
26	Chapter 26	214
27	Chapter 27	223
28	Chapter 28	234
29	Chapter 29	242
30	Chapter 30	250
31	Chapter 31	260
32	Chapter 32	267
33	Chapter 33	280
34	Chapter 34	292
35	Chapter 35	299
36	Chapter 36	308
37	Chapter 37	316
38	Chapter 38	329
About the Author		338
Also by Richard D Ross		340

Preface

Characters

Macrae-Claybourne Logistics
James Macrae – partner
Sarah Macrae – wife of James
Children of James and Sarah – Mason, Mia and Olivia
Chris Claybourne – partner
Jenny Claybourne – wife of Chris
Children of Chris and Jenny – Jackson and Bailey
Martin Farley – Director Legal Affairs
Laura Wesley – Chief Financial Officer
Rob Bisset – VP Operations
Janet Rushton – VP IT
Chad Greening – Director of Sales and Marketing
Jusuf Kahya – General Manager, Istanbul terminal, Turkey
Angus MacNiel – owner Halifax Port, Nova Scotia, Canada
Bryn and Catrin – Sarah Macrae's parents

Macrae Holdings LLC
Richard Macrae – Chairman, father of James
Mary Macrae – Richard's wife, mother of James

MI6
Jack Fox – Director, MI6

Jeremy Hirons – MI6 Special Agent
DI Stella Hudson – West Midlands Police, working with MI6

Other Characters

General Wu Shen – Chinese general / Head of MSS

Peng Zheng – Chinese Embassy, London – Head of Security (MSS)

President Jiang Zemin – Chairman and President of China

Huang Genjo – prominent Chinese dissident

Lingdao (Colonel Liao Min) – operative of General Shen

Tang and Jin – military assistants to Lingdao

Nick Northrop aka William Brocklehurst – mercenary working for General Shen

Wilfred Stevens – general manager Birmingham Public Works Dept

Ben Armstrong – Owner Pair-Tree Capital

Kevin Tan – Zemin's trusted agent from his Shanghai clique

Meili Shabani – PR representative, Shanghai Port Authority

1

Chapter 1

Spring 1996

What was that sound?

In the early hours of the morning, Huang Genjo felt his eyes flicker in the cold and damp semi-darkness as his subliminal survival instincts clicked in.

Something's out of the ordinary.

Lying on his back on the hard wooden bed frame, he winced as he tried to turn himself over to help decipher the sound trying to penetrate his state of semi-consciousness.

Something's definitely not right.

He raised his hand slowly and rubbed his crusted eyes to help his other senses try to comprehend the muffled sound.

It sounds like someone's trying to quietly enter my cell, but there's no sound of keys clanging? No, can't be!

He froze.

To the outside world, the location and presence of the most feared and infamous prison in China doesn't exist. To those that do know of its existence, just outside Beijing, the separate grey brick-built prison buildings are surrounded by several high walls and electric fences. Foothills to the east rise up behind the entire complex. Multiple steel gates divide the cell blocks from the front gate, while the whole structure is hidden from the road by surrounding orchards, tall birch trees and farmland.

After six years of solitary confinement in his tiny prison cell engulfed in the stench of sweat and human waste, Huang only ever heard screams or cries of people in distress after the constant beatings that went on daily. He had no idea who his fellow inmates were. The shrill yelling voices of the guards only used the names of either 'spy,' 'traitor' or the prisoner's assigned number. No real names were ever used. All this to demean and depersonalise each one of them. Huang had succumbed after multiple beatings and constant starvation. Such was the shrouded secrecy of the notorious Qincheng jail.

As the solid metal door slowly opened in the half light, Huang used his feet on the bedframe to push himself away from the sinister silhouette of a tall heavy-set man filling the doorway. He covered the top of his head in his hands and cowered as close as he could to the far wall of the cell in a foetal position.

Oh God! Please! Please! No more questioning!

As his eyes adjusted, the man entered the cell, leaned down towards him and put one finger in front of his mouth, making a low-pitched shushing sound. He raised his other hand and indicated for Huang to get up and follow him. Huang stiffened harder and tried to curl himself tighter into a ball, but the man continued to beckon him forward and signalled him to take hold of his hand.

CHAPTER 1

I don't have a choice.

In response, Huang stretched out his hand and tried to uncoil himself to lift his body off the bed. He faltered and fell forward, but the man caught him and steadily helped him move towards the door.

Outside the cell, another man was waiting in the shadows of the solid concrete walls, holding a corpse under his arms. The man dragged the body into Huang's cell, laid it on the bed, then closed and bolted the cell door quietly.

This doesn't make any sense.

Huang felt the heavy-set man's arm move around his back to help him move forward. His limbs protested with every step he took. Side-by-side they moved along a caged walkway and then up two flights of stairs.

The rest of the prison remained in semi-darkness, but the constant crying, screaming, muttering, shouting and calling out that prevailed during the day was more subdued at night. The heavy-set man opened a barred door with a key, ushered his follower through and then held onto Huang while he locked the door again quietly behind him. He then led them through another heavy-steel outer door where they found themselves in a high-walled yard.

Am I really outside?

He could scarcely remember what the outside world was like. In the endless solitude, he'd trained himself not to think of his memories. He'd simply paralysed his brain. It was the only way he could function without going insane. The spring air felt chilled. He thought he caught a whiff of undergrowth and fruit trees. Bewildered by what was happening to him, he tried to inhale deep breaths to try to jump-start his senses. Memories of beauty had long been erased. He knew better than to speak or ask questions. That lesson had been learned a long time ago.

Even though Huang had tried to keep in shape during his solitary confinement, his limbs continued to complain and resisted his efforts to push forward. He clung to his companion and was helped to cross the yard as quickly as they could through an outer door.

This is surreal. How can there be no guards, no security? There's not even any dogs or searchlights. Something has to go wrong!

A dark-coloured truck with a box van body stood in a narrow lane. Huang looked up to see the rear roller shutter was open.

'Come on, my friend, you need to step up inside!'

Huang tried to grip the steps and climb up, but he felt too weak. He turned to the two men and without asking they hoisted him up inside the truck.

Once inside, they pushed him forward through a collection of oil drums and tarps to the front of the truck body.

'Sit there and don't make a sound!'

He sank down to the floor, closed his eyes and gasped for air. His whole body started to shake, so he bent his knees towards him and clasped them tightly with both hands to try to steady himself.

This has to be dream. How could it possibly be real?

As his nerves steadied, he opened his eyes to see he was among several other emaciated men, all cowering closely together. In the half-light, Huang assumed they had all been Qincheng prisoners. It wasn't difficult to spot the same look of terror in each of their thin, pale faces. No one spoke. The roller shutter was pulled down, the engine started, and the truck was driven away. Huang rocked back and forth with the sway of the vehicle, the smell of sweat and filth-covered bodies rancid

CHAPTER 1

in the tight space – laced with the smell of fear.

Have I been rescued or am I about to disappear for ever?

———————————

General Shen paced up and down in his secret apartment, his clammy hand clutching the burner phone tightly by his side. He was loosening his necktie with his other hand when he felt the phone vibrate. He immediately accepted the call but remained quiet. A deep voice simply said, 'Grebes.'

Shen took in a deep breath, knowing this was the correct password. 'How did it go?' he asked.

'Mission accomplished, sir,' replied the deep voice.

'No complications?'

'No, sir. None. No alarms and no interruptions from the guards.'

'Were all the dissidents you took replaced with bodies?'

'Yes. No one will know they're missing.'

'Good. Standby until I give you further orders for the next stage of the mission.'

Shen sat down on his sofa, rested his head and stretched out his legs, trying to feel weightless. He let out a huge sigh. This was the end of the beginning of his mission and undoubtedly the riskiest for him personally. Had this failed, he would easily have been the prime suspect with the power to pull off such an audacious operation as this. As the relief in his body surged through him, he started to feel light-headed. He'd always imagined himself as a visionary and becoming the supreme ruler and leader of China in the same mould as the first Emperor of China, Ying Zheng in 221BC. In contrast, his boss, President Zemin was just too timid, merely extending Deng Xiaoping's former policies. Zemin also had too much respect for Western culture and business. China needed to push back hard on all the imperial powers that had intimidated his country for centuries.

He put his hand on his heart and whispered to himself, 'My time has come!'

Chapter 2

Against a clear azure-blue sky, the kestrel soared in wide circles using the thermal updrafts from the cliffs below. Her outstretched wings and tail feathers remained rigid but quivered ever so slightly in the uneven air currents. The kestrel's downturned head stayed perfectly still, enabling her to spot the slightest of movements of any prey below. In the blink of an eye, she swept her wings back and made a steep dive down towards the thick gorse and bracken undergrowth. At the last second, she extended her fierce talons, seized her prey and veered back off into the sky.

James Macrae had watched the whole episode unfold as he sat on his patio facing out to sea in Wales. Together with his family, he'd also been the target of an unseen enemy scrutinising them carefully from a safe distance far away. Unlike the prey today, however, he'd managed to identify his enemy in time, turn the tables on them and inflict some heavy damage back on them in return.

His wife Sarah came out to join him. She tilted her face up to the sun, savouring the warmth. James looked back up at her and marvelled how she had recovered from the sinister events of last year.

'I've got good news!' she said, smiling down at him.

James tilted his head. 'Oh?'

'Yes! I've got the contract for the plans to restore Highclere Castle!'

James jumped up and hugged her. 'Oh, that's great news. Congratulations! You worked so hard on that proposal.'

'I'm so happy. I wanted that project so bad!' she said, shaking her head.

'Well, it couldn't have come at a better time. Our week off here has both done us good. When we get home, you can get to work on your new project, and I need to get back to the office as well. Chris and I have some new ideas for the company.'

'Great! I'm off to pick up the kids from my parents and then we'll come back and pack up ready to go back to Birmingham tomorrow.'

James sat back after Sarah had left and reflected on his mood. On the one hand he was happy he and Sarah were moving ahead with their lives, but he was still angry about what had happened to them. China had set out to ruin him and take over his ports for future naval bases. Fortunately, with the help of the MI6 Director, Jack Fox and one of his agents, Jeremy Hirons, he'd managed to fight off Hugh Stanfield's company, Euro-Asian Freight and then Pair-Tree Capital and its owner Ben Armstrong. Even the kidnapping of Sarah, the murder of his parents and other attempts of sabotage to his company had failed to secure them his ports. Now that Stanfield, Nash and Pair-Tree Capital were gone, the question was: would they still pursue him for possession of his international seaports?

CHAPTER 2

....

'General, come to my office.'

'Yes, President Zemin.'

General Shen put down his phone and got up from his chair immediately. He made his way to the president's office on the Zhongnanhai government compound in Beijing. It was 7:00am. He straightened his uniform before entering the quiet sanctuary of the president's office, sinking into the plush carpet as he stepped towards his desk. It was more like a stately home library than an office, with polished mahogany bookshelves surrounding each wall. Apart from a large collection of books, multiple photographs recorded personal visits of the president to the country's various regions. It created an image of a leader very much in touch with his people.

Zemin got up from behind his desk and ushered Shen to the small conference table to the side of the office. Shen sat down while Zemin remained standing above him.

'I want to start off by letting you know I'm giving you the joint responsibility of the Ministry of States Security – MSS – as well your existing position of heading up the military. This will give us a quicker time to respond to any internal or external events that could offer either a threat or an opportunity for his country.'

Shen remained outwardly calm. Inside, he tried to cope with the surging elation bubbling up. 'I don't know what to say, President Zemin. This is a surprise. I was not expecting this.'

'Well, you've earned it. You're not afraid to speak your mind and I need more people around me like that instead of nodding dogs.'

Shen smiled in response. Had the president listened to him in the first place and paid the full asking price for Macrae-Claybourne Logistics, he believed China would have owned all their shipping terminals by now in Istanbul, Piraeus, Genoa, Valencia and Yanbu. This added responsibility would now give him a huge leg up in helping achieve his ambitious vision.

Zemin took off his suit jacket and placed it on the back of the chair facing Shen. He sat down, pushed the heavy black-framed glasses back on his nose and carried on. 'Now you have this joint responsibility, I want to share my ideas on China's expansion for world domination. This is our number one objective, endorsed by both myself and the Communist Party. We are entirely aligned with each other. Our silk-road policy of expansion will continue.'

He paused, staring Shen straight in the face. Leaning towards him, with both hands on the table, he raised his voice, 'Before we start, we need to get a few things straight. Just to be clear, I will not tolerate any show of outward force or violence either to a country, a group of people or an individual to achieve our common objectives that can be attributed back to us. We must move forward using every subtle means at our disposal.'

Shen leaned hard on the side of his chair and shifted his position. 'Does that include Taiwan?'

Zemin glared back at Shen. 'Taiwan is another matter! They are still part of our territory and, make no mistake, we will eventually unify them with the mainland! I'm not going to put a stop on any actions against them.'

Shen nodded. 'Understood.'

Zemin continued. 'It's now more important than ever for China to be well-behaved in all other areas since we want

CHAPTER 2

Hong Kong back under our wing next year. The Americans have given us a stern warning and the British are threatening to stall the return of the colony to us after the murder of James Macrae's parents and attempt to kill him on British soil. They say they have categorical proof it was China who organised this as a lever to take over their European ports! We, of course, have dismissed the accusations of using mercenaries to kill the Macrae seniors and Pair-Tree Capital to buy into the European terminals. This is mere propaganda from the UK as a way to retain their power over the territory. Our negotiations are continuing as we speak, so no violence! Is that understood?'

Shen looked straight back at Zemin, his gaze intent and unwavering.

'Yes, sir. I understand completely and give you my assurance that no one under my command, either in the MSS or the military, will resort to any kind of violence to achieve these aims. Now Li Ming is in Qincheng jail, that should take care of that concern.'

'Good! Now we've got that out of the way, I want you to listen to my strategy going forward.'

Shen remained quiet and alert.

'We've been closely watching Russia's remarkable behaviour on the world stage, in particular Boris Yeltsin. He is following in the footsteps of Mikhail Gorbachev after he ended the cold war. Yeltsin is transforming the perception of Russia as a deadly enemy into a much kinder and more cooperative world neighbour. With the transition of their centrally planned economy to a market-based economy, they have opened up their borders to foreign trade and investment. In addition, Yeltsin has met with US diplomats and President Clinton and agreed to slow down the arms race and promote democracy, security, and peace. The Russians also had separate meetings with all the G7 leaders before their formal annual meeting in Naples.'

He paused to let his words sink in.

'So, what does this tell you, general? Do you think Russia has developed a completely new personality and is everybody's friend now?'

'Certainly not, President Zemin. I'm still getting up to speed with the latest intelligence, but I don't believe for a second that Yeltsin will pursue democracy, security and peace. On the contrary, he is securing his position as president by removing opposition. Already several powerful industrial and political opponents have met with tragic, fatal accidents. What he says and what he does, or will do, will be entirely different. He's clever and if he manages to manoeuvre Russia into the G7 and become an eighth member, that will be a masterstroke. In fact, there is a meeting of the G7 in Birmingham, England in two years' time. It's highly likely Yeltsin will be a member by then.'

'Exactly! So, if we copy Yeltsin's strategy of going to charm school, we can also appear to be everybody's friend. We're already a member of Asia-Pacific Economic Cooperation (APEC) group, so if we behave responsibly both in a political and monetary sense, we may be able to follow Russia and join the G7 later. Perhaps we can meet the G7 members before their meeting in Birmingham like Russia did before. That way we can begin to improve China's standing in the world after being widely chastised for our harsh clampdown on the opposition in Tiananmen Square. Once we've achieved that, we can begin to manipulate future world events in our favour.'

Shen nodded as if to say he understood. Zemin lifted his

CHAPTER 2

glasses and rubbed his eyes with his thumb and forefinger. He continued, 'With this in mind, let's discuss specifically where we go from here. Turkey, as you know, is already a member of NATO. They joined NATO to help ensure their independence against any threats from Russia and they have also applied to join the European Economic Community, though this has not yet been approved.'

Zemin paused again and adjusted his seating position. He put his forefinger in the air.

'Stay with my line of thinking, general, because we still want port terminals in the Mediterranean. Our attempts to take over Macrae-Claybourne Logistics have failed twice, so we need to change our strategy.' Zemin allowed a few moments to let his words sink in.

'I'm proposing a series of visits to Turkey by you and our Foreign Affairs minister. In these meetings you will offer Turkey financial loans to help them develop their country economically, as well as supply them with Chinese military equipment to strengthen their independence and security. My goal is to invest in the ports of Ambarli and Izmir, preferably Ambarli. If we take over this port, it's only twenty-five kilometres from Istanbul, which would give us a comparable base to that of the Macrae-Claybourne terminal. With this base, we will then have a foothold in south-eastern Europe to control Russia's access to and from the Black Sea. We can expand our silk road policy and later build our naval bases to dominate southern Europe and North Africa.'

Shen sat still and then leaned forward on his chair, placing his hands on the table.

'I agree, President Zemin. This is an excellent strategy and may sway Turkey to follow us rather than the European Union.

Our military hardware is just as advanced as anybody else's and improving all the time. Not only that, but it will also cost them less to buy from us. We can lend them significant amounts of money to expand the port facilities and when they can't pay us back, then we can take over the port rather like we did in Sri Lanka when we took over the port of Hambantota. We could also steal Macrae-Claybourne customers by offering lower rates and maybe weaken them that way.'

'Excellent, general. Then we are on the same wavelength! Continuing Deng Xiaoping's policy of capitalism balanced with communist rule, our economic strength is growing exponentially. All other nations will be envious of the size of our massive domestic consumer market and will want a piece of it. This will give us a wider latitude in our foreign policy to take advantage of our so-called new friends. I will continue to visit foreign powers to demonstrate our goodwill going forward. On some of these visits, I will need you to come with me.'

Shen sat quietly and steepled his fingers to his lips. 'That might not be such a good idea, sir.'

'Oh, why's that?'

'Well, after Stanfield and Nash were arrested the first time, I'm sure they will have identified myself as their handler. Whenever I travel these days, I use a false identity, although MSS has informed me that the British and Americans have now developed facial-recognition software programmes.'

Zemin nodded in recognition of the fact. 'Alright, I will give you a new title for our trips.'

Zemin pursed his lips in thought. After a few moments, he nodded several times. 'You will now become the Minister for Trade and Development, drop the military uniform and wear a business suit. As a designated member of the Chinese government, you will receive full diplomatic immunity from all other nations.'

'Very well, President Zemin. I will draft out a step-by-step plan together with the foreign minister for your approval regarding Turkey. I will make a visit as soon as possible to set up relations with their equivalent personnel. Once we have everything set up and approved, then you can make a state visit there and formalize everything.'

'Bravo, Shen! I'll make a politician out of you yet!'

Shen left the office thinking and smiling inwardly.

You have no fucking idea what's going to eventually hit you!

———————————-

The London head of security of the Chinese embassy, Peng Zheng, picked up his raincoat and left his office for a late lunch. It was a damp and heavily overcast spring day. Walking purposely northwards on Portland Place he then turned right onto Devonshire Street past the stately Georgian offices and residences each with their distinctive dogtooth brickwork. He made no attempt to evade any followers, should there be any. At Great Portland Street he turned left and crossed to the other side of the busy road using the nearby pedestrian crossing and entered the Peyton and Byrne Bakery where he purchased a takeout tuna fish sourdough roll and a small arabica coffee. After leaving the shop, he waited for a break in the traffic, crossed the street and entered the Portland Hospital. Inside, he made his way past the elevators towards the fire escape stairwell and climbed to the third floor. With no signs of a follower, he exited the stairwell, then crossed the ward floor to the elevator and descended to the second floor. He sat in a visitor waiting area and ate his lunch, checking everyone around him. When he'd finished, he placed his empty cup and wrapper in the waste-paper bin and took the elevator to the seventh floor. He walked along the corridor of the offices and located the door to the roof. There was no one around. He reached the flat roof, and, observing it was empty, took out his burner phone and punched in a number from memory. He spoke in perfect English.

'Congratulations on your new position. I look forward to working with you.'

General Shen answered back in perfect English.

'Thank you. I look forward to working with you too. I will be short. My intent is to make you my number two, but, before that, I want you to stay where you are for the time being. We need to make certain preparations well ahead for some important events that will take place in the future. There will be a G8 meeting in Birmingham in two years' time. We will need to use your special operations team to have certain undercover people in key positions well before this meeting to further our secret agenda.'

Chapter 3

'Do you want me to lock up, boss? There's only me and you left.'

Inside the Birmingham municipality garage, Ted Norris, the workshop supervisor, uncurled himself from leaning over the chassis rail and driveshaft of the dump truck he was working on. He came out from underneath the propped-up tipping body and wiped his greasy hands on a rag from his overall pocket.

'Don't worry, Colin, I'll see to it. I'm nearly done. Just close the yard gates and I'll lock up. I just want to finish tightening up this hanger bearing before I go home. It's my little girl's birthday today so I'll be getting off soon. How about yourself? Got any plans for this weekend?'

'Na, not really, though I said I'd help a friend stick a new clutch in his car.'

Ted shook his head and chuckled. 'How come us guys always repair everyone else's vehicles except our own?'

'You got me! Anyway, see you on Monday.'

'Cheers, Col. Have a good one, mate!'

As Colin left the works central depot, it was already dark. All of the office and public works staff had left. He drove his car outside the yard gates, jumped quickly out and pulled them back together.

The Birmingham Municipal Works garage and yard was situated close to the city centre in a run-down industrial area in Digbeth. A damp, chilling wind circulated amongst the tired brick-built structures, outbuildings and chimneys, whose original red brick facades were now darker shades of grey and black due to grime. Crumbling cement particles from the eroded brick joints powdered the base perimeter of their walls.

The twelve-bay workshop and office stood to the rear of a large flat tarmac ten-acre site. Its brown and cream overhead doors were closed to the elements, giving anyone inside some relief from the cold, penetrating humidity. The extensive fleet of city dump trucks, gulley suckers, backhoe loaders and other various types of excavators were all neatly reversed into their allocated parking spaces. Their wet bodies and accessories dully reflecting the yard's subdued orange sodium lighting back through the soaking drizzle.

A dark figure emerged from the shadows in the yard, opened the workshop side door and slipped inside. He remained perfectly still for several more moments, then lowered the hood on his tight black jacket so as not to interfere with his 20/20 vision. He wore a dark woollen hat underneath. Even though his breathing was controlled, his senses remained on high alert. His eyes scanned side to side, taking in any possible movement inside the workshop. From his previous research he knew that outside normal working hours, the industrial

CHAPTER 3

area remained quiet. He carried no weapons, preferring to improvise at every location he worked. Having your own weapons, in his mind, was not a good idea. The risk of having them in your possession was too great if you were ever stopped. Moreover, DNA or fingerprints on the weapon could be damning even if it was disposed of afterwards. Always the chance it could be found. Escape plans and plausible excuses were always well thought out beforehand, if ever he was stopped. He was a planner, a thinker and a structured improvisor.

Satisfied, he checked his gloved hands and stealthily moved further inside the workshop and peered around the cab of a truck. He saw the workshop supervisor leaning underneath a propped-up tipper body. The sound of the workshop air compressor running would enable him to creep silently up on his target. He spotted a heavy iron bar on a work bench, quietly picked it up and moved slowly up behind the supervisor. At the last minute, Ted turned around and saw the intruder. He tilted his head quizzically, trying to understand what was happening but before he could make sense of the situation, the iron bar smashed down on top of his head. He let out a dull groan and slumped over the chassis rail. The wrench from his hand fell, bouncing onto the oil-stained concrete floor. Once the hollow, metallic clanging sound of the tool had died away, there was just the sound of the air compressor running.

The intruder pulled the body up but left Ted's head face down on the flat top half of the chassis rail with both arms hanging forward over the rail. He knocked out the body safety prop and let it fall down to the floor. Next, he clambered up into the cab of the truck and released the hydraulic lever controlling the tipper body. The body immediately fell back down to its normal horizontal position neatly squashing Ted's head in between the heavy steel body and the frame of the truck. He pushed the lever back to the Up position.

The intruder jumped out of the cab, found a wrench and slackened off a hydraulic hose just sufficiently enough to prevent sustained pressure from holding up the hydraulic ram of the tipping body. He cleaned and returned the wrench and flat bar to the positions he had found them in on the bench. The air compressor cut out leaving the place completely silent.

As silently as he came in, the intruder left. A key figure had been removed for the master plan to click into gear.

Chapter 4

'Hey, James, welcome back! How was your week off?'

James pushed his chair back from his office desk, looked up and smiled at Chris. 'It was great, thanks. Good weather and it gave me time to relax and think! How about you? How was your weekend?'

'On the go, running the kids around to their various activities as well as some renos on the house. Never ends, does it!' He spread out his hands and shrugged. 'Well, I'm glad you're back! We've been busy here, but we can update you in the management meeting this morning.'

'Looking forward to it.'

James and Chris sat down with their managers in the boardroom to start the meeting. The chatter was already buoyant around the table.

James shuffled his papers and put them to one side. 'Good morning, everyone! Let's get straight down to the division reports. Chad, let's hear from you first.'

Chad Greening, Director Sales and Marketing had been with

the company for over twelve years. Single and well respected, he knew the shipping industry inside out. He put both of his hands face down on the table. 'I'll get straight to the point. In the last six months our sales revenue from marine operations is up by over twenty-five percent and our net profit is up over thirty percent. Land operations profitability is also up by over twenty percent.'

Chad paused and saw the smiles around the table. He grinned back. 'I'd like to think it was all because of my magnetic personality and charm, but, credit where credit is due, our new logistics software has led to a greater utilisation of our equipment. There's nothing like it out there to compare with our system.'

Chad continued, 'There's also no doubt that the troubles in Shanghai, Rotterdam, Marseilles and Zeebrugge terminals also fell in our favour, but the efficiencies of combining sea and land operations has shortened delivery times. We have a lot of happy customers right now.'

James let out a long breath and looked over at his partner Chris. Combining Macrae Shipping with Claybourne Cartage had been a master stroke. Their friendship and trust had grown exponentially.

'Congratulations, Chad, to you and your team. Thank you!'

James turned to Janet Rushton. She'd now been with the company four years and had been pivotal in holding off the multiple threats to the company's IT infrastructure. It had been a huge move for her and her family to relocate from London to Birmingham, but she and her family had settled in well.

James continued. 'Thanks, Janet, to you and your IT team too for our entirely new and revolutionary logistics system.

It's clearly been a big contributor towards the growth of our new company.'

Janet beamed. 'Well, we're not finished yet. There are more developments to come but, before I update everyone with that, I want to tell you that we have promoted Lee Yuen to the position of Director IT, to replace Lisa Taylor who sadly ended her own life for reasons we can't imagine. His insight and vision for a fixed operations system working in tandem with our operational logistics requirements is a game-changer. Not only is he a futurist, but he is also a brilliant programmer. I've never seen anyone that can write code so efficiently. Whereas most programmers take say six lines of code to write one operation, he does it in two!'

James smiled. Only he, Chris and Janet knew the part Lee had played in figuring out that Lisa Taylor, the former director of IT, was the traitor who leaked their software secrets to the Chinese. Also, they were the only ones that knew the truth about how they had sabotaged the Shanghai, Rotterdam, Marseille and Zeebrugge terminals. It would remain that way. 'So, Janet, tell us about the new developments.'

Janet continued. 'All of our mobile equipment on land and water needs planned preventive maintenance to maximise our uptime. That's the same for all our fixed equipment in each terminal, such as gantry, stacker or straddle cranes. We're now creating a system of predictive maintenance for each piece of equipment. Our planners using the logistics system, therefore, will only see what equipment is fully serviced and operational to be available for the necessary movement of goods within our care. Too often in the past we've had to scramble last minute to find available equipment to move goods. This will enhance both customer satisfaction and our profitability.'

'What's your time frame for completion of this?' Chris asked.

'We should have a beta version in six months.'

'That's great news, Janet. Thank you, and to all your staff as well!'

Janet smiled and sat back.

'So how about operations, Rob?' James asked. Rob Bisset was VP of Operations and had been with the company for over twenty years. He was a gifted linguist and the 'go-to' guy for the company. He also had a very dry sense of humour.

'Good news again!' He paused and looked around the table. 'I must say, I feel a little bit like Elizabeth Taylor's eighth husband. In other words, I know what to do but how do I do it differently?'

Everyone laughed.

'So, yes. Good news. Apart from the new service and parts system that we've been working on with Janet and Lee, the percentage of our uptime has increased. With no interruptions from sabotage, our operations have been running seamlessly. Pete, who handles all the land transportation equipment, reports the same results as well.' He paused.

'Perhaps the biggest development has been the launching of our two new Panamax 1 container vessels giving us more cargo capacity. These two ships with their new lower emission technology engines are using fewer gallons of diesel per hour, saving us big money. Again, with world trade picking up after the recession and more business coming our way from new customers, the utilisation of our equipment is running at eighty-five percent. We have never seen results like this before. Together with Pete, we will be requesting more equipment to be included in next year's budget.'

James spread his hands out either side of him. 'You know it makes a huge change to receive such good news. These last couple of years we've had some strong head winds, so I'm thankful to you all. Chris and I had this vision over two years ago and with all your hard work, you have brought a dream to reality.'

James turned to Martin Farley, Director of Legal Affairs. Martin was now in his early fifties and had been a family friend with James's father, Richard. Well versed in international law, he was vital to the company as their corporate lawyer.

'So, Martin, what's your good news?'

Martin lifted his head and nodded. 'As you know, regarding the libel suit against Mercantile News, after seeing the chaos in the other ports like Shanghai and Marseilles, we decided to drop the case. Once all the negative press came out about the failure of their logistics system, we figured we'd be better off distancing ourselves from them altogether. The fact that our system works flawlessly and theirs is a total failure is proof enough that we never copied their system.'

James smiled widely. 'Yes, that was a good call!'

Martin continued. 'Since Pair-Tree Capital's involvement with China has been exposed, the European Union has asked for our assistance to help sort out Zeebrugge, Marseilles and Rotterdam. They can't afford to have these ports down. They are too important for international trade. They know China paid well over the odds to take them over so, with some financial help from Brussels, they have invited us to take a share in them. The ports' existing capital resources cannot finance the upgrades that are so desperately need. So, that sure falls into the category of good news!'

'It sure does. Chris, you and I will need to analyse what's involved here but it is certainly worth pursuing.'

'So lastly, Laura, with all this good news, how does our financial position look?' As CFO, Laura had been instrumental in helping identify Hal Spencer, the former CFO, as the traitor who had leaked information to Euro-Asian Freight.

Laura pulled her manila folder closer to her. 'At the risk of being called a party-pooper, I must caution everyone regarding budgets. I'm obviously delighted that the business is forging ahead, but I need everyone to be aware of the dangers of over-trading.'

James and Chris both quietly repositioned themselves in their chairs.

Laura continued, 'With the launch and commissioning of the new container ships, this new head office – together with other capital spending – puts a strain on our lines of credit. As we expand even more, we need to be aware that we have enough financial liquidity to pay expenses on time. Salaries, benefits, taxes and payables must all be paid promptly. So I ask all of you to be mindful of your divisions' expenses and be aware that we don't have a bottomless pit of available cash when you put your new equipment budgets together.'

James nodded. 'Good advice, Laura. You need to keep us on an even keel. So, how are relations with our bankers these days?'

'I would say they are good, however, since your father's friend, Henry Harrison, Chairman of MidCom Commercial Bank passed away, there doesn't seem to be that same sort of warm friendship as before.'

James frowned. 'Umm, maybe you, Chris and I need to do some schmoozing with them, although you'd think it should be the other way around.'

Chris jumped in. 'I think we should invite other bankers to give us proposals to handle some of our business.'

Laura smiled.

James nodded. 'Okay, go ahead, Laura, and let's see what kind of response we get.'

Once the meeting had finished, James returned to his office. A copy of the *Telegraph* newspaper lay on his desk. An article on the front page caught his eye.

China threatens Taiwan

1d ago. *China fired three Chinese M-9 ballistic missiles from China's Huanan mountains toward Taiwan. They splashed down in the shipping lanes adjacent to Taiwan's two principal seaports: first Kaohsiung in the south, then Chilung in the north, then south again to Kaohsiung. The US has said that if any missiles strike Taiwan, there will be grave consequences.*

James just shook his head. *Not good, but at least they were not the target.*

5

Chapter 5

'Let me take care of the discussions regarding trade and the armed forces. The Turkish politicians think they are the ruling party, but, trust me, it's the military that really rules the country.'

The Chinese foreign minister nodded and unbuckled his seat belt now the pilot had turned off the sign. He looked directly back at General Shen. 'I agree, Wu. Now you are the Minister for Trade and Development, that's only right. I'll do all the high-level *puff and stuff* that us seasoned politicians do so well. We'll make a good team, you and me. I deliver the velvet; you produce the nuts and bolts!'

Shen knew he could trust the Chinese foreign minister. He'd had him under surveillance for quite some time and knew that he was one hundred percent loyal to his country. He decided to elaborate on his plan for Turkey in more detail, rather than blind-side the minister in front of everyone.

Shen leaned further towards the minister and lowered his voice. 'Apart from general exports and trade development,

CHAPTER 5

I want to steer the Turkish delegation down the path with a focus on three main areas. Firstly, we need to help them develop their mining and exploration into REEs, or Rare Earth Elements. Turkey has Uranium deposits in Western Anatolia. They also have deposits of thorium, barite and fluorite in the Eskişehir region.'

'Umm. I see. That makes sense since these REEs are useful to us for military, industrial and renewable energy applications,' said the minister, nodding in agreement.

'Exactly. I regard these raw materials as strategic and critical according to their supply risk and economic importance. Even though China supplies eighty-five percent of the world's REEs, the more we can stockpile and monopolize these elements, the more power we have to use this as a hybrid method of warfare against the rest of the world. In an ideal situation, we can starve them of these REEs and halt their production of advanced weapons, communication equipment and renewable energy.'

The minister leaned his head to one side and tugged on his earlobe. 'Brilliant! What's your second focus?'

'Secondly, if I can get close enough to their military decision-makers, I want to supply Turkey with Chinese military hardware at a vastly reduced cost than they can buy from their NATO partners. Of course they won't be our latest secret weapons, but they will be advanced. In return I want them to show us all the latest NATO weaponry so we can either copy it, find ways to neutralize it or enhance it.'

'Shen, I'm impressed. Honestly, I've had my eye on you for some time. Most of our personnel don't seem to rise above the weeds and see the big picture, whereas you have the ability to rise above all of the others and recognize an opportunity as though it was a sphere right in front of you that you can scrutinize with three-hundred-and-sixty-degree vision.'

'That's kind of you. Thank you.'

'No, you deserve it. Your rapid rise through the military is impressive to say the least. Apart from the military background, I understand that you also majored in Economics and Maths.'

'Yes, I did. To me these are the keys for building wealth and can be used as weapons against our enemies. There are more ways of weakening our opponents than just military might.'

'You are certainly right there. Now, what's your third focus?'

'Their seaports. The Turks are starved of cash right now, so we can move in and finance their development. When they are so much in debt, we will have to take them over. Of course, the ports will be designed in such a way that they will provide us with naval bases in the future so we can control Southern Europe, North Africa and most importantly, Russia's access to the Black Sea.'

They both chuckled quietly as the captain throttled back the jet engines and announced they were on their final descent to the Turkish capital for their trade mission visit.

The motorcade made its way from the airport and stopped in front of the Grand National Assembly of Turkey. Shen looked up at the long three-storey government building constructed out of light brown stone and fronted by an extensive and majestic front-pillared portico. Large courtyards and manicured gardens surrounded the building complex. As he exited his vehicle, he could immediately smell the newly mown grass.

Inside the large, high-ceilinged conference room, the fifty-strong combined Turkish and Chinese delegations sat silently facing each other around a long, oval polished maple wood conference table. A large painting of Mustafa Kemal Atatürk, the founder of the modern-day Turkish Republic looked down on them from the wall facing the head of the table. A Turkish and Chinese flag stood proudly either side of the portrait mounted on brass poles. Names and positions of the delegates, as well as a microphone, were placed in front of each of them.

The Turkish foreign minister quietly cleared his throat, turned on his microphone and stood up to welcome the Chinese delegation. There was a rustle around the table as each person adjusted their seating position to pay attention to the minister. He spread his hands out and broadcast a warm smile around the table.

'Gentlemen, on behalf of the Republic of Turkey, it is truly an honour for us to receive you here today in Ankara.' He paused momentarily. 'Our old Ottoman and Chinese empires were once close neighbours from the Göktürk era when we were a nomadic confederation of Turkic people in medieval Asia. The Silk Road, at that time, facilitated our trade relations. I can say that this is a particularly good time for us both to revive that cooperation between our two countries and economies. I believe we can both benefit from closer economic and diplomatic ties. As our founder, President Atatürk, once said, *A man who doesn't think differently from his time and environment can't grow beyond his time and environment.*'

'And upon that note, I declare the meeting open.'

The Chinese foreign minister stood up and straightened his jacket.

'Thank you, minister, for your warm welcome. Indeed, we are old neighbours and from today we will revive that close relationship. We are also delighted to be in your presence and believe we have many splendid opportunities awaiting us. Both of our countries are opening up our borders to trade, so we can certainly jointly explore what exports and imports we can exchange between us to help make our countries even stronger.'

The Turkish minister bowed his head in acknowledgment as the Chinese Foreign Minister continued.

'In addition, you have a unique position in the world straddling both Europe and Asia. That, in itself, underlines the importance you play on the world stage. Of course, you are now part of NATO as well as having a customs union with the EU, but that does not mean we cannot be friends and neighbours. In fact, I can already say that we are bringing with us today easier access to finance and credit from our country. For that is an essential prerequisite for any trade friendly business environment. On that note, let me introduce you to Mr Wu Shen, our Minister for Trade and Development. Over the next few days, he will lead our delegation in detailed discussions of credit available for large capital projects, import and export of products between our two countries and availability of military hardware. Thank you again, minister, for your kind words and warm welcome. Let us both *grow beyond our time and environment!*'

Over the next two days separate smaller meeting were held by specialists in each of their economic and trade areas. On the second day, in late afternoon, Shen was in a meeting dealing with finance, when a Turkish official entered the meeting and spoke quietly with him.

'Excuse me, Mr Shen, but I have an important message for you.'

CHAPTER 5

Shen took the envelope and read the contents.

He stood up. 'Excuse me, ladies and gentlemen, but I will have to step outside the meeting. Please carry on.' The confidential message was an invitation to attend a one-on-one meeting with the General Chief of Staff of the Turkish Armed Forces at their headquarters in Ankara.

After a short ride by a military limousine, Shen was ushered into a large office on the top floor of the main military headquarters, a massive plain building with small square windows neatly punctuating the walls at even intervals. Aside from a large office desk, a sofa and two armchairs stood to the side on a large sumptuous and richly woven Turkish silk rug.

'Good afternoon, Mr Shen, or should I call you General Shen?'

A mid-height generously proportioned man in smart full military uniform came towards Shen with his hand extended. His thinning grey hair and full beard suggested he was probably in his late sixties although Shen knew from intelligence reports that the exact age of Adnan Gulnaz was sixty-two.

Shen reciprocated the smile. 'General Gulnaz. It's a pleasure to meet you in person at last. I'm guessing we know more about each other than we care to admit.'

Gulnaz released his tight grip of Shen's hand and roared with laughter, rocking back on both feet. His piercing gunmetal eyes were trying to weigh Shen up. 'Of course we do! I can say I've admired the rapid progression of your career. You're moving fast!'

'You are too kind, general. It is I that should be praising you. You are a pillar of stability behind the multifarious politicians you have in Turkey.'

Gulnaz laughed again. 'Ah, politicians! All of them ebb and

flow champions like the tide in the Bosphorus Strait; the only difference is they choose to change direction when it suits them. Come on, Shen, politicians come and go all the time while we military men are here to stay. Without us, these men have no foundation.'

Shen tilted his head slightly to one side. He was taken aback by how outspoken Gulnaz was, even though he agreed with him. He decided to be more tactful and replied accordingly. 'Yes, they can be a bunch of stuffed shirts but thankfully we are occasionally rewarded with some that are stable and sensible. It's a blessing when they are on the scene.'

'Come, Shen, let's sit down and discuss the real issues. I haven't got time for all this political bullshit. I'll tell you exactly what we need.' No sooner had Gulnaz sat down than he leaned forward from his armchair and anchored his attention on Shen. 'Give me your latest multi-launch rocket systems and short-range missiles. We also need long-range air defence missile systems that are anti-stealth so they can intercept not only aircraft but all types of drones, missiles and precision-guided bombs.'

Shen raised his eyebrows and tilted his head back. 'You don't mince your words, do you?'

Gulnaz nodded curtly.

Shen tried to slow down the sudden onslaught. 'You surprise me, general. As a NATO member I thought you had all this equipment already.'

'Ha! We may be a member of NATO but they don't trust us.'

Shen spread both his hands out either side of him as a 'tell me more' gesture.

'Here's why. Because we are a Muslim country, they don't sell us the latest military hardware and then they demand top dollar.' He paused and looked Shen straight in the eye. 'I believe your equipment is at least a match, if not better than the current Patriot System we have.'

Shen continued to play dumb. 'Wouldn't buying arms from China put you in an awkward position with the other NATO members?'

Gulnaz narrowed his eyes. 'We will cite competitive reasons. The simple answer is, we need foreign defence technology at the least possible cost.'

Shen nodded in agreement. 'I believe we can help you secure our technology, certainly at a competitive cost. We could also offer you flexible finance terms, but—'

General Gulnaz lay back in his chair and laughed. 'How did I know that *but* was coming?'

Within seconds he sat forward again and pierced Shen with a dispassionate look, transforming himself into the true head of a country with a single-minded agenda. 'I'll tell you how you can sell us arms.'

Shen continued to remain calm. 'I'm all ears.'

'Okay, you want to get your hands on the Patriot missile technology and systems even though they might not be the latest spec. Right?'

'Right.'

'Done deal, but... Now it's my turn...in addition to your latest multi-launch rocket systems, short and long-range missiles, I want five million US dollars transferred into a personal account I have in Cyprus.'

Shen gave a tight-lipped smile. 'I hear you, but since we are being so forthright, I want your approval for the trade, commerce, and finance agreements we have made between our two delegations in the last few days. I presume you were listening in on all the meetings, even though you weren't there in person.'

'You mean you want me to sign off on your plans and finance arrangements for the port of Ambarli; your rail expansion for your new silk road initiative; your mining investments in the development of rare earths and your exports of data-processing machines, mobile phones, cruise and merchant ships?'

Shen was not shocked to hear such detail. Gulnaz clearly had a firm hand on the controls for his country. Shen kept his face expressionless.

'That would be ideal.'

'First things first. Two and half million dollars must be in my account before I sign off on these intended projects. Then the balance must be in place before I release the Patriot technology to you.'

'Agreed.' Shen sat back quietly and rubbed his chin without saying any more. He'd been shocked at how forthright Gulnaz had been, more like a bulldozer. He decided he would do the same and throw out an outlandish suggestion to see where it landed. He leaned forward again and raised his head. 'There is a way you could earn more; shall we say commission?'

Gulnaz's eyes widened. 'And what is that?'

'Take over the port of Haydarpasa, the Istanbul marine terminal owned by Macrae Claybourne Logistics.'

'Ahh. Not so easy, general. If Turkey was to make a state takeover of any foreign business in the country, then all our foreign investment would cease. Precisely the opposite of what we need right now.'

'Okay, I understand but give it some thought.'

'I will.'

Chapter 6

'I know you!'

Huang Genjo tried to steady the constant shaking he was enduring. He slowly put his hand to his forehead to shade his eyes from the bright sunshine and peered at the wizened man standing in front of him.

'Yes, I know you. You're Huang Genjo! I didn't recognise you to start with, but now your features are becoming more familiar.'

Huang stammered. 'I'm sorry, who are you?'

'Y-you don't recognize me? I know I lost a lot of weight, and my hair has gone, but I'm Yan!'

'Yan?'

'Yes, Yan Li Jie.'

Huang stood back and put his hand to his mouth. He cried. 'Oh my goodness! Yan!' and continued to sob. Yan stepped forward and gently hugged his fellow student.

'It's okay. It's okay...'

Huang sighed. 'I'm so sorry, Yan, I just didn't recognise

you.' He looked down at his dusty feet and slowly said, 'I guess none of us are the same after six years of hunger, isolation and torture.' He paused almost as an afterthought. 'How our dreams of freedom were dashed so quickly away that day in Tiananmen Square. All we were doing was protesting the government. We weren't even violent.'

Yan frowned. 'Was it worth it?' He let out a loud sigh. 'I wonder? Let's go and find out who the other four are. I'm thinking they were protesting students just like us. Maybe we can find out what we're doing here.'

All six men were attempting to exercise their stiff limbs in a dry and dusty walled yard. Since arriving by truck from Qincheng Prison, they'd been confined there. Slowly they'd been fed solid food and water and their bodies were now starting to fill out again.

Yan and Huang shuffled over to the others, who seemed to be avoiding any kind of communication with anyone. Each person preferred to stare downwards, engulfed in their own little world. Prison had taught them that.

Yan was the first to speak. 'Hello, are you also students who were taken prisoner by the army after Tiananmen?'

The others still said nothing, so Huang spoke. 'It's okay. This is Yan and I'm Huang. We are two students from Tsinghua university.'

One of the others slowly looked up and spoke. His eyes were darting from side to side. 'I'm Haoyu and we are from Peking University.'

The group of six slowly came closer together, carefully eyeing each other up. Like Huang, the five men's gaunt sunken faces and hollow, empty eyes were gradually filling out. Their hair had been cut and was now black and starting to shine.

CHAPTER 6

Communication between the group had been sparse, each scared to talk to each other in case they were immediately thrown back into Qincheng; vivid memories that could never be erased, not even from the subconscious.

A medium height, well-built man with long black hair, thick black moustache and goatee beard came across the yard and joined them. Immediately the group stepped back and looked down into the dust. The man held his hands up either side of him. 'It's okay, I'm a friend.'

No one said anything, so he continued in a quiet voice. 'You can call me Lingdao. I'm here to help you, in fact, I'm one of you. Like yourselves, I was there that day in Tiananmen Square, but I managed to avoid being caught. I'm still an anti-government activist and am now working with a powerful group of Chinese dissidents who desperately want us to form an alternative to this Chinese tyranny. We need a free and democratically elected government of China, and it will be easier to organize this if we are outside the country. You were chosen to join this group overseas. It's because of this group, we were able to organise your escape from Quincheng.'

Huang looked up feeling more confident. 'But why us?'

Lingdao smiled back. 'Because you were all strong opinion leaders and well-organised activists in your universities. Listen, I know you're scared now, but, trust me, your bodies and minds will heal, and you will become valuable members of our cause.'

Lingdao could still feel the palpable apprehension in the group. He continued, 'Please... Feel free to talk to each other. We are all trusted friends here.'

Huang moved his foot around in the dust. 'What happened to our other friends and families?'

Lingdao frowned, tilted his head down and then looked up. 'It's been six years since the massacre. Hundreds of people were killed that day and over seven thousand wounded. I'm afraid many of our friends were executed after their arrest and our families have been purged.'

The group turned away and wept.

Another man approached Lingdao. 'You have a telephone call. It's important.' Lingdao left the group alone after excusing himself and returned inside the building to his private office, carefully closing the door behind him. He picked up the phone knowing it was General Shen on the secure line.

'Lingdao speaking.'

How's it going?'

'Stage one is nearly complete, general.'

Chapter 7

William Brocklehurst sat in his parked car and carefully read his résumé once more. Not that he needed to; he'd memorised it perfectly well beforehand. In a sense he was an actor taking on a new role, except this time he was now Nick Northrop, a former army officer of the Royal Electrical and Mechanical Engineers (REME). The project he'd been given was very important to him since he was being paid a great deal of money. The task would take approximately two years to accomplish under cover of his new identity. Essentially, in espionage terminology, he was to become a 'sleeper'. Another large lump sum would be paid to him at the end of this period if he successfully assassinated the intended target. It was right up Brocklehurst's street. In real life he'd been a British Army officer serving with the Staffordshire Regiment. Already trained as a mechanic, he'd served in Northern Ireland and the Gulf War. Afterwards he'd become a mercenary soldier, a paid killer.

His instructions had been given to him through a third-party handler, the same person that had issued instructions for him to kill Richard and Mary Macrae, the parents of James Macrae the year before. It was also the same handler that had instructed him to kill the Birmingham City Municipal Works superintendent two weeks earlier. To the outside world, the former mercenary soldier William Brocklehurst did not exist any longer. After killing the Macraes, Brocklehurst had slipped the country and rejoined his former comrades in Angola, fighting the rebel group UNITA. It was here that Brocklehurst had faked his own death and simply disappeared off the radar.

Now Nick Northrop, his résumé was impeccable. His handlers had also told him that the central army database had been 'modified' to include his new identity, should any interested party want to check him out. His former shaved head and out-of-control moustache were no longer. He was now clean-shaven and sported a neatly trimmed head of light-brown hair. The Staffordshire knot tattoo that had been on his right wrist had also been removed. With his new identity passport and the requisite stamps to authenticate his travels with REME, driving licence and various club memberships, this man with a slim build and rounded, weathered face looked like a perfectly respectable and reliable pillar of society. Northrop cleared his throat, took in some deep breaths and entered the Birmingham City Council offices. It was a grand, impressive building designed along Corinthian lines, located in the centre of the city.

A secretary approached him in reception. 'Mr Northrop, Mr Stevens can see you now. Please follow me.' He was led into a heavily wood-panelled office on the first floor. The building resembled more of a museum than a thriving office serving

CHAPTER 7

the second biggest city in England.

'Good afternoon, Mr Northrop. Please come in.'

Northrop quickly took in his surroundings. His interview for the position of superintendent of the Birmingham Municipal Works department was being carried out by the general manager of the works department. Wilfred Stevens stood up to greet Northrop. He was a taller man in his sixties with thin grey hair and matching handlebar moustache. The smart dark-blue pin-striped suit matched his eyes, which were bright blue and seemed to absorb everything in front of them.

They shook hands firmly. 'It's good to meet you, Mr Northrop, or should I call you captain?'

Northrop smiled and spread out both of his hands. 'Well, I don't need to be called captain anymore. I'm trying to adjust to civvy street in more ways than one.'

'Okay, "Mr" it is. As a former sapper myself, we have much in common.' He waved his right hand to the chair in front of his desk. 'Please, sit down and tell me about yourself.'

Northrop sat bolt upright. 'As for my background, it's pretty simple really, Mr Stevens. After leaving school I became an apprentice mechanic at a local dealership but got tired of working on just heavy trucks. I wanted something more challenging. So I joined REME to widen my experience, to work on more interesting vehicles and to have the chance to travel. Bottom line, I've worked on all kinds of heavy trucks, tanks, personnel carriers, helicopters, and fighters. Apart from hydraulics, my speciality is electronics and diagnostics.'

'Excellent. Where were you posted?'

'As with all REME recruits, I did my training in Chatham but saw service in the Falklands War and the Gulf War. I've also done stints in Germany, Mali and Cyprus. By this time, I was in supervisory positions in charge of training. I live by the saying, *it is what it is, and it takes what it takes.*'

Stevens leaned back in his chair. 'Jolly good! I have the same saying myself!' He paused and adjusted his half-moon reading glasses to refer to the résumé in front of him. He looked directly at Northrop over the top of his glasses and smiled. 'Excellent! Quite honestly, your knowledge, skills and experience are perfect for the opening we have. I have to say, army recruits are the best. As a former officer myself, I respect the training and discipline that comes with the job. We know what it takes to get the job done, don't we?'

Northrop smiled back. 'We do, sir!' He paused for a few moments. 'So, Mr Stevens, tell me more about the position.'

Stevens frowned, sighed heavily and laid his glasses carefully on the desk. 'Quite honestly, this position's only just come up. The former superintendent had an unfortunate accident while repairing a vehicle and died while working late on his own in the workshop.'

Northrop recoiled backwards and winced. 'Oh, I'm so sorry to hear that. That's awful.'

'Yes, it is. He left a wife and two children.' Stevens took a moment to steal a glance at the ceiling. 'Anyway, I need a replacement to supervise the shop and train our new apprentices. It's a position that needs someone with your skills and the ability to ramp up our operations since we're expanding and will soon move into a brand-new workshop and yard in another location in the Digbeth district.'

Northrop nodded. 'That sounds right up my alley, sir. I can easily handle that.'

'I believe you can,' said Stevens, nodding. 'Do you have family?'

CHAPTER 7

'I don't. I'm afraid army life didn't suit my former wife. In all honesty, I don't blame her. With all the constant upheaval of moving from base to base it's difficult for a partner to make friends. Just when you've done that, you lose them when you move on. Add that to her never knowing if I would ever come home again. Every time I left on a mission it just, well, became too much for her.'

Stevens nodded quietly in understanding. He looked back at his visitor and mulled over a few thoughts in his mind.

Northrop raised his eyebrows but remained silent.

Stevens continued. 'I don't know if you're aware, but the G7 meeting will be held here in Birmingham two years from now, in May 1998. All the leaders of the G7 will be here, even possibly Russia and China as well. Birmingham will have to look its best and of course security will need to be taken care of well before that. We have a mandate to ensure all buildings, roads, sewers and canals and the whole city centre are safe and secure. The workshop supervisor position would play an important role for this to happen. Of course, all this would be carried out jointly with the police and special security forces. Could you handle that?'

Northrop blew out his cheeks. 'I didn't know about the G7 meeting. That would be a huge event and responsibility. Yes, I could handle that.'

'Well, us REME men know what we're doing. Right?' He nodded at Northrop.

Northrop had remained sitting upright. Instinctively he let out a 'Yes, sir, we do!'

Stevens carried on. 'As I said, your experience and background could not be better suited for the job of supervisor. I have already checked out your record with the Army Central database, so I'm prepared to offer you the job based on a probationary three-month period.'

'Yes, sir! I'm ready to go to work. Thank you for the opportunity. I won't let you down.'

Northrop left the council offices satisfied that he was making progress on his mission.

The fox was about to enter the chicken pen.

Chapter 8

'Hey, Chris, remember I told you I did a lot of thinking while I was away recently?'

Chris looked up from his office desk. 'Yeah, I do. Why, what's up, mate?'

'I was thinking of the shipping side of the business.'

Chris tilted his head and said slowly. 'Okaaaay, what's coming next? You'd better grab a chair!'

James pulled up a chair to the desk and leaned forward. 'Here's the thing. Our company's strong in Europe but we don't have ports in North America or the Far East. Now we have the best logistics systems worldwide, wouldn't it make sense if we could expand there?'

Chris took in a breath. 'Yes, but only if the opportunity came up at the right price and on the right terms.'

'Right. Well, I think it has.' He didn't wait for Chris to reply. 'I was looking at North America. Now Canada, the US and Mexico are all part of the North American Free Trade Association or NAFTA, if we could take over or buy into a port there, it would give us a gateway into the whole continent.'

'Yes, it would, however all the main eastern ports are spoken for after the fiasco of Pair-Tree Capital. I can't imagine there are any bargains to be scooped up there right now.'

'Right but look further north – Canada. They're in NAFTA and now there could be an opportunity in Halifax.'

'How come?'

'Well, I approached the owner of the Port Authority, Angus MacNiel, after reading that the last recession had set the Port back with a dramatic fall in imports and exports. I'd met him before at EXPO in Genoa a couple of years ago. It seems that high interest rates and the price of oil, due to Saddam Hussein's invasion of Kuwait, didn't help either.'

'Okay, so where does that leave us?'

'Angus is inviting us to over there to discuss becoming a partner in the business. He believes it's worth exploring as our capital and logistics management capability could help revitalise the port.'

Chris clasped his hands together and rested his chin on them for a few seconds. 'Well, it's certainly worth pursuing. We can't lose anything by going over there and having an open discussion.'

James nodded in agreement. 'Halifax has some advantages. It's one of the deepest and largest ice-free harbours in the world. Also, the most easterly North American one, being the first inbound and last outbound port to Europe. This could give us a tremendous opportunity for expansion and also strengthen us against the Chinese meddling in our affairs.'

'Okay, set it up, James. Let's go take a look. I have to go now; Jenny and Bailey are here. Bailey's going to spend some time with Laura and find out more about accounting. She's sixteen, loves maths and thinks she might want to pursue that as a career.'

As James turned around, Chris's wife Jenny came into the office. He got up from his chair. 'Oh hi, Jenny! Good to see you!'

'Hello, James, good to see you too!' They hugged. 'How's Sarah and the family?'

'Oh, we're all good. Sarah's working flat out on another historical architecture project. I don't know how she does it! So, how about you? What are you up to these days?'

'Well, that's why I'm here. I'm dropping Bailey off for a couple of hours in the office and Chris and I are heading up to the Birmingham Children's Hospital and then we'll all have dinner together. I'm going to go back to the hospital, part time. While I was off, I still kept up my certifications as clinical psychologist and they desperately need more staff.'

'Sounds like a great plan! When I get home, I'll talk to Sarah; we should all get together again soon.'

———————-

'Look, I've had just about enough arguing and bickering between you three. Now just stop it! It's bedtime!'

James arrived home from the office well after dinnertime. He could hear Sarah upstairs, trying to corral Mason, Mia and Olivia to finish up and prepare for bed. Constantly yawning, he kicked off his shoes, loosened his tie and dropped his briefcase on the kitchen table. He opened the fridge to see what there was to eat and saw a dinner covered in clingfilm. Sarah came back into the kitchen, carrying some dishes. James leaned forward and kissed her on the head. 'Sorry I'm late. Something came up. How are you?'

'Tired! It's been a long day.' She placed the cups and plate into the dishwasher and slammed the door closed.

'Yes, of course. Sorry I wasn't home earlier but an opportunity came up for us to buy into a port in Canada. They're five hours behind us, so our days don't exactly coincide. I'm going over there next week with Chris to see if this is a viable venture.'

'James, I need more help here. Now the kids are getting older, they're getting more difficult to handle. I'm also having a tough time trying to get my new job off the ground. Wrestling with my job and all the family matters is becoming more of a challenge, and you seem to be working longer and longer hours. It all seems to fall on my shoulders these days.'

'I know, but it will pass once we get the new company up and going properly.'

Sarah sighed. 'I hope so. I don't understand why you don't rely on Rob Bisset more. After all he's supposed to be in charge of operations.'

James yawned again. 'Oh, I'm sorry. Yes, he is.'

Sarah pressed her lips together. 'Listen, remember we have parents' night at the school on Thursday next week.'

'I should be back by then. I'll heat my dinner up.'

───────────

'What do you think will happen to us next?'

Huang Genjo posed the question to his fellow students sitting around in a circle in a small room next to the walled yard they exercised in. Haoyu, one of his comrades from Peking

CHAPTER 8

University, spoke up first.

'I'm thinking Lingdao must be waiting for instructions before we can finally escape from China.'

Very quietly, Yan spoke next. 'Do we trust him?'

Huang looked around at the five other students. Their bodies had filled out and they looked healthy enough on the outside but, like himself, he suspected they were damaged mentally. No matter how hard he tried, he couldn't bring himself to feel safe and secure. He wondered if he would ever trust anyone ever again. No one replied to the question, so he spoke up, 'What choice do we have? Lingdao and his two assistants got us out of Qincheng, and we're being fed and looked after. At least the idea of forming an opposition to the government outside China is a good one. Maybe our protests weren't in vain after all.'

No one added anything further when Lingdao entered the room. 'Sorry, I couldn't help overhearing your conversation. I know it's early days, but you can trust me, otherwise why would we have gone to the trouble of getting you out of prison? Our cause is just. We must bring an end to this tyranny.'

The group all nodded slowly. Huang looked directly at Lingdao, whose smile revealed a set of shiny white teeth contrasting with his darker skin. Huang couldn't decide what nationality he was. He may have had Chinese ancestry, but he looked more Indian. It was the sort of face that could probably blend in with a number of different nationalities, yet his Mandarin was perfect.

Lingdao continued. 'Very soon we'll be leaving here and boarding a Chinese freighter bound for Europe. Our plan is then to stowaway on a British ship and seize command of it in British territorial waters. This way we will achieve maximum world publicity for our cause and force the British to take us all in as refugees.' He looked down at the group and could see the apprehension in their faces. 'I know, you're wondering why we would come up with a plan like this?'

Huang replied. 'Why couldn't we just present ourselves to the British authorities and seek asylum that way?'

Lingdao nodded back at him. 'An excellent question. The problem is there are thousands of refugees crossing the English Channel in small boats every year to try to enter the country. We, and our message would be lost in the crowds. No, by creating a hijacking, there would be front-page headlines streaked across the globe within hours. Imagine the headlines: *Tiananmen protesters hijack a British ship and seek asylum to form an alternative Chinese government.*' Lingdao let his words hang. 'Think about it. We need maximum publicity for our cause which will also help raise more volunteers and funding. This is how we can achieve it.' He left them to think about it.

Lingdao returned to his own room. He closed the door and waited for the arranged call from General Shen.

Shen did not waste time. 'How are the dissidents?'

'We're making progress, general. They're gaining strength day by day. Of course, they're all wary about what's happening to them, but I believe they're starting to trust us.'

'Good! Now, in three days' time, arrangements have been made for you and your two assistants, Tang and Jin to take the group to Tianjin port where you will board a Chinese freighter bound for Livorno, Italy. Make sure all the dissidents are committed to the project. If there are any doubters or troublemakers, get rid of them before you leave!'

'Will do. Have the final arrangements been made for the last leg of our operation?'

CHAPTER 8

'Yes. Our London intelligence unit has provided us with the details. The vessel you will hijack is one of Macrae-Claybourne Logistics oil tankers, the *Constellation II*. You will be able to gain access into the ship from the rudder trunk. I will have a plan of the ship provided for you. The ship completes regular round-trip voyages picking up crude oil from the port of Livorno going to Southampton, England for refining at the Fawley Refinery to produce propane and butane gas.

'Have there been any changes to our original plan and objective?'

'No, there have not. Our ultimate goal is to determine exactly how quickly British Special Forces can react to a direct threat to one of their ships in British territorial waters. Once we know their battle tactics and timing, we can hone our own military skills to deal with them when the time comes.'

Chapter 9

As the Macrae-Claybourne company Gulfstream IV jet levelled out, the lush green fields and rocky coastline of southern Ireland were replaced by the vast blue North-Atlantic Ocean, forty thousand feet below. James finished his coffee and smiled at Chris.

'How long do you think it'll be before your son, Jackson, will want to come into the business?'

'Good question, James. If he had his way, he'd already be working with us. We've butted heads a few times, but now he's coming up to eighteen he sees the value of going to university first. He seems to be leaning towards Business and Economics. How about your brood?'

'Not sure yet. Still a bit early. Olivia's always the comedian, Mia's our resident actress while Mason's more serious. Funnily enough, he's just read a book on Canada and thinks he'd like to work in a diamond mine. He's heard that workers in the mine work for three weeks straight and then have three weeks off. That's great as far he's concerned.'

CHAPTER 9

Chris laughed, 'He probably thinks he can keep all the diamonds he finds as well!'

James smiled back. 'He does!' He paused momentarily. 'Mia's probably the one who has the clearest picture. She takes a great interest in Sarah's historical architecture projects. Mia's always watching Sarah working on her draughting table and then with CAD on her computer. She loves the look of old buildings and, more importantly, the history behind them. I must say Sarah's enthusiasm for her job is contagious.'

As the Canadian coast approached, the jet flew over Cape Breton Island on its final descent into Halifax. James and Chris peered through the windows, looking down on the waves cresting and crashing on the rugged rocky coastline. Closer to the airport they were also able to see the port of Halifax. The harbour appeared to be relatively spread out, but it was well protected from bad weather by McNabs Island and promontories of land to north and south.

Chris looked over towards James. 'There appear to be reasonable rail and road links to the rest of the country. Looks like there's some land there that could take some more warehouses and cold stores.'

James pointed through the window. 'There's room to expand the docks to the south as well. Hmmm. We'll just have to see what they have in mind.'

A Canadian coastguard and naval base was located further along the coast. Once over the city, the Gulfstream jet flew over thickly forested evergreens before landing gently on the runway from the south-west.

———————

'Good morning, gentlemen! James, Chris, so good of you to come over so soon! It's good we can all discuss this proposal face to face. After reading about your recent merger and systems integration, your business appears to be setting an example for us all.'

Angus MacNiel, the Port Authority chairman and owner stood tall in casual khaki pants and a blue open-neck dress shirt. With a full head of ginger hair and a weathered complexion, he appeared to have spent many years by the coast. James put him in his mid-fifties. His welcoming smile, white teeth and brown eyes gave a reassuring confidence.

'Thanks, Angus. It was good of you to invite Chris and I to meet with you. We look forward to our stay here to learn more about you, your business, and your future plans.'

The three men stood around the board room table. A large window overlooked the port busy with incoming and outgoing freight. Straddle cranes weaved back and forth, loading double-stacked containers onto intermodal rail cars.

Angus stood pointing at the plan of the port spread out in front of them. 'My belief is we need additional quays that can accommodate the biggest post-panamax container vessels as well as the largest supertankers. Halifax would be the only port in eastern Canada that could accommodate this size of vessel. It would also be stiff competition for any port in the US, especially now that NAFTA has been signed.'

After three hours of discussion, they walked the length and breadth of the facilities, inspecting all of the equipment and available land. James and Chris both turned up their coat collars in the stiff easterly breeze. They took photos and notes as they went along.

Standing with his back to the sea, Chris pointed to a piece

of open ground. 'You know what, Angus, you could easily add more grain conveyers here to speed up the loading of bulk cargo and decrease turnaround times. With additional warehouses backing onto the rail heads, loading and unloading times for breakbulk goods would also improve.'

'You're right, Chris. It's capital, your knowledge, and a completely new logistics computer system we need. There's also something else you need to know. Canada is the fifth largest producer of natural gas in the world. Believe it or not, most of it goes by pipeline to the USA. If we could develop a compressed natural gas terminal here, we could start massive exports to Europe. Not only could this be a huge export for Canada, a good profit centre for this port, but it would help Europe lower its greenhouse gas emissions from the use of coal.'

'Now that is interesting!' James exclaimed. 'Alright, Angus, let Chris and I put our heads together and draft out an expansion plan for your consideration. Once we've come collectively to an agreement on what we think is needed, we can hang some estimates on this and try to come up with a share that's agreeable to all of us. Of course, we'll need to sign a non-disclosure agreement. Once that's been done, we can do due diligence and share financials. Does that sound reasonable?'

Angus nodded. 'It does. I'm hoping we can do something together. I think we'd make a good team.'

James stood quietly for a few moments, tapping his index and middle fingers on his lips. 'Just thinking, Angus. Have you ever had any dealings with a Ben Armstrong? He owned both Portland and Wilmington Ports, although I think he's a minority partner now?'

Angus shook his head more in disappointment than in denial.

'Funny you should bring his name up. He barged in here not too long ago sensing we needed help. He offered a solution with such a low-ball offer that I was insulted. It was afterwards that I heard he was in trouble on several fronts, both moneywise and losing whatever partners he had.'

'Hmmm... Interesting. If we can reach an agreement, we could certainly pull business from his terminals. Maybe if this goes well, we could move in and take him over.'

Chris shook his head. 'Hang on, James! Let's slow down, shall we? One step at a time. We have to work out what's needed here first before we go charging off in another direction!'

Angus raised his eyelids but remained tactfully quiet.

James frowned. 'Okay, Chris. You're right. I do need to slow down.'

Angus looked relieved and coughed. 'There's something else that I believe could be important to you. Canada is part of APEC, the Asia-Pacific Economic Cooperation Organisation. That would give you a window to see the strategic vision and economic direction for that region.'

'That's good to know, Angus. Thanks for allowing us the opportunity to partner with you. Truly, we do see the potential here. Chris and I'll get back to you as soon as possible.'

As James and Chris got back in their rental car, Chris exploded. 'What the fuck, James! We're trying to make a serious deal with this guy and there you are giving the impression it's already done. Then you go off blabbing on about taking over Portland and Wilmington. For god's sake, we're still building our business back home. Let's make sure we are on a solid foundation before you set off on some illusory crusade.'

CHAPTER 9

Chris shook his head, getting redder in the face. 'Sometimes you really piss me off, James! Do you want to build a solid business or is it revenge you are seeking on Ben Armstrong and the Chinese?'

James remained quiet in the passenger seat. In a quieter voice he said, 'Let's go to the hotel and put our heads together. I didn't mean to upset you.'

They drove in silence to the Marriott Hotel and checked in. An hour later they met back in the bar and sank a couple of beers.

'Sorry about this afternoon, Chris. If I'm honest, I'm still having difficulty with how we've been victimised by the Chinese. What they've done to us is unforgiveable and I know we've inflicted some heavy damage to them in return, but it always feels like I have a shadow following me. I suppose subconsciously I'm looking to take a swing at them whenever I have the chance, but you're right, it shouldn't jeopardise our business or our relationship.'

'Okay, James, apologies accepted. Let's forget it. Listen, I've been thinking about APEC. If we can make a deal with Angus, this will give us an opportunity to find out what's happening tradewise on the other side of the world. From what I know about APEC, they have business advisory panels where representatives of the private sector of each member country meet regularly and are represented at the APEC ministerial meetings.'

'That certainly would be good. If we could somehow swing ourselves into that, we could keep a closer eye on our competition, especially the Chinese.'

Chris twisted the glass in his hand. 'Before we commit to anything here, I think we should stay an extra day. I'd like to explore what trucking companies operate out of the area. If we're to move forward with Angus, it would make sense to have an integrated transport solution for our customers. From what I can see, I believe there will be a growing opportunity for Halifax to handle exports of oil, natural gas and other refined fuels, to key markets across the world.'

James rested his chin on his hand. 'Okay, I'd better call Sarah and let her know.'

'Are you sure you want to do that? It's one o'clock in the morning there.'

James looked at his watch. Yes it is. I'll have to let her know in the morning. I'll miss parents' night at the school, so I'll probably be in the doghouse. I know she really wanted me there.'

Chapter 10

President Zemin got up from his desk. 'Sit down at the conference table, Shen. We're having a working lunch. Time is short before my visit to India to try to settle the border dispute along the Himalayan frontier.'

Shen saw two plates of steaming gaifan sitting there. There was a choice of beef or chicken with the rice.

'Okay, Shen, help yourself. While we're eating, I want to synchronize our calendars with our plans over the next two years. It's important we stick rigidly to this plan to ensure our integration with the other world G7 members so they can learn to trust us. As I've said before, once we've achieved that, we can begin to manipulate future world events in our favour.' Zemin picked up his chopsticks and dug into the chicken and rice.

Shen dabbed his mouth with his napkin. 'Your approach, President Zemin, is excellent. We'll be right on the heels of Russia. How fickle these Western leaders are, wanting to believe that we are their friends! Little do they know what

Russia and we have in mind for the future.'

Zemin finished chewing and took a drink of water. '*Softly, softly, catchy monkey* as they say! Okay, here's the agenda. Firstly, there's a G7 meeting this month in Lyon, France. Russia will attend and continue their informal meetings with the members as they've done since 1994. We've not been invited to this meeting; however, I've received notification that it is possible we will be invited to the following G7 meeting in June 1997 in Denver, Colorado for informal talks, rather like Russia has done. If so, I'll want you there with me. It's also highly likely Russia will formally join the group then to become the G8.'

Shen sat forward in his chair and placed his hands on the table. 'Do we know for sure that we'll be invited to Denver?'

'No, it's not a hundred percent at this stage.'

'Understood.' Shen placed a question mark against his own note.

Zemin continued, 'Secondly, if all goes well and we behave ourselves and become model world citizens, Hong Kong will be handed back to us on the 1st of July 1997. You need to be at my side then too.'

Shen nodded his understanding, making a further note.

'So, that brings us to the following year, when there will presumably be a G8 meeting in Birmingham, England. With Russia being a full member of the G8 by then, I'm assured we will definitely be invited to attend the meeting on an informal basis. I think we can rely on this.'

Shen made a further note. His face remained impassive. Inwardly, he'd already come to the same conclusion months ago. His vision of becoming the supreme ruler and leader of China comparable to the first Emperor of China, Ying Zheng in

CHAPTER 10

221BC was coming closer. Like a chess game, his long-range plan for achieving this would reach its climax in Birmingham in two years' time.

Zemin ticked off the note on his pad and took a bite of rice. 'So, let's deal with APEC next. Now you are Minister of Trade & Development, at least to the outside world, I want you to attend each of the APEC meetings with me. Get to know who our friends and enemies are and find all their weak spots. We may be able to leverage them at some point in time. Now the next APEC Meeting is in November this year in Manila. Let's get you into that meeting.

'Excellent, President Zemin. I will step up our MSS activity in backchecking all the attendees at these meetings since the representatives from each country constantly change. I believe that APEC also invites specific industry leaders and subject matter experts to help shape future policies. We will have to keep an eye on these attendees as well. This may be an area where we can exert some strong influence on the direction China wants to follow.'

'I will leave that to you, Shen. Let's get to it!'

Shen left the office feeling elated and bloated at the same time. Trying to contain his excitement while eating the heavy lunch had given him heartburn. He walked outside in the gardens for several minutes trying to digest not only his food but also to assess his short and long-range plan using his trusted inner circle of contacts. So far, his preparations using Peng Zheng in London and planting the 'sleeper' in Birmingham were falling into position.

―――――――――――

Yan pushed his arms out straight from the deck rail of the Chinese freighter and looked up into the blue sky. 'I'm starting to feel better. It's good to smell the fresh sea air and see the horizon opening up to us.'

Huang smiled back at Yan. 'Yes, it seems like Lingdao's promises are coming true after all. I'm beginning to believe we can really set up a new political organization that could rival the current regime in China once we're established in the United Kingdom.'

Huang and his five comrades had left the port of Tianjin five days earlier and were now heading south through the gentle rollers of the South China Sea. The freighter ploughed on at a speed of just over twenty knots and their voyage was expected to take just over three weeks. They had been confined in a cargo hold but were allowed on a small area of the deck at certain times when the crew were not there.

By now, all the group were convinced that the intentions of Lingdao were to be trusted. Tang and Jin, his two assistants, were equally friendly and continued to encourage the group that they would be the centrepiece of world headlines for weeks, if not longer. Surely refugee status in England would be granted to them to set up opposition to the Chinese government.

Once during the night on deck, Huang looked up at the vast glittering canopy of stars above him. The shimmering reflected light was intense against the void of blackness beyond. He was joined at the rail by Lingdao.

'Hard to comprehend, isn't it, Huang?'

'It is! No one on earth will ever make sense of this, at least not in our lifetime. I honestly never thought I would ever see a sight like this again having given up all hope. Now,

CHAPTER 10

experiencing this glorious sight, smelling the fresh sea air, tasting the salt, hearing the waves and feeling the cool breeze around my head feels like a miracle. It's almost like I've been born again!'

Lingdao placed his one hand on Huang's shoulder. Weeks ago, Huang would have recoiled sharply, but he remained still and calm. Lingdao spoke softly, 'I hope we will see many more years of experiences like this. We must just be patient and stick to our goal so we can all be granted asylum.'

'I can scarcely believe this but tell me why we must be armed and carry out a hijacking? Surely we could just ask for asylum?'

Lingdao sighed. 'We've thought about this a lot. Trouble is, with thousands of would-be refugees all trying to enter England every year, there will be no big headlines unless we try something different. We need to jump to the front of the queue, otherwise we'll be insignificant.'

'But what if someone gets hurt?'

'They won't, but we have to convince the crew that we are taking over the ship. If we don't do that, we'll all become prisoners to be returned to our homeland. With the takeover of the ship, it will be front page news across the globe.'

11

Chapter 11

'How's it going, Colin?' The workshop technician slid out on his creeper from underneath the chassis of a street sweeper. He wiped his greasy hands on a rag and looked up at his new boss.

'It's gonna need a new steering box.'

'Let me take a look.' They changed positions and Northrop slid underneath the vehicle and inspected the box. 'You don't need to replace it just yet. There's enough adjustment in the bearings to tighten them up and remove the play in the steering.'

'That's a relief. They're a pig of a job to change them on this model. Your predecessor, Ted, would have changed it rather than adjust it. Seemed we always replaced components before it was necessary. I know he was constantly under fire for blowing the workshop budget to hell every month.'

'Well, that's easy to do, but I'm old school. If it's safe and it has to be safe, then why change a component if it's not necessary? If it ain't broke, don't fix it.'

'Isn't that the way, eh? I sure wish they made kitchen appliances like that. I've just had to change my stove and fridge at home, and they weren't even seven years old. More like a giant con if you ask me.'

'Yeah, funny how the guarantee just runs out before they fail. Anyway, once you've finished this job, I need you to come with me and take a look at the new workshop.'

After half an hour, they jumped into the mobile service van and set off to the site of the new Birmingham Municipal central workshop. Colin looked over at his boss. 'You know, Nick, it was a sad loss after the accident of Ted Norris, but I have to say that you've made a good impression with everyone. We're all admiring your knowledge and drive. It's become infectious with us techs. I guess you've worked on just about everything?'

'That's kind of you to say! I've always felt that a group always functions better when everyone is treated the same and we share our knowledge and skills rather than trying to compete with our co-workers.'

'I agree, Nick. I just wish we could attract more recruits into this line of work.'

'You're right, Colin. I'm planning some open days when we can bring in secondary school students for them to see what we do and how we do it. They'll be able to see how technology and computer diagnostics is changing our trade.'

'That would be a great idea!'

They pulled into the new yard and entered the extensive, nearly finished workshop and parts building. 'Okay, Colin, tell me how you think we should set out the flow of parts from the warehouse and how we should organise the work bays.' Northrop already knew exactly how it would be organised, but he wanted to build up trust with Colin knowing he would have to use him later to achieve his secret mission.

———————————-

Jusuf Kahya, the general manager of the Macrae-Claybourne Istanbul Terminal drove his Toyota Land Cruiser off the E5 highway and took the slip road to the port of Ambarli twenty-six kilometres southwest of the city. It was an unseasonably warm and clear day for October with the sun breaking through the partly cloudy conditions to give the Sea of Marmara a warm, enticing glow. He did not care to look at the sea that day since he was focused on the Marport terminal within the port complex. He parked his vehicle on a side road overlooking the port. It appeared to be under heavy development and construction.

Jusuf picked up his binoculars and carefully scrutinised the area. From the outset it was clear that heavy investment was being pumped into expanding the container and ro-ro terminals, adding to the bulk and liquid cargo facilities already in existence. Six new outreach cranes were being erected along two new quays. Rail lines were also being laid alongside the cranes and were being linked to the main rail network. Dust rose up from the constant back and forth of graders and concrete mixers. He'd heard there were some changes being made to the port which had lagged behind for many years through lack of funds. This, however, was not a small operation. On the contrary, it was an undertaking of major proportions, certainly not one that could have been afforded without massive help from the outside.

CHAPTER 11

He moved his binoculars and scanned the interior of the port and saw a dozen new mobile cranes that would eventually handle the containers to be transferred from the railheads to the dock area. They were all neatly grouped together awaiting the completion of newly constructed berths. He jotted down some notes and took photographs. He would need to report this immediately to his boss, James Macrae.

―――――――――――

'So, what do you think, Chris?'

James and Chris stood poring over the proposed plans and estimates for the Port of Halifax on their own boardroom table.

'Well, after several attempts at organising the berths for the type of ships and cargo that are needed, I'm comfortable with this design. At least utilising the current facilities as best as we can, it means the investment will be lower than we originally thought.'

'I agree. I particularly like how you've interlaced the land transfers of marine cargo to rail and road with the minimum of transfers. Couple this with our software logistics system and the port will be way more efficient than before. I believe Angus MacNiel will be pleased.'

'So how do you want to play the money side of things as well as the ownership share, James? Do you want to low ball Angus and then negotiate from there?'

'I've thought about that, Chris, and I believe Angus has laid his situation out realistically and fairly. My impression is that he's honest and sincere. How about you?'

'I did some digging on him and he has an excellent reputation, so I have a similar point of view. We should go in with a completely fair offer both to him and ourselves. I believe he will make an excellent partner and we will have a foothold in North America.'

'Okay. Let's get Martin Farley to draw up a draft agreement to present to Angus.'

The door opened and Rachel, their secretary, stepped in the boardroom. 'Sorry to interrupt you, gentlemen, but Jusuf Kahya is on the line from Istanbul.'

'Thanks, Rachel, we'll take it in here and put him on the speaker.'

'Hi, Jusuf, it's just Chris and me here. How are you?'

'I'm good, but I need to let the two of you know we may have a fight on our hands going forward.'

James looked quizzically at Chris, who just spread his hands out either side of him.

'Go ahead, Jusuf. What's happened?'

'I've just returned from a visit from the port of Ambarli. From what I could see there's some serious money being invested in the port. It's clear they are expanding the container terminal and installing the latest handling equipment. Their dry goods and liquid terminals are also being upgraded.'

James sat frowning, elbows on the table, gently banging his fists together in thought. 'I suppose we shouldn't be surprised, Jusuf. That port has not received any investment for years. Sooner or later, it was going to need some kind of revitalisation.'

'No, James, this is not like that. As you know yourself, Turkey has struggled economically for years, but if you could see the scale of construction and development there you would

CHAPTER 11

be shocked. The port is roughly doubling in size and the new equipment cost must be in the multi-millions. I'd heard something was going on down there, so I went and checked it out. I'm telling you, even I was stunned! This is serious, especially if they start targeting our own port and customers. Remember, they're only forty kilometres south of us and now they're creating a completely integrated hub.'

'Jusuf, it's Chris. How come they seem to have all this money all of a sudden?'

'That's easy. Are you both sitting down?' Chris and James looked at each other, both with their eyes wide open. Jusuf carried on. 'Here's what I think; a full trade delegation came over here from China earlier on in the year. It's rumoured they are expanding their silk road and investing heavily in the infrastructure of the country. Not only is money flowing into Turkey, but the speed of these developments is astonishing. God knows what Turkey has promised China in return, but this is the current thinking and it's the only explanation I can come up with for this latest development. We need to consider how we react to this from our own company point of view.'

Chris and James both nodded. James cleared his throat. 'Okay, Jusuf, I'll come as soon as I can so we can make plans. Thanks for letting us know.'

After the call, Chris called Rachel. 'Rachel, can you see if you can find any details of a Chinese trade delegation visiting Turkey this year.'

James frowned at Chris. 'I didn't see this coming.'

Chapter 12

Huang and his fellow group of dissidents were confined below deck in the dark and damp cargo hold for some time as the Chinese freighter approached land. They huddled together trying to console their fellow student, Haoyu, who constantly whimpered. It was clear his mental state was deteriorating rapidly. Lingdao also appeared to be agitated, constantly telling him to be quiet.

The vessel pitched and tossed through the rough Tyrrhenian Sea northwards towards the port of Livorno on the north-west coast of Italy. As the ship laboured past the Island of Elba in the darkness, one hundred kilometres south of Livorno, it seemed ironic that this was the island where Napoleon Bonaparte, also a prominent political revolutionary, was exiled between 1814 and 1815.

The freighter tried to increase its speed so it would not miss its time slot for docking at Livorno. If they missed that, this would be a major setback for the mission. All plans had been made to coincide the docking with the arrival of

CHAPTER 12

the *Constellation II*, the Macrae-Claybourne oil tanker. As the group clung tightly together in the pitch-black darkness, Haoyu became silent.

Huang began to hear the revs of the diesel engines slow down. The ship had ceased its slow pitch and roll, but it felt a long time before it gently jolted against what he presumed to be the dock. They waited in the darkness below until a shout from above signalled them to go above deck. When light finally shone through into the cargo hold, they all stood shakily trying to maintain their balance. All except Haoyu. He was dead.

Lingdao looked down on the slumped body. 'Okay, wait here till I get back and get these crew coveralls on!'

After several minutes, Lingdao was back. 'We'll have to leave Haoyu here. He will be taken care of.' He paused for a moment and put his finger in the air. 'We all have to act normally. Remember when people act openly and confidently, they appear normal, and no one questions them. It's only when we behave furtively that suspicions are aroused. Act as though you are regular deck hands and don't speak to anyone. If we're stopped, I will do the talking. Now follow me!'

He led the group of five together with his two assistants off the ship down the steep metal gangway and onto the concrete quayside beneath the giant outreach cranes stretching out either side of them. After so long, it felt strange for Huang to walk on solid ground, his brain still trying to compensate for stability with the constant uneven movements of the ship. He felt his heart starting to race and his legs felt heavy and stiff. He noticed the others in his group starting to sweat, several of them darting their eyes back and forth. This was the first time they were out of China since Qincheng. They could easily be questioned by the Italian police and sent back home where they would certainly face the death penalty.

Under bright sodium lights all kinds of trucks and forklifts buzzed around them. The port was a noisy living city operating twenty-four hours per day with pungent diesel fumes and salt-coated dust pervading the air. They each carried duffle bags containing dried food and water. Lingdao and his two assistants, Tang and Jin appeared to carry heavier bags.

'Wait here. I'll be right back.' Within minutes Lingdao was back driving a white Fiat minibus. Huang was astounded. How was it that this man could know so much? It wasn't just his knowledge of the ship they would take over, but how did he know so much about docking times and schedules? And just when you thought that you'd have to run and hide within the port, he rolls up driving a minibus!

After getting into the bus, Lingdao drove them along the jetty and entered onto a perimeter road that was busy with other port vehicles entering and leaving the docks. He seemed to know exactly where he was going. Huang just sat there with a slack jaw. They drove past vast warehouses full of crates and other assorted goods; rows and rows of twenty and forty-foot containers and along another quay where they entered an area of oil storage tanks. He drove confidently down a narrow service road in between the giant circular tanks. The road was lined full of metal pipes leading from the docks to the tanks. They passed a sign that said, 'St Stefano Basin' where three large oil tankers were moored securely alongside the quay. Their giant hulls were all painted black giving the whole scene a sinister feeling. Fixed pipes running up to the ships were connected with them by a series of flexible pipes acting as umbilical cords to load the crude oil from the adjoining storage tanks into the vessels.

CHAPTER 12

Lingdao parked the bus next to a portacabin marked *Security*. Huang and his group all widened their eyes in disbelief. They knew enough English to know what *security* meant. Would this be the end of their journey? Instead, a security officer came outside the office and met Lingdao. Lingdao gave him a thick package. The officer opened it, peered into it, nodded and went back inside. As he opened the door, they could see there were a group of security officers seemingly on a break. Huang and his group sat in silence until Lingdao returned.

'Follow me!'

They exited the bus and followed him down a metal step ladder at the side of the quay and onto a small open launch with a covered cabin at the bow. The five men were ushered to the front of the craft under the canopy. No words were spoken. Lingdao and his two assistants cast off and steered the boat slowly and quietly alongside the hulls of the tankers until they came to the *Constellation II*, the Macrae-Claybourne tanker that they would take over nearer the coast of England. In the shadows of the ships' giant hulls, they remained out of sight of the decks. Being in a secure area, most of the shipping company security personnel were stationed at the top of the gangways on the land side of the ship.

Huang was the first to clamber unsteadily off the launch. He stretched his hands out to try to cling to the top of the huge rudder protruding above the water at the stern of the ship. As he lunged upwards to grab the top, his feet slipped, and he was left hanging by one hand swinging perilously between the gap of the launch and the rudder. Tang darted forward and quickly hoisted him higher so could get a firm purchase on the vessel. One by one, Tang helped the group up into the rudder stock, the narrow passage containing the thick steel rod that connected the rudder to the steering gear in a room above. They dragged their duffle bags behind them. Once they were all on board Lingdao, took off quietly in the launch. Huang assumed he was returning the launch to its original berth.

Lingdao tied the launch up where they had found it. He checked his watch. It was 12:30am, which would mean it was 11:30pm the night before in London. He took out his burner phone and called Peng Zheng on his secure line.

'In position and down to five members. I had to terminate one of the group.'

'Okay. You have the go-ahead to complete the operation to measure the exact tactics and response times of the British authorities. Once you've taken control of the ship, kill all the dissidents before the British forces regain control of the vessel to make it look like they killed them. To do this, you already have the same pistols the British Special Services use, the Sig Sauer P226. We can't afford for any of the students to report they were sprung from Qincheng jail or be able to identify you. Arrangements have been made to get you, Tan and Jin off the vessel before the counter terrorism forces arrive. I will need you then to lie low here in the UK afterwards awaiting further instructions.'

Lingdao returned to *Constellation II* and joined the group in the steering gear room. He was soaking wet and must have accessed the rudder by swimming from the dock.

The steering gear room was located aft and on the starboard side of the ship. It was a large room containing the steering rams, hydraulic pumps and valves as well as an emergency generator. A constant hum from the primary generators reverberated throughout the hull. The floor felt hot and sticky. Adjoining the stuffy room was a separate stock room that contained large fifty-gallon drums of oil and hydraulic fluid. Wrenches and specially shaped tools were hung on a large tool board fixed to one of the walls. A large amount of fire extinguishers were grouped together just inside the stock room.

Lingdao signalled for the group to move to the rear of the stock room and huddle behind the drums. They managed to all squat down and used their duffle bags for pillows. Huang shot a quick glance at Lingdao, Tang and Jin in the subdued light of the oil store. His head was full of doubts. How come Haoyu had died so suddenly? How could the Italian security officers look the other way? How did Lingdao know so much detail about the port, timetables and routes of ships? He surmised the only explanation for their safe passage was bribery and a highly developed organisation, certainly more than a group of enthusiastic dissidents. Who were the powerful people behind their escape from Qincheng and how could they manage to get this far without such intelligence and confidence? It all seemed so perfect, almost like a precise surgical military operation. The journey on *Constellation II*, once they left the port, would take approximately seven days, that is, if they weren't discovered first.

Peng Zheng picked up his secure line in the Chinese embassy located in Portland Place, London and called General Shen. It was 6:45am in Beijing.

'Our hijacking operation will soon begin. We will then know

what methods the Brits use to counter this type of external threat and how long it will take them to respond. Once the tanker has been taken over by Lingdao and his team, the British reaction time should be their fastest, given they have an SAS and SBS base close by. This will set the benchmark we need to measure ourselves against to find out how much time we have when we eventually take over their other strategic seaports around the world.'

'Keep me posted, Zheng. I need every detail. Monitor all news channels and have your UK inside contact note each timeline. We need to precisely know their reaction times, both planning, launching into action and completion of the exercise.'

Peng Zheng held the secure line phone close to his mouth. 'I will, General Shen. My men are already in position.'

───────────────────

'Shush...'

Huang and his comrades had been woken gently by Lingdao. His head felt muzzy in the poorly ventilated stock room. They had spent much of their time dozing off while hiding in the oil and equipment stock room during the voyage. A look-out was always posted giving them an early warning should anyone enter the steering gear room. When all was quiet outside the stockroom, they were able to stretch and take a few steps to ward off stiffness.

Lingdao and his two assistants held their pistols close to their sides. He whispered, 'Okay, now's the time to spring into action. Remember your instructions and stay calm. Each of you, grab those lashing bars off the tool board and bring them with you. Use them as a weapon if you have to. Most of the crew will be in the mess room at this time. Group one, led by Tang will take them over, herd them into the bosun's locker and lock them up in there. Group two, led by Jin, will round up the crew in the engine room and I will then lead group three with Huang and Yan to take over the bridge.' They split up and followed their memorised plans.

Huang felt his breathing quicken and his hands starting to sweat. He noticed that his friend, Yan, looked agitated, his eyes darting in all directions. Conversely Lingdao looked calm, his actions being decisive and methodical. Lingdao, Huang and Yan followed group two who already had the engineers in the engine room under control. Inside the cavernous room were two enormous throbbing diesel engines, the size of which he had never seen before. Two massive rotating propeller shafts were surrounded by generators, compressors, valves and a patchwork of horizontal and vertical pipes. The heat, vibration, noise and smell of diesel was intense.

Huang gulped for air and struggled to follow Lingdao up a flight of metal steps and along a maze of suspended metal gantries and crosswalks high above the turbines. After climbing another set of non-slip metal steps, they emerged slowly through an outside hatch onto the main deck just below the bridge at the stern. The sudden light made their eyes narrow to crinkled slits. They waited for their eyes to adjust to the harsh daylight. The sea air felt fresh. Lingdao checked both port and starboard deck walkways. All was clear. He then led them through another watertight hatch and took another flight of stairs and burst onto the bridge.

'Hold it right there!'

The captain turned around, both his bushy eyebrows shooting up. 'What the…?' Lingdao anchored his gaze on the captain pointing his gun at his head. 'Shut up and listen. We're taking over your ship. Do as you're told, or you will die.'

Huang and Yan covered the two other officers on the bridge with their lashing bars held ready.

Captain Moretti, a thickset man with a full grey beard put up his hands. 'Don't harm my crew! Please stay calm, we're in a busy waterway with one million barrels of crude oil aboard and if this ship is wrecked it would be a major disaster. He turned to his other officers. 'Keep on your stations and keep her on course but slow her down to fifteen knots.'

'We don't care about you or your ship. We want asylum!'

Lingdao shifted to the side and noticed the navigation officer slide his hand behind himself and press a button on the control console of the ship. He knew exactly what the officer was doing. It was an alarm signal to the rest of the ship as well as the radio room. He knew within minutes that the coast guard would know that the ship had been hijacked.

The captain stood firm. 'What is your name?'

'It doesn't matter what my name is. I am now in charge of this ship!'

'Listen, if you want asylum, we will take you to the authorities when we reach port safely. There is no need to resort to violence. How many of you are there?'

'I don't believe you! You could be fined and return us to our homeland. Many people like us disappear as crews capture their stowaways and just throw them overboard to die so we don't cost you any money or hassle.'

Captain Moretti shook his head. 'I know that is true, but Macrae-Claybourne Logistics is not one of those companies. I give you my word.'

CHAPTER 12

Lingdao raised his voice. 'I don't believe you. Hold your ship's present position!'

'I can't do that! It's too deep to anchor here and if we stop the engines we will drift onto the rocks on the east coast of the Isle of Wight.'

'So, keep the ship on low speed and circle until I give you further instructions. Remember I have your crew under my control and if you don't do as I say, they'll all die!'

Lingdao turned to Huang and Yan. 'Come, follow me!'

They followed him off the bridge and swiftly descended the stairs to the aft deck. Just as Huang came through the deck hatch he heard several gunshots from inside the ship.

He looked at Lingdao. 'What's going on?'

Lingdao shoved Yan against the deck rail and levelled his gun to his head. He fired and Yan dropped straight to the deck. Huang froze momentarily. 'What the...?' Then he flung himself at Lingdao, swinging his lashing bar towards Lingdao's head, but Lingdao side-stepped him and pushed him down. He dropped the lashing bar and fell flat on the deck. He looked up. 'I don't understand.'

Lingdao smiled and fired his gun. Huang felt a jolt of pain in his chest and blackness engulfed him.

Chapter 13

'You sound worried, James. Is everything alright?'

James put his cell phone down slowly on the dashboard. He continued to look blankly at the windshield instead of through it. Sarah stole a quick glance at him while she drove her Land Rover Defender down the A34 towards Newbury. They were on their way to visit Highclere Castle where Sarah had started her project to authenticate plans to restore the ceilings and walls in both the Great Hall and the Library. She'd been so taken aback by the elegance of the castle, nestling in the beautiful rolling hills dotted with lush green pastures and forests, that she wanted James to take a day off work and see it for himself. They had scarcely had any time together for a while.

James gave a half-smile back to Sarah. 'How come I can never hide anything from you?'

Sarah laughed. 'Woman's intuition! Don't forget we've been together for sixteen years. If I don't know you by now, I never will!'

'Ah, that's it, is it? Then how come I can never figure out

CHAPTER 13

what you're thinking!' Before Sarah had time to respond, he quickly jumped in again to counter a jab that he knew would come. 'Just joking!'

'So come on. What's up?'

'Maybe I'm just being sensitive, but remember I mentioned when I was visiting our Istanbul terminal last week that I saw a lot of construction and development at the port of Ambarli, just south of us?'

'Yes I do.'

'Well that was Jeremy Hirons of MI6 on the phone calling me back after I told him about my visit. I mentioned I suspected the Chinese were pumping a huge investment into the port.'

'Well isn't that just fair competition? You will always have competition and it's no secret anymore that the Chinese are expanding their silk road.'

'Normally I would agree but it's more serious than that. There was a Chinese trade delegation that visited Turkey earlier this year and the minister for Trade and Development was a man by the name of Wu Shen. Jeremy just confirmed that this man is also known as General Shen. He's the man who controlled Hugh Stanfield. Also, the same man that was responsible for sabotaging our company and the very same man that was handling Ben Armstrong of Pair-Tree Capital. I can't help thinking we're in the crosshairs again.'

'Will they go after him?'

'They can't. Apparently, he now has diplomatic immunity. Personally, I'd love to get my hands on him after what he's done to us!'

Sarah sighed aloud, gripping the steering wheel tightly. Her bottom lip started to quiver. She was quiet for a few moments and then burst out. 'You know, James, we can't go on living like this. We must put all this behind us. God knows, we owe it to our family! I wanted today to be special; for you to see what I was doing at work and to have a lunch together to sort out our problems.'

James crossed his arms. 'I know, I know but...'

'No buts! Leave it alone or you'll wreck all our lives, okay?'

James uncrossed his arms, looked away and rolled his eyes. 'Okay.'

They crossed over the A34 on a single lane bridge and pulled up in front of an estate surrounded by rough Cotswold stone walls. Sarah lowered her window. The day was clear, and the air was fresh. Two large stone pillars supported a set of heavy, ornate black wrought-iron gates at the entrance of the five-thousand-acre estate. Sarah produced her credentials to the uniformed gateman, and they were allowed to enter. They drove forward on a winding narrow lane through a wooded area that eventually opened out into undulating hills punctuated by green fields and Lebanon cedars. She pulled up on an incline next to a meadow full of sheep. Down before them stood Highclere Castle.

James gasped. 'Oh my god. It's beautiful and in such a wonderful and grand setting. Someone must have had a great vision to create a building like this. It's like a pillar of stability and tranquillity with all its magnificent turrets and spires.'

Sarah smiled. 'Can you believe the first records of this estate go back to 749. The architect who designed the Houses of Parliament then remodelled the house in the Elizabethan style. That's why I love it so much!'

James gave Sarah an appraising glance, marvelling at her enthusiasm. Architecture was her passion.

He shook his head. 'So what needs doing to it? It looks

perfect from here?'

'It does until you get inside. The castle has over two hundred rooms, many of which are uninhabitable. Water has damaged the ceilings in the Great Hall and Library. I have a feeling this will be my biggest project yet. Let's go and I'll show you.'

James and Sarah entered the Main Hall after passing through a grand entrance hall. James craned his neck back and just stood there with his mouth and eyes wide open. He turned around to take in the full scope and size of the room. 'Phew! That ceiling must be fifty feet high. No wonder they called you in with all these Gothic marble arches and intricate detail and look at that majestic oak staircase leading up to the galleries!'

Sarah beamed. 'Glad you came, James?'

James just shook his head. 'I've never seen such splendour! I see now why you are so taken with this project.' He was about to add something else when he felt his cell phone vibrate in his pocket. 'Excuse me a moment. I need to step outside.'

James was back inside after five minutes pacing from one foot to the other. 'Sarah, we have to go!'

Sarah was busy talking to two contractors who were overseeing the delicate carvings and stonework. She spun around suddenly. 'What?'

'We have to go now!'

She turned back to her surprised co-workers. 'I'm so sorry. Please excuse me for a moment.'

As she stepped towards James, she tilted her head. 'What's the hurry, James, can't it wait? We just got here!'

'No! I'll explain on the way.'

'Way where?' She stamped her foot on the oak floor. 'You know, James, I'm sick of this. Every time I get something good in my life, like this project, you and your company have to take priority and to hell with everything else!'

'I'm so sorry, Sarah, but this is a life-or-death situation. One of our oil tankers has been hijacked just off the Isle of Wight! The hijackers are armed and the crew's in danger. Chris is already heading down there.'

Sarah put her hand to her open mouth.

James flushed as he carried on. 'Listen, a police escort is on its way to take us to Poole, Dorset. That's where the headquarters of the SBS, the Special Boat Service, is. They're planning a commando raid and I can help them with my knowledge of the crew and the ship.'

Sarah looked up. 'James, I'm so sorry!' She stood silent for a minute and then let out a long breath. 'Look, you'll have to go on your own. Even if I did go with you, there's nothing I can do. Remember, once I'm finished here, I have to pick up the children from school. Chris can bring you back.' She leaned over and kissed him. 'Good luck! Call me as soon as you can.'

As low grey clouds swept in from the west and rain started to fall, James arrived at the SBS naval base headquarters in Hamworthy, Poole. The police car bringing him at high speed had taken just under an hour to complete the journey. High-wire fences capped with coils of barbed wire surrounded the base of non-descript low-rise buildings. They were stopped at the gatehouse but quickly given clearance to enter the base. As they pulled up in front of a plain red-brick, two-storey building, they were met by a tall, well-built man in army fatigues and were led through a series of hallways to emerge into a large operations room. Sea and weather charts covered one wall while a blown-up plan of *Constellation II* covered another wall. A group of SBS men wearing dark green berets with dagger cap badges stood scrutinising the plan.

'Mr Macrae. I'm Colonel Jarvis of the MoD. We have a situation developing on one of your cargo ships, *Constellation II*, just off the Isle of Wight. Your captain, Moretti, has issued a mayday distress call to the coastguard to say that a group of armed stowaways have taken control of the ship. The ship has since started to weave in a haphazard manner off its course. We are not only worried about the loss of life, but if this ship goes aground on the Isle of Wight, it will be one of the biggest environmental disasters of all time.'

James took a deep breath and remained standing. 'I see.' He shook his head and looked directly back at the colonel.

Jarvis continued. 'The local police were alerted and, in turn, have contacted us in the ministry. The home secretary and prime minister are being contacted as we speak. We need your advice on the layout of the ship and the personnel involved. We are already preparing plans for an assault to take over the ship once we are given the go-ahead from Westminster.'

James clenched his fist. 'I see you already have plans of the ship. You need to know this is an older tanker and is due to be replaced by the end of the year. Because she only tramps between Southampton and Livorno, both being fully secure ports, for these reasons, we did not allocate the expenditure to install security grills in the rudder trunk or between decks. Access within the ship is open on all decks and will be an advantage for your men.'

'Good to know. How many crew on board?'

'There will be the regular twenty-two personnel. The master, Vincenzo Moretti, three officers, four engineers and electricians and fourteen ratings.'

'I see. What we do know so far is that the captain and two of his officers are confined to the bridge. We also understand the third officer has locked himself in the radio room. From what we can gather, the rest of the crew has been taken prisoner and confined in the bosun's locker. We do not know how many hijackers there are.'

'Have they made any demands?'

'They are claiming they are seeking asylum. Your captain has been able to let us know that he offered to bring them safely ashore, but they refused to lay down their arms, fearing they will be dumped overboard. Please stay here while I address the men.'

Colonel Jarvis turned around and addressed Officer Commander Alan Jones and the members of the Counter Terrorism Squadron, a Special Forces unit of sixteen men. Each man was already kitted out for action for the well-rehearsed classified protocols.

'While it is clear that the captain and crews' lives have been threatened, we still do not know if this is a clear case of hijacking or an attempt by these individuals to seek political asylum. Whatever, once we get the go ahead from Westminster you are to treat this as a potential hijacking. The lives of the crew and the safety of the ship are our concern. There will be two assault groups. Commander Alan Jones will lead the first group towards the bridge and ensure the safety of the captain and his officers. The second group will make their way from the stern to flush out the stowaways from there.'

James stood wide-eyed to the side of the men decked out

CHAPTER 13

with their black SBS frogman kits, M16 assault rifles and underwater pistols. He had been allowed in for the briefing in case there were any questions.

The phone rang. Colonel Jarvis picked it up and turned to face his men. 'Okay, we have the green light!'

In a rapidly darkening sky and deteriorating weather conditions, the two SBS groups split up and took off on two separate Merlin helicopters. Sheets of torrential rain cascaded down at ever-changing angles as the wind twisted and turned from the west. Two Chinook helicopters also took off, diving into the pummelling rain, ready to lower two rigid inflatable boats for additional SBS members to carry out an assault on the ship from the sea using grappling irons. This group would also seal off the rudder trunk in case any of the stowaways tried to exit the ship through there. Snipers were added to the assault force circling in Wildcat helicopters to provide additional assistance to the raiding crew should they need it.

As the two Merlin helicopters approached the ship in the darkness, the rain and wind intensified. Captain Moretti, still on the bridge, had been instructed to turn off all lighting on the ship. A three-mile radius surrounding the ship had been cleared of all other shipping while police boats circled the ship from a distance. Their blue lights were flashing and acting as a distraction to the hijackers. The Merlin helicopter with Officer Commander Alan Jones descended quickly out of the low cloud ceiling and hovered over the forward mooring deck of the rolling and pitching vessel. The pilot, a veteran of the SBS, instinctively compensated for the heavy gusts of wind that tried to toss the helicopter off its position. The SBS members stealthily fast roped themselves onto the deck. They quickly spread across the breadth of the ship and crouched low, carefully studying their surroundings. Within seconds of the first Merlin descending, the second Merlin helicopter descended low over the aft mooring deck.

There was total silence within the group. With practised procedures, everyone knew their positions and responsibilities. Once the deck was secured, the first group descended below through the forward hatch leading down to the A and B decks to make their way to release the crew incarcerated in the bosun's locker. Alan Jones crouched low with his back to the hull amid ship scanning and listening. The muzzle of his M16 assault rifle followed exactly the same careful arc as his eyes. His HPK11 pistol was ready on his hip. This was his preferred weapon of choice at close quarters as it was virtually silent when used out of water and had a range of fifty meters.

Apart from the sounds of the circling Wildcat helicopters there were no other sounds except the heavy rain pounding the deck and superstructure of the vessel. No gunshots and no shouting. Within minutes additional SBS members ascended from their inflatable boats using their grappling irons. They took up positions around the deck. Both SAS groups appeared on the deck. Commander Alan Jones met the second group leader. 'Sir, the ship is secured, and the crew has been set free. All the hijackers are dead. Thing is, they were dead before we got here. None of us has even fired a shot. Doesn't make any sense!'

There was a yell from the aft deck. 'Sir, this one's still alive, barely.'

Chapter 14

'The state of this old workshop is the best I've ever seen it.'

Nick Northrop smiled and nodded his head. 'Thank you, Mr Stevens. We have everything ready in the new location. I'm just waiting for your go-ahead.'

'Let's go into your office before we continue our tour of the new facilities.'

Wilfred Stevens took over Northrop's office chair and beckoned him to sit in front of his own desk. He took off his glasses, polished them meticulously and put them down. 'Nick, I have to say that I am most impressed with your transformation of this department since you started. Not only is workshop efficiency up by over thirty percent, but you are also constantly under budget. If I couple that to the number of accident-free days and general morale, then this is a breath of spring air around here. With your military background, I knew you could do it!'

'You're very kind, Mr Stevens, but I'm just doing my job.'

Stevens picked up his glasses from the desk and twirled them around. He opened his mouth to say something but put on his glasses instead.

'Come on, Nick. Let's go and inspect the new workshop.'

As they pulled into the entrance, Stevens tapped Nick on the shoulder. 'Stop here a moment. I need to see the whole empty yard before we bring in all the equipment and clutter the place up. Fifteen acres can look pretty small once all our gear is moved in here!'

The black tarmac yard was laid out in a one-way system of white lines and arrows with the entrance and exit, both controlled by a single gatehouse. Separate parking spaces were allocated for vehicles awaiting service, work-in-progress vehicles and those that were ready for operation. The large central workshop with its twenty drive-through, eighty-feet bays; each had plenty of shunting space around it. Each bay had fifteen-feet roller shutter doors and was well equipped inside with workshop tables and computer terminals. Space was available for all the technicians to bring in their own tools and storage cabinets. Bright-white lights shone down from the roof giving the whole workshop a light and airy feeling. A large 'safety first' sign dominated the wall to the office and parts department.

'You've done it again, Nick. This is thoroughly well organised. I know I resisted your idea of a fully staffed gatehouse since I consider them unproductive workshop staff. I'm a stickler for only having the barest of overheads, as you know.'

'Yes, I'm sorry that I pressed you so hard for this, but, with so much dishonesty these days, you can't be too careful. What with the high cost of equipment and tools, we can't afford to have anything stolen.'

'Yes, you were right. This is another age.' Stevens rubbed

CHAPTER 14

the back of his head. 'Nick, I may be retiring soon. Mrs Stevens has had Alzheimer's disease for a number of years, and her condition has now started to deteriorate rapidly. Of course we have known this for a while, but her memory and mobility have gone downhill so fast in the last month, I will need to be there for her.'

'I'm so sorry to hear that, Mr Stevens. Is there anything I can do?'

Stevens swallowed hard and looked at the floor. 'Not on a personal front, Nick, but thank you.' He looked up again at Northrop. 'On a professional front though, I want you to apply for my job. You understand we must post the job publicly as per council policy and procedures, don't you?'

'I understand. And yes, I would like to apply for the job.'

'Good. Then that's settled. Since it is me that will make the final decision, with your background and after what you've accomplished here, you need to know that you will be my personal choice. Just sit tight for the time being. You know what these HR types are like. They seem to take all the time in the world seemingly to justify their existence. Never had a proper job themselves but tell everyone how it should be done – in theory. Can't stand them myself.'

Northrop laughed. Stevens smirked and then continued. 'So, who would you recommend for your replacement?'

Northrop thought for a moment. 'That's an easy decision. I would recommend Colin, the workshop foreman. He knows what he's doing, he's smart and he has the confidence of all the other techs in the shop. There's something else as well. He's prepared to work long hours which is more than I can say for a good many others.'

'Right then. Make sure Colin applies for that position when

it is posted. Okay, next things. The council wants every department to start preparing for the forthcoming G8 visit to Birmingham. I want you to accompany me when I tour all the canals, bridges and sewers in the city centre. You will need to know where everything is. Once that is done, we will liaise with both the police and Special Forces several times before the arrival of the delegates.'

'Very good, Mr Stevens. You can't be too careful these days.'

———————————————

Peng Zheng left the Chinese embassy and headed west on Weymouth Street. He then turned north on Harley Street and doubled back to Portland Hospital using a series of side streets. He made an arranged secure call to General Shen.

'General. We have all the information you requested.'

'Go ahead.'

'Our mission was a complete success. The British believed the Macrae-Claybourne ship was being hijacked and launched a commando raid to protect the ship, just as we had planned. We now have exact response times and know their protocols in dealing with this type of situation. When the time comes for us to act at other ports, we will know exactly how to deal with them.'

'I take it that all the dissidents are dead?'

'Yes, sir. It will take the British a while to work out exactly what happened.'

'Excellent. We will now lie low until after the return of Hong Kong to our country.'

CHAPTER 14

———————————————

'When are you coming home, James?'

'I don't know, Sarah. I'm still here at the SBS headquarters in Poole. The ship's been freed from the hijackers, and she's now safely docked in Southampton. All the crew are safe.'

Sarah replied in a rather gruff tone. 'Well at least that's something!'

'What's wrong? You don't sound very happy.'

'I'm not happy, James! I'm tired and I've had an awful day!' She stopped and bit her lip hard.

All Sarah heard was a loud exhalation of breath on the other end of the phone and then the final, convenient reply: 'Look, I have to go. I'll see you when I get home.'

Sarah shouted back, 'Whatever!' and slammed the phone down.

James stood there completely gobsmacked.

'James, is everything alright?'

James let out another huge gasp. He turned towards his partner.

'Oh hi, Chris. Glad you're here. No. It's just that Sarah wasn't happy and was very short with me.'

Chris tilted his head and squinted. 'That's not like you two. You're the perfect couple!'

'Not tonight we're not. I'll have to sort a few things out when I get home.'

Colonel Jarvis approached them. 'Gentlemen. We're ready to start the debrief.'

James and Chris sat at the back of the operations room. Jeremy Hirons from MI6 had also joined the group.

Jarvis strode to the platform at the front of the room and picked up a clip board. His voice was strong and firm.

'Okay, men, our mission may be over, successfully having saved all members of the crew and ship, however there are more questions than answers at this stage. A full ministerial inquiry will be held later, but let's deal and record the facts that we know so far.' He looked down at the clip board and then focused on his group.

'A distress call came in from *Constellation II*, a British ship in British waters, at precisely 11:35am this morning, asking for immediate assistance. The ship was situated six miles off the east coast of the Isle of Wight. The call stated there were several armed assailants who had hijacked the ship. One group of three armed males stormed the bridge and announced they were taking over the ship. Another group, also armed, took the engine room crew prisoner while a third group overcame the rest of the crew and locked them in the bosun's stores.'

Jarvis paused and then continued to summarise the facts. 'The Hampshire constabulary began coordinating a response with the Maritime and Coastguard Agency and the UK Border Force. A three-mile exclusion zone was established around the ship by 12:30pm while coastguard helicopters circled the *Constellation II*. The vessel was moving aimlessly, raising fears on shore that the captain had lost control. The police then requested military assistance, and by 5:00pm the home secretary and defence minister gave the go-ahead for an operation by the Special Boat Service. We commenced the operation at 6:30pm, storming the tanker by sea and air.'

The colonel referred to his clipboard again. 'Our operation took nine minutes to complete. There was no resistance since all the hijackers were already dead, except one. None of our forces discharged their weapons. The captain and his crew are still on the ship as the police are treating it as a crime scene.'

Jarvis walked from one end of the platform to the other. 'So, here's the first question. Why were the hijackers all dead before we arrived? They appeared to have been shot. Autopsies will be carried out. Any theories?'

Commander Alan Jones stood up. 'Sir, we found a Sig Sauer P226 in the hand of one of the dead men. I'm sure the autopsies will tell us what type of bullets killed the hijackers, but the only weapons my group had with them were M16 assault rifles and HPK11 pistols.'

'Duly noted, commander.'

'Sir, another question that bothers me is that, once we released the crew, they stated that there were a total of eight hijackers. We swept the ship and only found five men. This tells me three men must have escaped before we set up the three-mile exclusion zone. Why leave the ship if they were seeking asylum and was it them that killed their comrades?'

Jarvis nodded again. 'Perhaps the one hijacker you found alive may be able to shed light on this mystery if he survives. Right now, he's in intensive care at Southampton General Hospital.'

'I have another question, colonel.'

'Go ahead, commander.'

'If the assailants wanted asylum, why didn't they stay on the bridge and instruct the captain to take them straight into port instead of ordering him to keep the ship circling?'

'That would have been the most logical thing to do, I agree. It's almost as though asylum wasn't their intention at all. Question is, what was their intention?'

James Macrae put up his hand to attract the attention of

Colonel Jarvis.

'Go ahead, Mr Macrae.'

James stood up. 'Commander Jones, do we know the nationality of the hijackers?'

'Not for sure at this stage, Mr Macrae, but they appear to be Chinese.'

James sat down, looked at Chris and gritted his teeth. He punched his open left hand. James turned to Jeremy Hirons. 'Jeremy?'

'I have no comments to make at this stage, James. My next visit is to the hospital. I will want to question the surviving hijacker first-hand as soon as I'm able. He may or may not have some of the answers we are looking for, if he's still alive.'

Chapter 15

With a loud bang, the Chinese freighter, *Xingshen*, nudged heavily into the quay in the port of Ambarli in the dark hours of the early morning. The whole vessel shuddered under the shock of the impact. Heavy rain pelted the metal decks and cargo hatches in incessant bursts and any noise from the dock machinery was immediately overwhelmed with the blistering pounding of the heavy drops of water. Deck hands struggled to handle the sodden mooring lines as heavy mist swirled around the port lighting fixtures, stifling their penetration into the dense atmosphere. A line of trucks waited patiently below to transport the eagerly anticipated cargo into a secure warehouse nearby.

General Gulnaz stood by the downward sloping windows in the main dock office peering as best as he could through the driving rain at the quayside below him. Only his chosen men were allowed to be present in the port that night. The ship had been delayed deliberately until tonight to unload. Its contents needed to be offloaded with the least risk of prying eyes or intrusive satellites. Large, heavy wooden crates lined with thick sheets of plywood began to be hoisted out of the cargo holds straight onto the flatbed trailers and trucks waiting below. To anyone who happened to look or cared to enquire, they would simply have seen a large consignment of machine tools being transported away.

Once the cargo had been fully offloaded, General Gulnaz made his way to the large warehouse located in the high-security area of the port. Inside, the air was heavy with the humidity rising from the concrete floor drenched with water from the parked convoy of trucks that had brought the cargo inside. A smell of wet rubber pervaded the air. Overhead cranes whirled above his head going back and forth, carefully transferring each crate onto the floor. He stood back, inspecting the cargo and issued instructions to his trusted men to open each crate. Checking the secret cargo manifest, he assured himself that the Chinese shipment of multi-launch short and long-range missile systems was complete. Knowing that he was already five million US dollars better off from the money transferred into his personal account in Cyprus, he had already approved plans for the expansion of China's silk road initiative involving the development of Ambarli port and a new rail network. Mining investments of rare earths, imports of data-processing machines and mobile phones had also been approved for China.

He stood back and took in a long breath. 'Okay, you can now load the Patriot missile and control systems onto the trucks and then transfer them immediately onto the Chinese freighter, *Xingshen*. Do it as quick as you can! The vessel needs to leave well before daybreak.'

Gulnaz strode around the warehouse, dividing the crates up

to be loaded onto several trucks which were then covered with different coloured tarps, each marked with different company names. One by one, at intervals, they left the warehouse and took multiple routes to the same destination.

Outside the port, a Toyota Land Cruiser was parked in the shadows of a narrow alley between two warehouses. The buildings were on higher ground overlooking the port entrance and exit. Jusuf Kahya sat low in the passenger seat straining his eyes as best as he could through the shifting mist and rain. Occasionally he would rub the inside of the windshield with a cloth to clear the condensation. Richard Macrae had hired him many years ago as general manager of the *Haydarpaşa* port in Istanbul. So, when the Chinese started their proxy war of sabotage on the company, Jusuf took it personally. It was as much his company as anyone else's. To this end, once he found out about the rapid development of the Ambarli terminal, he allocated a rotating team of personnel to keep an eye on the terminal and report on anything that would have been considered out of the ordinary. In addition, Jusuf had constantly monitored marinetraffic.com for any Chinese vessels that were approaching Istanbul. He'd spotted *Xingshen* several days before and queried why the ship, coming from Tianjin, had slowed down on its approach to Istanbul. There were no other ships waiting outside the port to unload, so why? When a low-pressure system moved in coinciding with a moonless night, he surmised that maybe they wanted to offload a cargo that might be considered sensitive or even secret.

It had been a long night and a couple of times he felt his eyes becoming heavy. He poured himself another coffee, at least what was left in his Thermos and rubbed his eyes. Trucks were now leaving the dock and taking different routes away from the port. He picked up his camera and took several photos of the trucks and then, to his surprise, he saw an image of General Gulnaz in his long-range viewfinder. The image was grainy, given the dense atmosphere, but it was definitely him. Jusuf knew enough that he was the man pulling the strings of government. 'Interesting, very interesting. What are you doing here at this time of the morning? And what was on the ship *Xingshen?*' He waited for the port to go quiet and then he drove slowly from between the warehouses without his lights on. He had decided not to follow either General Gulnaz or the trucks. That would have been too risky. Instead, he decided to call it a night and head home to his house in the Edremit district, east of the city. He took the E80 eastwards to cross the Bosphorus. Being the main artery across Turkey from Bulgaria in the west to Iran in the east, this six-lane highway was always busy, no matter what time of day it was. Visibility was poor as clouds of spray were thrown up by the many vehicles using the highway. His eyes felt heavy, so he decided to grab a fresh cup of coffee at the Yilmaz Truck Stop. As Jusuf squinted through his windshield, he spotted two of the trucks that left the port earlier pulling into the truck stop. He parked his Toyota and hurried into the café, making sure he was within earshot of the two drivers waiting to be served. All he could hear was, 'It should take us about three hours to get to the Köroglu Mountains.'

Jusuf drove home. He needed to call James and update him on what he had witnessed, but what was in the Köroglu Mountains? He knew the area well but there was nothing there.

———————————————

CHAPTER 15

President Zemin moved uneasily in his office chair and cast a wary eye at General Shen. 'What do you know about this reported hijacking of a Macrae-Claybourne oil tanker Shen?'

Shen remained still in his chair, looked directly back into Zemin's unrelenting stare and calmly replied, 'Sir, intelligence reports are just coming in on this incident.'

'Incident! Is this what you call it! This is headline news that could have negative consequences for our country! I need facts, now!'

'Sir, I have our London team working on this report as we speak. From what we know, a group of five armed men attempted to hijack the ship so they could be landed in Southampton, England to seek asylum.'

Zemin drilled down on Shen. 'Is that all? Don't we have more information than this?'

'Well, President Zemin, it appears there is a possibility these men might have been Chinese dissidents. We are trying to verify this. What we do know is that the ship was stormed by British Special Forces who then killed all the hijackers.'

Zemin scowled. 'This is embarrassing! It's also weak intelligence, general. We should know who these men are, especially if they are Chinese dissidents. Shake up the MSS! I need to make a statement as soon as possible denying any knowledge of this event. Understood?'

'Yes, sir. I agree we cannot have anything thrown in our way before we have Hong Kong returned to us. We must be perfect in every way.'

Zemin raised his voice. 'Get me that intelligence, now!'

'Yes, sir!'

Zemin looked down and jotted a note on the pad in front of him. Shen got up to leave, thinking the meeting was over.

The president looked up. 'Sit down, general. This meeting is not over. I need to know our present situation with Turkey.'

Shen remained straight-faced and sat down again. 'Sir, I have a written report prepared for our regular meeting tomorrow, but I can summarize the facts for you.'

'Do it!'

'We have delivered a full complement of our third-generation short- and long-range missiles to Turkey. They are accompanied with the corresponding guidance and control systems. Of course, they are not based on our latest technology, but the Turks do not know that. We cannot afford for them to share any knowledge of our advanced systems with NATO. In return, their Patriot Missile system and controls are being transported by ship back to us. We can then reverse engineer all their components.'

Zemin nodded sternly. 'Good! Now, what results do we have from the trade mission that you attended in Ankara earlier this year?'

Shen perked up. 'More good news on that front. We have accelerated the upgrades to the port of Ambarli with the installation of new quays, integrated rail systems and handling equipment. Plans are also forging ahead for the silk road high-speed rail system to link Asia and Europe. We are also increasing our exports of computers, machine tools, yarn and iron and steel.' Shen paused. 'Of course, you are aware of the payment of five million US dollars to General Gulnaz.'

'I should be, I authorized it. Very well, Shen, let me have the written report tomorrow.'

Shen stood up again to leave the president's office. As he approached the door, he casually mentioned, 'We have piled substantial debt onto Turkey. They will continue to run a trade deficit with us for years. We'll then need to move in and take full control of all their facilities as payment.'

Zemin continued to look down at his desk already absorbed in a bunch of papers.

———————————————

James drove slowly home through the narrow Worcestershire winding lanes. The late afternoon sun was already low in the sky and the air was starting to turn chilly. Tall hedgerows cast dark, sinister shadows across his path. The musty smell of wet autumn leaves managed to find its way into the car, only darkening James's mood. Not even the song 'Start It Up' by blues singer Robben Ford could lift his spirits.

He'd stayed in Poole the previous night and then returned to Birmingham with Chris the following morning. They'd both been allowed to speak with Captain Moretti, however, there were no further revelations on what had happened on board to lead to the deaths of the stowaways. The one surviving member of the group would probably be the only way to unlock the truth as to what had taken place. Both James and Chris had been sworn to secrecy about this fact.

He'd tried to call Sarah several times, but she'd not picked up. After the abrupt conversation on the phone the previous night he wondered what kind of reception he would receive. He turned into the gravel drive, parked his car in the garage and grabbed his briefcase. As he walked through the mud room into the kitchen, Sarah had her back to him packing some clothes into a bag. Mia and Olivia sat opposite her with long, glum faces.

'Hi, everyone, I'm home!'

There was a stony silence like a heavy wet blanket smothering the entire room. He moved closer to Sarah to give her a hug. She turned halfway towards him and exclaimed, 'Don't touch me!' As she turned, he could see that her eyes were red and puffy. Her stare bore into him like a set of laser guided missiles. She spoke directly to the girls, 'Mia, Olly, please leave us.' Mia and Olivia slumped out of the kitchen and went up to their bedrooms.

James's eyes widened. 'What's wrong?'

'Yesterday, you left me high and dry and then I got a call from the school to pick your son up after he was suspended. Mason got into a fight at school. It seems he was the instigator and the other boy had to have medical attention. I had an earful off the boy's parents and the headmaster!'

'What! I don't believe it!'

'Well, you better believe it, because it seems this isn't the first time Mason has been unruly.'

'What's brought all this on all of a sudden?'

Sarah raised her voice. 'I'll tell you. It's because Mason doesn't have a father around much these days!'

'Oh! That's unfair. I've been working my ass off trying to get the new company off to a good start and I couldn't have foreseen what happened yesterday.'

'That's right, you've been too focused on your work, and forgotten about your family. If you aren't obsessed with the Chinese undermining you at every opportunity, then you charge off to Canada to open a terminal there. When was the last time we went to Wales?'

James just stood with his mouth open.

CHAPTER 15

'No! You can't tell me, can you? All you do is come home late at night, flop into a chair and then leave early in the mornings. No wonder our children are out of control, they don't have a father!'

'Look I'm sorry. It's just that...'

'Just what! You wanted to know what's wrong. Well, I'll tell you what's wrong. Today, your son was expelled from school!'

'Our son!' He stood motionless for a moment. 'It can't be as bad as that, surely!'

'Really? Of course, you wouldn't know. You're never here! While you've been away, I've spent all yesterday afternoon, last night and this morning arguing with the headmaster. I could have done with some support yet again, but oh no, you're so involved with your beloved company!'

'That's not fair. I had no choice but to leave you yesterday. It was a matter of life or death.'

'Yes, but that's not the only time, is it? Every time something good happens for me, you have to bloody well wreck it. When I want to spend time with you or just even talk to you, you always just have to do this, and you just have to do that!'

'Oh, come on, I've got a business to run! I've worked my ass off to get the new company off the ground.' He was about to continue when Sarah turned full bore on him and cut in. She slammed her hand hard down on the kitchen table.

'You have a company to run! Ha! What about me? I have a company to run as well. I also have to look after our children and the house. I've been trying to tell you about the problem for months, but you never listen to anything I say any more. Either you're preoccupied with work or you're chasing Chinese shadows.' She wiped her eyes with the tea cloth.

'Look, I'm sorry. Can't we work this out now?'

'No! We can't. Today was the last straw!'

James took in a deep breath. 'Where's Mason?'

'Where do you think. In his room!'

James clenched his jaw and went upstairs.

He knocked on the bedroom door. 'Can I come in, Mason?'

There was no reply, so James slowly entered the room. Mason was sitting on his bed looking at the floor. It was obvious he'd heard the row downstairs.

James sat down next to him. 'Do you want to tell me what happened?'

Mason looked away from his father. 'Not really. There's no point.'

'Well, there is for me. I'm going to go to the school and sort this thing out.'

'You're too late. The decision was made by that idiot of a headmaster that I've been expelled.'

James let out a sigh. 'So, what happened?'

'That's easy to answer. I stuck up for a younger and smaller boy who was being constantly bullied by one of the older boys. We got into a fight, and I broke the older boy's nose and knocked him down.'

James remained quiet and nodded. Mason looked up at his father. 'He asked for it, Dad, honest. He's nothing but a bully and a sneaky coward. He went off squealing like a little pig to his parents and the headmaster.'

'So why didn't the headmaster and parents believe you?'

'The headmaster did question the smaller boy, but he denied he was ever bullied because he's so scared of the big boy.' Mason grabbed the bedspread and wrung it in his hands. 'Then the mother of the bully came down to the school spitting blood, defending her poor son. She was hysterical. I suppose it's not surprising because she's known everywhere as a prize bitch.'

James shook his head and drew in a breath. 'Oh dear. I better contact the headmaster straight away.'

Sarah appeared in the doorway. Her voice was quiet and resigned. 'It's too late for that. I spent most of yesterday, last night and this morning arguing for an inquiry into this, but the headmaster just won't budge. One, he's adamant that Mason was the instigator and two, he's intimidated by the bully's parents. Seems they are big donors to the school.'

James stood up and shouted, 'Well I'm not taking this lying down.'

Sarah shook her head. 'There you go again, not listening to me. This is not all. Mia and Olivia have been picked on for being Mason's brother and sticking up for him. The school's doing nothing for them. I told you James, I can't take this anymore. It's over. I'm going to separate from you for a while and take the children with me to Wales.'

James stood there; his mouth wide open. 'Bloody hell, Sarah! You can't do that! You can't just up and leave!'

'I can and I will!'

James put both of his hands on his head. 'Oh god, how did this go wrong so fast?'

Sarah gave him a dismissive flap of her hand. 'My parents will move with me into the house, and I've made preliminary enquiries into a private school in Caernarfon for the children to attend. I'll be able to work in my studio above the garage to complete the work for Highclere Castle.'

James felt tears forming in his eyes and moved towards Sarah with outstretched arms, but she ducked around him. She turned to Mason. 'Come on, Mason, the girls are already in the car. Let's go.'

Chapter 16

'Has our hijacker recovered consciousness yet?' Jack Fox, the MI6 director, asked.

'No, sir. Not yet.' Jeremy Hirons stood up from his bedside hospital chair. He looked down at the still unconscious patient lying flat on his back. An oxygen mask covered his face, while a blood pressure monitor measured readings constantly. 'He was operated on last night; the bullet was extracted and has been sent away for a ballistics report. He's lost a lot of blood, but the doctors believe he will make a full recovery.'

'Good. Make sure no one knows that this man is alive. We've released a report to say all the hijackers were killed. From the evidence we have from the police report, it's clear there were eight hijackers in total. The ship has been swept clean which means the three fugitives escaped before we imposed the three-mile cordon around the vessel.'

'Have you received the ballistics report from the SBS yet, sir?'

'I have and it confirms that none of the Special Forces fired any of their arms. These stowaways were dead before the ship was stormed.'

Jeremy paced around the private hospital room. 'Based on this information, I believe this was a targeted crime, the purpose of which I'm not clear on at this stage.'

Jack Fox nodded. 'I agree. Stay there, keep the room guarded and as soon as this man wakes up and he's given clearance to leave, let's move him to the safe house. For all we know the three other fugitives could be in the UK now, following up on their operation. There's more to this than meets the eye.'

———————————————

'Holy shit, James, you look like crap! What's wrong?'

'Come into my office, Chris.' He closed the door behind him. James stood still and stared down at the floor. 'Sarah's left me and taken the children off to Wales.'

Chris's mouth opened. He stepped towards him and put his hand onto James's arm. 'Oh god, James, I'm so sorry. I know Jenny had mentioned that Sarah felt under pressure with her job and looking after the family. It'll be alright, mate. She'll come round! Is there anything I can do?'

James felt tears forming in his eyes. 'Not really. I'm resolved to leave things as they are, at least for a short while. Sarah needs a break from me, in fact, she deserves it. Whatever has happened is, honestly, my fault. I've had all night to think about it and I see that now. I've ignored the family and spent too much time focused on the company. I know we have a lot to deal with in the next little while, but I'm going to have to find a way to get Sarah back and lead a more balanced life after that.'

Chris puffed out his cheeks. 'This is the last thing I ever expected to hear from you two. Do you want me to get Jenny to call her, James? Maybe we can help smooth the waters between you?'

James put his hand on his heart and looked closely at his partner. 'That's kind, Chris, but let's just leave things as they are for the time being. It's more complicated than that. Sarah's angry because I haven't been there for them, and Mason was expelled from school yesterday. There's a lot to unravel, but I believe it will take time. Sarah needs space too.'

'Alright, James, but let me know if there's anything, and I mean anything, I can do. Come to think of it, you and I need to let others take up some of the workload that we've set for ourselves. We've both been driving hard recently.'

James frowned. 'That's for sure. I know we have great staff who we can hand work off to but Rob Bisset and Janet have their hands full implementing the next step in our new logistics system. Let's face it, that's our competitive edge right now. As for Canada, only you and I can drive that new opportunity forward. Maybe, once we're over that, we can delegate more and take some breathing time.'

Chris nodded in agreement. 'You know, it's not just that either. Any time a perceived threat comes from China, or from anyone else for that matter, you and I need to be in the front trench ready for anything.'

'That's just it, and with the hijacking and news that Jusuf is bringing in from Istanbul, how can we delegate that? We both need firm hands on the tiller.' James looked up for a minute. 'That reminds me, Jusuf is waiting for a return phone call from both of us.'

CHAPTER 16

Chris pressed his lips together. 'Alright, let's call him back now. Then you and I need to leave for the airport for our meeting with Angus MacNeil in Halifax.'

James and Chris sat around the conference phone in James's office. Jusuf's voice was firm and clear.

'So that's what I witnessed last night outside Ambarli terminal. To me, to dock a ship as they did last night in those adverse weather conditions after delaying her entrance to the port during good weather leaves me wondering what was being offloaded, or even loaded for that matter. Couple that to the presence of General Gulnaz and then the trucks departing to an area of mountains and forests where there's absolutely nothing. Something's clearly not right.'

James looked at Chris. 'I agree. It does sound fishy. Keep on it, Jusuf, but for heaven's sake, be careful. Our enemies are both cunning and dangerous.'

James pressed the button on the conference phone to end the conversation. 'What do you think, Chris?'

'I don't like it either. A Chinese freighter, strange time of day, General Gulnaz and trucks going to an obscure destination. Hmmm. I think you need to call MI6. This is something they should hear about. Maybe they can make more sense out of it than we can.'

James picked up the phone again. He tried to call Jeremy Hirons but had to leave a message. Five minutes later he received a return phone call.

'James, Jack Fox. Jeremy's tied up right now. We're still trying to figure out what happened on the *Constellation II* hijacking. Is that why you're calling?'

'Hello, Jack. Partly, to see if there have been any further developments with your enquiries?'

'Not so far, James. We're waiting to speak to the one survivor. Of course, you're sworn to secrecy on this. Officially there were no survivors.'

James replied immediately, 'Of course.'

Fox continued. 'We're also appealing for anyone who took photos or video around the ship that day, particularly before the cordon was put in place.'

'I see. Let me know if there's anything further we can do from our end. Now, the other reason I called is there's been some suspicious activities around the port of Ambarli in Istanbul.' He hesitated for a moment. 'That is, Chinese involvement.' James relayed all the information Jusuf had passed on.

Fox grunted. 'I see. What was the name of the mountain destination those trucks were headed for?'

'The Köroglu Mountains.'

'Alright James, we'll keep you posted on the hijacking inquiry and look into what's going on in Turkey. This could be yet another attempt by the Chinese to redress the balance of power.'

As James slowly put the phone down, an acute feeling of sadness and depression overcame him. He felt alone and adrift, dreading going home to an empty house.

———————————————

'The preparations for the G8 summit in Birmingham must be well organized in advance of May 1998. We, or should I say you, will have a lot of work to do in the meantime.' Wilfred

CHAPTER 16

Stevens looked at Nick Northrop sitting opposite him in front of his office desk. He tilted his head and gave just a hint of a smile at his subordinate.

Northrop raised his eyelids, quickly analysing the subtlety of the message. 'Does this mean, you have chosen your successor, Mr Stevens?'

Stevens smiled back. 'It does. You should receive official notification in a few days. I'm happy to say the decision to promote you to this position was unanimous. The HR people are clearly on your side. This means you will have a team of people behind you from the get-go. That's going to be very important for us to arrange all the security precautions well before the G8 meeting.'

'Thank you, Mr Stevens. I'm very grateful. So, what are the next steps?'

Stevens picked up his glasses and started to suck on one of the temple arms. He took it out of his mouth, looked at it and frowned. 'Can't get used to not being allowed to smoke my pipe anymore in the offices! Bloody rules and regulations!' He regained his composure and adjusted his seating position. 'At the start of next month, you and I will work alongside each other for the next three months. After that time, I will retire, so it should mean you're on a solid footing.'

Northrop smiled. 'I'll be glad of that and look forward to it. By the way, how is Mrs Stevens doing?'

Stevens exhaled quietly. 'She's holding her own but there's still a marked deterioration in her condition. I'll be sad to leave here, but I know I'm doing the right thing.'

Northrop leaned forward and locked eyes with Stevens. 'You'll be missed by a lot of people.'

Stevens made a mild gesture of opening his hands and

then carried on. 'Okay, next things. The decision for your replacement was not an easy one. We had some excellent applications that HR wanted to push, but I insisted that Colin should replace you in the interests of continuity. It also demonstrates that longevity of service working for the municipality can be rewarded. So, Colin, it is!'

'Thank you, sir! I'm glad. He'll do an excellent job and we already work well together.'

'Right, that's settled then. Now, let's take a walk. I've received the preliminary agenda for the G8 meeting, so I want to start by scoping out the area we need to start working on for security purposes.'

Wilfred Stevens put on his raincoat and trilby hat. Northrop grabbed his jacket and followed him down the staircase underneath the central dome of the council offices. They emerged under the massive columns of the grand entrance overlooking Victoria Square. The paving slabs were starting to steam under the sunshine that had replaced the recent early morning shower.

Stevens stretched his arm out and pointed towards the town hall, a magnificent white limestone building designed in the early 1800s along the lines of Roman architecture. 'Right, let's imagine a large oblong area stretching out to the west to include the International Convention Centre and the canal network alongside it. To the east as far as Snow Hill train station. We will need to check everything that is under and above this area. That means sewers, tunnels, waterways, bridges, roads and pedestrian areas. I have all the detailed drawings and plans in my office. We will need to assign staff to regularly check this area and install security seals on all drainage, sewer covers and access points. You'll be working closely with the police and the army.'

Northrop surveyed the area, turning a complete circle. 'So, what does the agenda for the meeting look like?'

'Well, it's only preliminary at this stage but the G8 leaders will arrive on Friday fifteenth May. There will be a reception and dinner here. On Saturday, the leaders will go to a retreat. I believe it will be at Weston Park in Staffordshire to the north of here. We don't need to concern ourselves with that since it is out of our jurisdiction. Then, that evening they will attend a reception, dinner and concert back here in the symphony hall located next to the convention centre. Most of the leaders will be staying on the top three floors of the Grand Hotel, two minutes' walk from here east on Colmore Row. Then, on Sunday, they will reconvene at the convention centre in the morning before they issue their press release. After that they will leave the city, flying from Birmingham International Airport to their various destinations.'

Northrop turned around again and nodded. 'I see what you mean about the oblong area. It's conceivable then that the leaders could walk everywhere except to the retreat in Staffordshire?'

'Yes, that's a possibility. I know some of the leaders like to mix with the public. President Clinton is a case in point, and I believe Boris Yeltsin is another. Our Prime Ministers also love the spotlight so yes, I think you're right.'

'So will all the leaders stay at the Grand Hotel?'

'Not sure yet, but it's all been provisionally booked. I do know President and Mrs Clinton will stay at a separate boutique hotel. Come on, let's walk around to the Grand Hotel and the surrounding roads.'

As they walked along Colmore Row, they passed St Philips

Cathedral on the right, set amongst a lawn-covered graveyard shaded with a canopy of maple and linden trees. Stevens looked hard at the area. 'You see this churchyard, it's right opposite the hotel and would be a potential area for protesters to gather and disrupt the hotel guests. I understand there could be a large number of people gathering to demand the cancellation of debt for poorer countries. The police believe there could be several thousand protesters.'

Northrop frowned. 'In that case we'll need ample fencing to seal off areas to keep them away from the G8 leaders and their wives. I'm beginning to see now why this planning will take well over a year to fine tune.'

'It's good you're a military man, Nick. You will understand better than anybody what needs to be done.'

Northrop smiled to himself. Not only was he now a party to organizing security for the G8, but he could plan his ultimate mission, ensuring complete success. His secret employers and his bank balance would be very happy.

Jack Fox sat alone looking out of his office window on the twenty-second floor of the MI6 headquarters, located on Westminster Bridge Road in central London. The sky was heavy with a cloak of dark-grey clouds enveloping the whole city. Gone were the bright colours of summer. They'd been replaced by dull autumn shades of grey, black and brown. He looked over the rooftops below him, split by large arteries of rail lines feeding into Waterloo station. Traffic

CHAPTER 16

over Westminster Bridge, approaching Big Ben and the Houses of Parliament, moved at a snail's pace. That pace reflected his mood. Results from the enquiries into the hijacking of the Macrae-Claybourne oil tanker were frustratingly slow. Nothing added up. He'd read the internal SBS and police reports but, in both cases, there were more questions than answers. On top of that, there were new reports coming in of increased Chinese activity in Istanbul. He couldn't help thinking that the Macraes were being targeted yet again.

Jeremy Hirons entered the sound and sight-sealed office. 'I've got some news for you, Jack.'

Fox smiled for the first time that day. He knew he could rely on his friend of many years. They'd come up through the MI6 ranks together, both of them enduring some challenging scrapes when operating in the field. Together, they were on first-name terms but when outside the office, they were always formal. If Fox ever needed to bend the rules to achieve his goal, Jeremy was his man.

'Shoot, Jeremy. We need some better news. I've got the PM all over me pushing for more information on this Macrae hijacking business. As we draw closer to returning Hong Kong next year, the pressure's on us to expose any wrongdoing by the Chinese before ownership reverts back to China.'

'Understood. I've just returned from the safe house. Our surviving hijacker is a man by the name of Huang Genjo, at least, that's what he calls himself. It's a long story, but he claims he's a Chinese dissident and was imprisoned after the riots in Tiananmen Square. He was locked up in Qincheng Prison for six years but was then sprung from his cell about two months ago, together with five other dissidents.'

'Interesting. As far as we know, no one has ever been able

to escape from that prison. This is a first.'

'It gets weirder. He claims a dead body was placed in his cell at the same time he was freed. His other five colleagues, if we can call them that, claimed their places were also taken by corpses.'

Jack Fox made some notes on his pad. 'Go on.'

'Huang says they were taken at night, and it seemed the regular guards were not even present. From there, they were taken to a secure house near Tianjin, fed and trained to take over a ship by some kind of a military man and two assistants, by the names of Lingdao, Tang and Jin. These three other men also claimed to be dissidents working on behalf of an influential Chinese group that wanted to set up opposition to the government in Beijing. Their aim was to seek asylum here in England.'

Fox frowned. 'Doesn't make sense. Why threaten the crew to try to hijack the ship. The captain would have brought them here anyway.'

'That's what I said to Huang. He claims that because several thousand illegal immigrants try to make it into this country every year, the publicity of this event would put a spotlight on their cause of setting up an opposition to the Chinese government.'

'Hmmmm, that makes sense. They certainly achieved headlines, but not the right ones!' Fox got up from his desk and stretched. 'So, this Huang also agrees there were eight hijackers?'

'Yes, he does. He said that there would have been nine but another student by the name of Haoyu died on the voyage from China.'

'I see. Did you show him photographs of the four dead

hijackers?'

'I did, and he says the other four were his fellow dissidents that were freed from Qincheng Prison. The three other men who disappeared were the leader and his two assistants. The leader, a man who calls himself Lingdao, was the man who shot Huang and his accomplice Yan after they threatened the captain on the bridge of the ship.'

'What did he tell you about this man, Lingdao?'

'I have descriptions of Lingdao and his assistants, Tang and Jin. Graphics are making up their images right now. It was interesting because Huang got the impression they were military men, even though they wore civilian clothes. They had the posture of being in the forces. He also says that their exercises resembled a military style.'

Fox nodded. 'Lingdao obviously isn't his real name since it means "leader" in Chinese. So, question one. Why replace the six dissidents with six dead bodies in Qincheng Prison?'

'That's an easy one, Jack. The story remains that no one has ever escaped from Qincheng and if none of the regular guards were present that night then this must have been an undercover operation from the word go. That raises another question. Who would have the power to do that?'

Fox rubbed his chin. 'That might be the key question to this whole event.' He carried on. 'Question two. Why did this Lingdao leave the bridge with this Huang Genjo and the other dissident? If you're hijacking a ship, that's your command centre and where your power is over the captain and the crew.' Fox made another note on his pad.

Jeremy referred to his own notes. 'Huang couldn't figure that one out either. The captain had said he would deliver them safely to the authorities and Huang believed him. He did say that Lingdao had seen one of the officers push the alarm button to alert the ship's crew and shortly after that Lingdao ordered Huang and his accomplice to leave the bridge. When they got back onto the deck, that's when they heard gunshots from within the ship and that's when Lingdao shot Yan, the other dissident and Huang.'

'That leads me to another question I have. How did the three men escape from the ship? They were several miles off the east coast of the Isle of Wight so they must have had help from another craft before we sealed the area. Did Huang make mention of anything?'

'No, he didn't but they must have been picked up by a speedboat. Bembridge would have been the closest town on the coast, and I know there's a harbour there. The police are already making extensive inquiries for anyone who might have seen anything.'

Fox rested his elbow on the desk and pumped his fist gently up and down. 'Why shoot the five dissidents, if all eight of them wanted asylum?'

Jeremy was quick to reply. 'To me, there's two agendas here. Huang and the original five colleagues were chosen because they were genuine dissidents. It wouldn't take long to establish that, since their photos would easily have been taken that day in Tiananmen Square. The other three men had another agenda.'

'I think you're right, Jeremy, and those three men think they've got away with it. First, they believe all five dissidents on the tanker are dead, so they think there are no witnesses to their crime. It was made to look like there were only ever five hijackers, since each of the three ships crew groups on the bridge, in the engine room and in the crews' quarters only

CHAPTER 16

ever saw either two or three hijackers at a time. They tried and failed to make it look as though the SBS had killed them all, using a Sig Sauer P226, widely believed to be used by the Special Forces. Thing is, the SBS didn't use that weapon and didn't discharge any guns.'

Jeremy stood up and moved around the office stroking his hair. 'So, two completely different agendas and an operation that would have been planned from someone high up in authority. If we can identify the three other men, maybe that will give us a clue who's behind this and why.'

Jack Fox remained behind his desk. 'You mentioned earlier that Huang said they boarded the Macrae tanker in Italy. Again, someone must have arranged with the regular dock staff there to look the other way. Had to, otherwise it would never have been possible to move from the dry goods harbour to the oil terminal and then access the ship via the rudder trunk. Let's get onto the Italians and see if we can get any footage from their security cameras. It's worth a shot.'

'Will do, Jack.'

Fox moved over to his whiteboard on the office wall, rubbing the nape of his neck. He drew a series of boxes and made headings of the points they had made in the meeting. 'You know how I like to think in pictures, Jeremy.' He started to join some of the boxes together with arrows. 'We know the Chinese have tried to take over the Macrae Shipping terminals before, what if this was a military exercise to see what we would do if a suspect ship approached one of our harbours and how fast we would react?'

Jeremy tilted his head and pursed his lips. 'It's possible. I mean, maybe they thought we would leave them alone and wait for a ransom demand rather than launch a full-blown military assault. At least they now know how we react to such matters and how fast. If that's the case, then this is definitely a military operation. There's only one guy who I can think of who would come up with an idea like this.'

Fox cut in. 'Don't tell me. General Shen.'

'Exactly.'

'Sit down, Jeremy. This is getting worse by the minute. There's more. While you were debriefing Huang Genjo in the safe house, James Macrae called with news on a shipment of suspicious goods arriving at Ambarli port in Istanbul in the dead of night. General Gulnaz was present and afterwards a convoy of trucks left for a destination in the Köroglu Mountains. I need you to fly out there and do some poking around. Liaise with Jusuf Kahya, James's general manager at their terminal. Call James and set it up.'

'Yes, I'll get right on.' He sat for a moment. 'Shen bothers me, Jack. As a military general he has the power to pull a lot of strings but he's also now the Minister of Trade and Development for the Zemin Government. That means he could be behind the Macrae hijacking and these new developments in Turkey. After all, he was there earlier on this year with a trade delegation from China.'

'We're thinking along the same lines. I'll step up our surveillance on the Chinese embassy here. We better make sure our theory is correct before we blow the whistle. The trouble is, time isn't on our side.'

Chapter 17

'You need to pull yourself together, James!'

James snapped back. 'What do you mean!'

Chris turned his gun-metal eyes on his partner and spat the words out. 'Bloody hell, can't you see it? You stink of alcohol; you look like shit, and you acted as though you couldn't care less in the management meeting.'

James ran his hand through his hair. 'Look, I've been up all night, alright? I feel like I'm drowning. Sarah and the children were my life and now they're gone. I've blown everything and now it seems I'm fighting the Chinese all over again. How much more can I take?'

'Well if you ask me, acting like this won't solve the problem! Right now, you're an embarrassment to yourself and the company!'

James gritted his teeth and clenched his fists.

Chris stood firm. 'Sorry, mate, but you needed to hear it from someone and you're my partner.'

'Look, Chris, you and I want this business to succeed, not just for us but for both our sons and daughters if they want it.

But what if the price of success is too high? Is it worth it if we lose our families?'

Chris gave James an unrelenting stare back. 'I'll tell you this. If you don't shape up, you'll lose both your family and this business for good!'

James looked back at Chris, somewhat mystified. 'Look, I'm sorry, but I've been trying to work out how I can get my life back together. Okay?'

Chris let out an exasperated gasp. 'James, you're my partner and my friend and I know how much you're hurting, but you must put this to one side for the time being. You said yourself Sarah needs some space, so give her some. We've also got a big meeting coming up in Canada and are about to make some very important decisions affecting our company going forward.'

James closed his eyes briefly, then looked back at Chris. 'I know. I know you're right. Again, I'm sorry. I seem to be saying that a lot lately, don't I?'

Chris gave James a pat on the shoulder. 'Go and get yourself cleaned up, mate!' He stood back and smiled. 'Come on, we can do this. This is a great opportunity for us to expand into North America with a complete logistics system that is a world leader. Let's hope Angus MacNeil agrees with all our plans and projections.'

James took in a deep breath. 'Right!'

———————————————

'There's definitely something suspicious going on in those mountains, Jeremy.

CHAPTER 17

'You seem very certain of this, Yusuf.'

Yusuf leaned forward in his office chair and looked hard at Jeremy Hirons. 'I am.'

'Okay, before I go and investigate the Köroglu region, take me over to the port at Ambarli so I can get a look at the changes that are taking place there.'

They hopped into Jusuf's Land Cruiser, drove east to the port and took up a position high above the terminal. Jeremy produced a powerful set of binoculars with a tripod stand. He carefully scanned the whole area with them.

'These new developments are bigger than I thought. Looks like they've more than doubled the size of the whole terminal. Seems to me it resembles more of a naval base than a commercial port.' Jeremy adjusted his focus and then started to press a trigger several times on the side of the binoculars. 'Tell me, are those railheads linked to the new high-speed network that's being developed to span Turkey east-to-west?'

'They are.'

'And will this railroad go close to the Köroglu Mountains by any chance?'

'The railroad actually goes to Ankara and to the east beyond, but to the south of the mountains.'

'So, access to these mountains can be made by rail to the south and road, using the E80, to the north.'

'That's right. You know, Jeremy, I've wracked my brains as to why those trucks were going there that night because it's quite a big and remote area.'

'Okay, Jusuf, let's go back to your terminal and then I'm going to go up there myself and take a look around.'

'I don't agree with you, James!'

Angus MacNeil stood tall after poring over the drawings of the proposed extension to his Halifax terminal that James and Chris had brought with them.

James and Chris seated across from him at the boardroom table looked quizzically at each other.

Angus beckoned them to the window overlooking the port. 'Come, see for yourself. If we expand the grain terminal which we discussed the last time you were here, we will need an additional two quays and surrounding area to house the liquefied natural gas (LNG) holding tanks and pipework.'

James drew in large breath. 'You don't think we can utilize the two new quays we've proposed to serve both grain and LNG exports?'

'No, I don't. You see, the US is becoming more self-sufficient in natural gas, which means we need to export more of our Canadian gas to other world markets. From my research, the price for energy is only going to go on increasing. This could be a massive opportunity for both this terminal and Canada.'

Chris turned around. 'But don't you just export grain mostly in the summer and autumn, giving us spare capacity for the two quays to use for LNG for the rest of the year?'

'I wish that were true but as one of the biggest grain exporters in the world, Canada exports huge quantities all twelve months of the year. So, if we are to capitalise on our expansion of the grain terminal and take advantage of the growing export market of LNG, then we need to invest more now, rather than later.'

James sat down again and fiddled with his pen. Chris sat down next to him. 'What do you think, James?'

James curled his bottom lip over the top one. 'I see what Angus is saying, but this will soak up more capital than we thought.'

Angus came and sat with them. 'I believe it will be cheaper in the long run to do all the investment now rather than piecemeal later.' Honestly, if I didn't see the potential, I would never have contacted you in the first place.'

James sank his chin onto his clasped hands. 'Could we get funding from the federal, provincial and municipal levels of government? After all, the construction and operation of these facilities is going to need more labour.'

Angus nodded. 'I've already asked our government representatives and they're looking into it.'

Chris frowned. 'If they work as fast as our government, we might be waiting a long time!'

Angus smiled. 'You might be right. Remember, we work slower here in the colonies than you do at home! There is hope though. After the recent recession, there's a push to reduce unemployment. One thing I can say is that the Liberal government here is focused on reducing unemployment and increasing exports. I'll let you know as soon as I know.'

James was quiet for a while. 'Let Chris and I talk this through tonight and then we can get back together with you tomorrow.'

―――――――――――――――――――

James and Chris walked from the waterfront up into the town of Halifax. They took the pedestrian walkway past St Paul's

Anglican Church and climbed up the steps to Argyle Street.

James looked around. 'Considering Halifax was founded in the mid 1700s and the municipality's growth in the 1800s, I'm surprised at the lack of historic buildings.'

Chris replied. 'Yes, it's all high-rise buildings. Not what I expected. Maybe there are older parts elsewhere.'

'Whatever, let's get some of that seafood we promised ourselves.' They made straight for the Five Fishermen Restaurant.

James looked up at the server. 'I'll have an Alexander Keith's IPA please.'

Chris looked up from his menu. 'Make that two. Nothing like trying the local brew.'

'Well, we have some serious decisions to make, Chris.'

'Yep, we sure do. Honestly, I thought we'd covered every angle before we got here. That was a surprise today!'

'For me too. I guess we don't have the same depth of local knowledge like we do back home. At the same time, I can't disagree with Angus's thinking.'

Chris took his beer off the server and took a gulp. 'Neither can I. It would be cheaper to make this investment now rather than wait. Trouble is, we don't want to overstretch ourselves financially, especially if we have to fight a price war with our expected competition in Istanbul. If we have to finance an additional two quays on top of the two quays we've proposed, then this deal is dead. We can't stretch ourselves that thin.'

'Ummm. Yes, you're right. At least the LNG tanks and pipework would be paid for by the gas company. That would not be an expense for us. Anyway, for now, let's get stuck into some food. I'm starving. I'm going for the seafood chowder to start and then the lobster. How about you?'

Chris looked over the menu again. 'I'm going for the crab

cakes and then this signature dish, the five fish experience.'

While they waited for the main course, Chris looked hard at James. 'Are you going to be alright, mate?'

'How do you mean?'

'Come on, you know what I mean. Sarah.'

James looked wistful. 'Honestly, I don't know. I did manage to speak with her before we left the hotel this morning. She's back in the house in Wales and she's managed to get the children into a good school. She hasn't changed her mind about the separation. She feels she needs it to sort her own life out, away from me and the business. I still love her, always will and, of course, I miss the kids. Even though I've apologised and promised to balance my work and home life, perhaps it's good to give us both some space.'

'You know what they say, James, *absence makes the heart grow fonder.*'

'Well, I hope it's right in our case because it certainly wasn't the case for Charles and Diana. They were separated for two years and now they've just got divorced! I'm certainly going to give our separation a try. After all, what else is there in life. All we want is to love and be loved.'

'Let's drink to that! Come on, let's get stuck in.'

They finished the dinner feeling slightly intoxicated, warm, full and happy.

Chris sat back in his chair, 'Bloody hell, no wonder this place has such a great reputation.

'Got that right! Let's get coffee and resume our chat over the expansion of the terminal. My mind must have been working subconsciously as I've got an idea.'

Jeremy Hirons pulled out of the Budget Car Rental depot at Istanbul's Ataturk Airport in his Toyota Camry and threaded his way out of the complex and onto the E80 trunk road east. He kept his driver's window in the up position. It would take him approximately four hours to make the trip to the town of Bolu where he'd booked himself into the Poi Oberj Kartalkaya, a moderately priced hotel that consisted of separate, self-contained chalets. The establishment was nestled in a forested hillside in the valley leading up into the Köroglu mountain region. He made sure he had his false passport in the name of Anthony Foley, an independent travel writer. There was even an article: 'Great Hikes in New Zealand' published in the magazine *Wanderlust* with his name and photo on it. His passport had the requisite stamps.

It was a pleasant afternoon with a high cloud ceiling, a light breeze and around twenty degrees Celsius. He wore a pair of stout hiking boots and was well kitted out for a walking holiday. In his rucksack, he carried his binoculars, camera, a bird-watching book and an English–Turkish Dictionary. The six-lane highway was moderately busy as it weaved its way eastwards through the outlying towns of Gebze and Izmit. As the towns fell away, the densely tree-lined road continued until Sakarya when the gradient started to increase. Hills began to appear either side of the highway.

Jeremy noticed there were several flatbed trailers carrying heavy loads of steel I-beams and rebars, apart from the normal dry van trucks and trailers. As the gradient increased, the speed of these heavy trucks declined. With more load on the engines, they started to emit black clouds of exhaust fumes. After travelling through an arid region, the valley sides came closer together and the area became greener. He turned right onto Kartalkaya Yolu Road after the town of Bolu onto a narrow two-laned road and started the ascent to his hotel. There were a few houses dotted either side of the route that resembled Swiss-style chalets. As he rounded a hairpin corner, to his surprise, he came up behind a slow-moving truck carrying a heavy load of steel. It was impossible to overtake the vehicle on the winding road. He stayed patiently behind the vehicle and when he arrived at his hotel he drove straight to reception.

'There's your key, Mr Foley. Enjoy your two-night stay. Is there anything else I can help you with?'

Jeremy smiled back at Taahira, the receptionist. 'Yes, there is. I'm here to write some travel articles on the region. Tell me about the Köroglu Mountains. What is there to do here?'

'Actually, it's a beautiful and remote area. Not many people visit it, but I've always thought it would be great for trekking and camping. It's heavily forested with lots of caves and rocky formations. There's some talk that a ski resort is being planned. We do get quite a lot of snow here in winter.'

'Yes, I'm looking forward to exploring the area.'

Jeremy set out early the next day and continued to follow the narrow lane higher into the mountain range. He took a packed lunch from the hotel. Taahira, the receptionist, was right. Not many people knew about the area; he did not encounter any other cars on the road. The road ascended even higher after a series of tight hairpin bends. Low stone walls marked the edge of the road as it dropped away steeply into the valley below. At the crest of the route, the road opened into a bowl of green undulating pastures surrounded by more peaks of rock and forest. Jeremy pulled off to the side of the road and got out of his car. The cool air caused him to breathe in deeply. He zipped his jacket higher and looked up at the thin strands of cirrus cloud streaking high against the clear blue sky. The sound of silence was palpable.

He took a walk around the car, studying the whole panorama around him. *What the hell is up here? Am I on a wild goose chase?* He got back in the car and studied the map again. According to his position, he still had some miles to go before he reached the summit. He pushed on and as the road ascended higher, he pulled off to the side of the road again and got out. As he was closing the driver's door he happened to look to his side and thought he saw some black smoke on the other side of some trees against a sheer wall of rock. Jeremy grabbed his binoculars and fired off some quick shots with the built-in camera. At the same time, he saw some birds pecking in the grass nearby. He took some close-up photographs of them with his other Nikon camera.

Back in his car, Jeremy drove to where he'd seen the black smoke. He knew it was diesel exhaust smoke. He approached the area slowly and backed up onto a small patch of grass in the trees to try to conceal his car. It wasn't possible to fully hide it, so he opened the trunk and pulled out the spare wheel and tools leaving them at the side of the car. He let some air out of his back tire. Next, he grabbed his binoculars and Nikon. Stealthily, he crept along the tree line towards the end of the track. The mountains cast a dark shadow over the forest enabling him to remain unseen behind the bushes and trees. To his surprise there were no trucks there. The track just seemed to peter out against a solid rockface. A barrier across the road warned people that this was private property.

CHAPTER 17

Jeremy checked his surroundings carefully. His hearing was on high alert. All he could hear was the buzzing sounds of insects and the odd bird chirping away. He ducked down and quickly crossed the track to the other side. This gave him a better angle to see the rock face. And then he saw it, an entrance to a large cave big enough to swallow several trucks and trailers. Inside the cave, he could see armed military personnel around what looked like a guard house. He fired off some more photos from his binoculars but thought better about trying to enter the cave. Perhaps he could climb above it and maybe see if there were any further clues as to what this place might be.

Jeremy crept silently towards the steep rock face out of sight from the front of the cave, carefully trying to avoid stepping on any dry twigs. He took in a deep breath, stretched out and clutched the branches of a bush and started to haul himself up the steep face. With each step higher, his fingers felt carefully above for firm holds as he tried to gain traction without dislodging any loose rocks. As the cliff became steeper, he pressed himself closer to the rockface when he felt his right foot give way. A shower of loose rock fell away beneath him as he clutched desperately onto the side of the cliff. He froze solid. He waited. Would there be a shout first or would he be shot without warning? The pain in both his hands and arms became intense. He moved his right foot further away to his side and felt for some sort of protrusion that he could at least take some of the weight off his arms. He could not find one so he used all his upper body strength to haul himself higher until he could find a foothold. He did and started to climb again, finally reaching a less steep part of the cliff. Since there had been no shouting or shots, he felt sure he had not been seen.

Climbing over roots and outcrops of rock he was able to ascend high above the cave. Once out of sight of the valley below he sank into the undergrowth and tried to regain his breath. It had been a close call.

As he recovered, he could hear a stream burbling away, so he headed for the source of the sound. The stream that was coming down from above suddenly disappeared into a giant cavity. He lay flat and inched his way forward to look down through the hole. It took a few seconds for his eyes to adjust to the subdued light, but once they had, he could see down onto the floor of the deep cavern. Shapes of missiles were clearly discernible. Steel beams had been constructed around them to provide a solid housing for their installation and deployment. Technicians were mixed with both construction and military personnel. He used his binoculars again to take shots of the interior of the cavern.

Scrambling down a less steep cliff away from the cave, Jeremy got back to his car as quickly as he could. He'd taken some more photos of birds with his Nikon camera. As he approached his car, he saw two armed soldiers inspecting the outside and inside of the car. He quickly dropped to the ground and hid his binoculars under a bush. He grabbed a couple of rocks and then strode confidently towards them with his Nikon camera around his neck.

'Good morning! Can you help me? I need to change my wheel.'

Both soldiers turned towards him, levelling their rifles.

'Eller yukarı. Izinsiz giriyorsun!'

Jeremy stood still. 'Sorry I don't understand.' He dropped the rocks.

The other soldier moved in close and peered at him with

a tight-lipped grin. Jeremy smiled, 'It's okay, I just need to change my wheel.' As he turned and pointed to the spare wheel on the ground, he felt the thrust of the soldier's rifle butt slam hard into his kidneys. A stab of pain shot up to his head and, as he doubled over, he felt another blow to the side of his head. The light disappeared from his eyes.

———————————————

'Good morning, Angus! Sorry we took off on you yesterday, but Chris and I needed to review our plans after our discussions. What you're proposing would mean extra funding from us that we hadn't bargained for. You realize, of course, that a further injection of capital from us would make you a minority shareholder?'

Angus smiled at James and Chris with both his eyes and mouth. 'I do. You two have been honest with me since we met. I believe I have also been one hundred percent honest with you too. That said, our independent financial evaluations of the existing business and the proposals practically match.' Angus took a drink of water. 'I guess I could have gone with your original plans and remained the major shareholder, but if we're to make this business a success then I believe this is the right decision.'

James and Chris looked at each other again and both nodded to each other.

'Angus, we think we've found a solution.'

'I hope so, gentlemen. I really want this to work. It's not just the modernisation of the terminal, it's also the opportunity to work with you both as partners. I meant what I said yesterday; I believe there is a bright and profitable future for this terminal.'

James smiled. 'We agree with you, but we don't believe you need the extra two wharves with all the additional space. Chris and I agree that only one is needed for the LNG terminal. With this and the grain terminal expansion we can handle the anticipated volume.'

Angus shook his head. 'I don't see how you can.'

'No, I guess you don't and please, I don't mean that in a mean sense.' James paused. 'Our logistics software system is very comprehensive and efficient. So much so, we can turn ships around much faster than anybody. We've kept this to ourselves since this is our competitive advantage.'

Angus furrowed his brow. 'So, you're saying the two new quays can handle the volumes of grain and LNG?'

James leaned forward. 'We are.'

'How can you be so sure?'

'Two reasons. With our integrated logistics system, we know we can handle the tonnage you're proposing. Secondly, we're already doing it at our terminal in Turkey.'

Angus gripped the table. 'I would never have thought it possible!'

Chris leaned back with his hands behind his head. 'Yep. It is!'

'So, Angus, should we get our lawyers and accountants together to draw up our proposed partnership?'

'Absolutely. I'm ready. Thank you, James and Chris. I knew I needed to do something drastic. One hundred percent of a failed business is not as good as a smaller ownership in a flourishing business!'

Chris laughed. 'Funny you should say that. That's exactly what James and I said nearly two years ago. Sometimes the sum of the parts is greater than the whole.'

Angus put his finger in the air. 'Before I forget, there's one more thing. I mentioned to you that we'd applied for federal funding to help with the cost of the port expansion. We still hope that will be forthcoming, but the ministry asked at the same time if I would like to join the Canadian group of businessmen attending the APEC meeting in Manila this November.'

James sat up. 'Interesting.'

Angus continued. 'There's only one spot available. How about if you go, James? After all, you will be the majority shareholder.'

James looked at Chris for guidance.

Chris smiled. 'I think that's a good idea. You can keep an eye on the Chinese.'

Chapter 18

'Let's call it a day, Nick.'

Just after 5:00pm, Nick Northrop finished working alongside Wilfred Stevens in his council office. Stevens had piled on as much information as he could, knowing he only had three months to do it. Essentially the general manager of the works department job was a clerical job, however the impending visit and all the necessary preparations for the G8 meeting gave it a completely new dimension. Stevens had gained a vast amount of security experience of this nature before when Queen Elizabeth II had come to Birmingham for the inauguration of the International Conference Centre in June 1991. Northrop had gone over all those security plans several times, hoping to find a weak spot.

'Okay, Wilf, I'll put away all the plans. You get off and see to your wife.'

Once Stevens had gone, Northrop adjusted the desk light and studied the plans of the International Convention Centre (ICC). He was focussing on the entrances on Centenary Square,

CHAPTER 18

Brindley Place and the Canal Complex. Satisfied he'd mentally noted several points of interest, he set off there on foot. It was highly likely the delegates would take this route from the Grand Hotel, past the Council House to the ICC, as it was known. The walk would take approximately seven minutes.

As he emerged from the Council House, the sun on his right was getting lower in the sky casting a long shadow of the Town Hall across the interlocking stones of Victoria Square. He turned to his right and followed the path as it narrowed between the two buildings. He noted the number of drains as he walked. He turned left at the great clock tower and took Centenary Way in between two modern glass-fronted, six-storey office buildings. Glass was a good friend if you were creating a terror bomb campaign, however this was not his goal for this mission. He came out on Centenary Square housing the Hall of Memory, a large war memorial commemorating over twelve thousand Birmingham Citizens that died in World War One. As the square opened out in front of him, he noted an absence of drains since the ground sloped well away to his left. He carried on past the ultra-modern library, adorned by a decorative metal framework and then, facing him, there was the entrance to the convention centre. On his route he had not seen any sites for commercial waste bins, one of his favourite methods for hiding explosives.

Hmm, not too much opportunity so far. Drains, maybe?

He entered the convention centre through the main entrance into a huge shopping mall that housed retail shops, and the indoor entrances to the symphony hall and the convention centre itself. The high-pitched roof was all glass. He looked up, deep in thought.

This would be a great place for another terrorist bomb, maybe a second bomb in quick succession after the first one between the previous office buildings. There's even more glass here.

He turned around full circle.

No. It's no good. This won't be a terrorist campaign. It has to be a targeted assassination. Planting a bomb in here is too random.

He carried on and exited the ICC, next to the Gas Street Canal complex. Brindley Place on the other side could be accessed over a pedestrian bridge.

He stood for several minutes facing the canal, trying to remember what Stevens had told him about the preliminary agenda for the G8 meeting. He'd said it was possible the delegates might have a lunch in a pub called the Malt House nearby. Northrop fully surveyed the former industrial area, now turned into a tourist attraction. The canal complex reminded him of Venice with its brightly painted barges and water taxis going back and forth. Cafes and patio bars adorned with the last flowers of autumn and coloured sun umbrellas were beginning to turn on their decorative lights. There were a wide variety of cafes and restaurants to choose from.

The Malt House was on the same side as the convention centre, so he turned right and followed the old narrow towpath alongside the waterway. He dawdled under a pedestrian footbridge constructed from heavy steel I-beams and concrete. Underneath the structure, wire mesh had been used to prevent pigeons from nesting and making a mess.

Perhaps a place to plant a bomb? The blast would be forced downwards on top of the pedestrians. Maybe.

He carried on for only a few more steps and there it was, The Malt House. A beautifully constructed building with its own courtyard and balconies facing the canal complex. There were two bridges either side of the pub and one of the

CHAPTER 18

waterways went underneath the building. Northrop peered into the tunnel. That would have been where the crew would have lain on boards and literally used their legs to sidestep against the narrow tunnel walls to propel the barge through to the other side.

Now this has possibilities.

Satisfied, Northrop retraced his steps after carefully casing the area. When he got back to the ICC entrance opposite Brindley Place, he looked down to the other end of the canal in Gas Street Basin. One building facing him had a large sign on the top – 'Macrae Holdings LLC'. He smiled to himself.

No one will ever know it was me that blew up Richard and Mary Macrae. Perhaps when this mission is over, my handlers might want me to finish the job!

— — — — — — — — — — — — — — — —

'He's not going to say anything now. Doesn't matter anyway. He's clearly a spy! Finish him off!'

Jeremy Hirons tried to open his eyes. Only one responded. The bitter taste of blood mixed with bile filled his mouth and burned his throat. He tried to lift his head up and open his jaw. The swelling on the one side of his face sent stabs of pain pulsating down his neck and back. In his blurred vision, he could just make out the shape of two men standing in front of him. He tried to raise his hand to wipe the blood from his mouth, but it was strapped securely to the arm of the chair.

A voice that sounded a million miles away kept asking, 'What were you doing up there?'

The other man threw his hands up in the air. 'Just do it!'

Jeremy tried to look up. 'Water, water.'

The second man sneered. 'I'll give you water!' and threw a metal bucket of cold water straight over him. Still with the bucket in his hand, the man couldn't resist clobbering his prisoner with it. Jeremy slumped forward again, blood oozing from his mouth and nose.

As the bucket clanged on the floor, the cell door opened.

'Stop this immediately!'

An army colonel came in and surveyed the prisoner. He turned to his men, shaking his head. 'You've gone too far this time! I hope it's not too late.' He put his hand on Jeremy's neck to check his pulse. 'He's still alive. Get some medical personnel in here now and get him cleaned up!'

The two soldiers looked disappointed. 'What's the story. Sir?'

'Our security services have thoroughly checked him out. He's a genuine travel writer from England, apparently commissioned by this magazine to do two articles. One on trekking in the Köroglu Mountains and, secondly, an article on bird species found here. His camera only contained photos of birds.'

Jeremy moaned and came to. The colonel bent down in front of Jeremy. 'Seems you are not a spy after all, but I have one further question. Why did you come at my men with rocks in your hand?'

Jeremy slobbered, trying to smile but it was impossible. Slowly he croaked, 'Chocks for wheel.'

The colonel turned to his men. 'What's he talking about?'

'He claimed he was trying to change a wheel, but we didn't believe him.'

CHAPTER 18

'It's plausible. Get him fixed up, give him his passport and get him out of here. We don't want the bloody UK embassy all over us.'

'James and Chris! We can't go on like this!'

Laura Wesley, the chief financial officer, sat back and crossed her arms. All the other managers around the boardroom table remained silent. There were some raised eyebrows.

'Laura, you have to find a way to finance the additions to our original plan for our partnership with the Halifax terminal in Canada.'

'I'm sorry, James, but we'll be over the top of our credit lines. It's as simple as that. I could not have been clearer in the last meeting! Before you left, I gave you my cost and cash flow analysis. There's no excuse!'

James sat back and exhaled loudly. He'd never seen Laura with such furious eyes before.

Chris chimed in. 'Look, Laura, it's highly likely we will be granted funds from the Canadian government for the expansion of the harbour, since these developments will mean an increase in their workforce. This could amount to several million dollars. If it hasn't come through by then, James will be in the Philippines in a couple of weeks with the very politicians that will grant the funds.'

Laura shook her head. 'But that's just it. There's no certainty. You remember at the last meeting; everyone was happy because the business was expanding so rapidly. I agreed, it was great news, but you also remember that we've spent millions on IT, we're financing the two new Panamax 1 container vessels and Rob and Pete are getting more equipment for our increased operations. Bottom line, we're expanding too quickly and over-extending ourselves.'

James lowered his voice. 'Laura, we have to find a way.'

'James, I know you and Chris are aggressive entrepreneurs, but you can't just go charging off and keep moving the goalposts on me. We're really stretched right now. I can show you after the meeting.'

James stood up and moved around the table, giving all the others in the management meeting a smile.

'This isn't unusual, you know. When companies expand, it's never a smooth line rising on a graph. On the contrary, expansion goes up in a series of steep steps. We go along the flat for a while, then there's a vertical climb up to reach the next step. Our part ownership into the North American market is essential as international trade continues to expand. With our own ships, terminals, warehouses and road transport, we vertically control whole industries that export their goods. Grain exports and liquified natural gas are two essential commodities that the world needs.'

He sat down again and looked at Laura. 'We hear you, Laura. Please don't ever change! We need firm hands on the finances. So we're not going to back off the accelerator, but here's what I'll do. I'll bring in a bridging loan from Macrae Holdings to cover the shortfall. We're solid.'

James and Chris finished the meeting and went back to Chris's office. Before they'd even had a chance to speak to each other, Martin Farley and Laura came in and closed the door behind them.

CHAPTER 18

Martin bit his lip. 'Look, I didn't want to say this in the meeting but there's a legal hold-up after your parents' death. It means you can't access funds from Macrae Holdings just yet.'

Jack Fox got up from behind his office desk and came to meet Jeremy. He gave him a gentle double-handed handshake. 'It's good to see you and have you back!' He stood to the side and looked at Jeremy's face. Black and purple bruises were still evident around his left eye and his face was still slightly swollen. Jeremy hobbled further into the office, leaning heavily on his walking stick. Jack took further stock of his loyal friend and co-worker. 'Bloody hell, they really did a number on you. I hope you were able to mend well in the last few weeks.'

Jeremy eased himself slowly down into a chair. Jack took his stick and placed it against the desk.

'Tell you the truth, I wasn't sure I was going to make it back, but physically there won't be any lasting damage. Luckily I was able to retrieve the binoculars and get myself to the British embassy in Ankara. Good job I had the embassy bring them over in the diplomatic pouch because I was searched again on my exit from the country.'

'Our embassy in Ankara launched a formal complaint about your arrest and interrogation. Needless to say, the Turkish authorities have dismissed any accusations as such. On the contrary, they say they rescued you after a nasty fall down a rockface while birdwatching.'

'Well at least that covers my tracks well enough. All part of the job.'

'Well, I can tell you, you did a great one. More than you realize.'

Jeremy glanced sideways and tilted his head.

'Look at these.' Jack handed him a folder marked top-secret.

One by one, taking his time, Jeremy gazed at each photograph that he'd taken with the binoculars. Not only did the binoculars take photos and video, but they were also able to measure and scale all the objects within the frame of the picture. They also captured the exact location of the subject by GPS.

Jeremy cleared his throat. 'This confirms what I thought at the time. Seems Ambarli port is being modified to accommodate Chinese naval vessels. This new quay measures three hundred and fifteen metres, enough to accommodate one of their aircraft carriers. The new cranes are higher as well.'

Jeremy picked up the magnifying glass off the desk. 'Yes, this port is definitely being set up as a military base. You can see the buffer zone they are setting up together with the bunkers to store the ammunition. They're even constructing blast barriers around the area.'

'That's the conclusion of the admiralty as well. Now take a look at the photos you took in the Köroglu Mountains.'

Jeremy scrutinised the photos carefully. 'Seems Yusuf Kahya and James Macrae were right to be suspicious of that shipment that arrived from China in the dead of night. These are Chinese CSS-2 medium and long-range missiles. They're certainly not the latest ones. You can also see the construction of this secret missile storage and launch area.'

Jack took back the folder from Jeremy. 'Yes. I wonder what

CHAPTER 18

the Turks gave China in return. That's the question.'

'Has the PM and Foreign Office seen these yet?' Jeremy asked.

'They have. We'll have to wait and see what will be decided.'

Jeremy stretched his back and winced slightly. 'Have we found out any more information from that Chinese dissident Huang Genjo?'

'We have. He's still in the safe house. We've ascertained that his story's genuine, so he will be processed for asylum and assume a completely new identity. We've also secured video footage from a tourist visiting Bembridge on the Isle of Wight of four people coming into the harbour by speed boat on the day of the hijacking. He was taking a video of his family on the quayside when this speed boat came into view at high speed. From the blow-ups of the stills, we've identified two out of the three hijackers. They are both known to us as Chinese ex-military foreign agents. Huang has confirmed their identities as the two assistants that accompanied the group out of China. This fellow, Lingdao was not on the boat, so we still don't have a shot of him or know who he is.'

Jeremy let out a breath. 'I suppose they've since disappeared off the radar?'

'Yes, no sign of them. We don't know if they've left the country or not. We have APBs out on them. That brings me to the next point, Jeremy. I'm putting you off on extended leave, at least until you're fully fit again.'

'No problem, Jack, I think I need a rest from the field!'

Fox continued. 'In the meantime, I want you to get hold of that Detective Inspector Stella Hudson from the West Midlands police who was involved in the manhunt for Hugh Stanfield. She's one hell of a detective. Make sure she has the necessary security clearance. We need her help to track these hijackers down and, at the same time, keep an eye on James Macrae and his business. Since the hijacked tanker is owned by Macrae, it's possible these three men are known to General Shen and he's still interested in this company.

19

Chapter 19

'We need to talk, Sarah.'

'There's nothing to talk about. I haven't changed my mind in the last month.'

'So I'm to carry on as if nothing has happened. Is that it?'

'If we have to do this now, let's go and talk on the patio. I don't want to have this conversation with you on the front doorstep.'

James shrugged his shoulders and followed Sarah around the house to the patio overlooking the sea. Normally he would have admired the view off the Welsh coast, but instead he focused on Sarah.

She turned around to face him. 'I told you, James, nothing has changed. I can't live like this. I mean, look at you. You were supposed to be here last week to pick up the children for the weekend but instead you cancelled at the last minute. It's the same old story over and over again. Okay, yes, you can pick them up this weekend and bring them home on Sunday before 7:00 pm, but remember, our children have lives too. I need to plan their activities for school and leisure, but you just can't be relied on. It was the same before and, obviously, nothing's changed!'

'Come on, Sarah. That's not fair. I've been to Canada on business and next week I have to go to the Philippines for an APEC meeting. It won't always be like this, I promise you.'

'Sorry, but I don't believe you!'

James looked down and scuffed the patio with his foot. 'Look, Chris doesn't have the same problem with Jenny!'

'So it's my fault, is it?'

'No, that's not what I said.'

'Sure sounded like that! And I'm not Jenny!' she hissed. 'For god's sake, James, our kids were going off the rails. I'm trying to get them straight again and so far; I think I'm on the right track.'

'Yeah, you love all this don't you! Big house in Wales...' He was about to carry on when Sarah bunched her fist but thought better of it.

'Don't you ever pull that one on me. I was doing perfectly fine before you came along, and I've got my own money. Now take the children and get out!'

As James drove away with Mason in the front seat and the girls in the back, he looked in the rear-view mirror, but the front door was already closed. There was nothing but silence in the car.

'So how do you like your new school?'

Mason slowly responded. 'I like it. It's better than the last one.'

'What about you girls?'

Mia and Olivia both answered at the same time. 'It's fun. We're even learning the Welsh language.'

CHAPTER 19

'Oh... How's your mom doing? Is she okay?'

Mason continued to look through the windshield. 'Mom says living with you was like a game of roulette. She never knew when she was going to see you.'

James felt more of an outsider than ever.

They drove on in silence for a while.

'Dad, this isn't the way back to our house in Bromsgrove.'

'No it isn't, Mason. We're not going back there.'

Mason looked at his father. 'So where are we going?'

Olivia shouted from the back seat. 'Are you kidnapping us, Dad?'

James couldn't help but laugh. 'No I'm not! We're going on a magical mystery tour.' He turned on the car stereo and the Beatles song blared out loud. Within seconds, they were all singing along with it.

James let out a huge sigh of relief. He'd broken the ice! For the next little while they had fun guessing where they were going.

'Welcome to Alton Towers, Mr Macrae. We have you and your family booked in the Chocolate Suite.' The hotel receptionist smiled at the children. 'You're going to love it! There are hidden chocolates everywhere.'

Mia looked up. 'What is this place, Dad?'

'Well, first of all it's my treat to make up for lost time. We're staying in the Chocolate Suite, but it's also a theme park. It's like Disneyland. There's lots of rides including roller coasters, river rapids and haunted castles. Come on, let's drop our stuff off in the room and get started.'

Mason and Mia both had wide smiles, while Olivia did a quick spin on the spot.

They ran into the suite and immediately started looking for the chocolates. There was even a little wheel connected to a bucket with a chain. As the wheel was rotated, the bucket filled with chocolates. It was all complimentary. James stood back in awe. How he wished Sarah could have been here as well.

By the time evening came, they were all screamed out, having attacked as many rides as they could. The roller coaster with the stall turns and corkscrews had been the most frightening but thrilling. They made their last ride of the day a ride on the river rapids. Even though they were given protective raincoats, by the time the ride was finished, they were all soaked. Their stomach muscles ached from laughter.

After they'd eaten in the hotel restaurant, they all went back to the suite. Mia and Olivia crashed soon after, totally exhausted. As Mason sat alone with his dad on the sofa, he spoke quietly. 'Dad, do you think you and mom will ever get back together?'

James put his arm around Mason. 'I hope so.' Staring straight ahead, he reflected, 'I don't blame her for the way she feels. It's true, I haven't been around much these past few months. My work has seen to that. Unfortunately, it's going to be like that for the next little while, but I promise you, once we've got everything set up, I will be here for you.'

He looked down. Mason was already asleep.

—————————————

General Shen hugged and kissed his elderly mother as he left her in the retirement home west of Beijing. As usual, his

CHAPTER 19

frequent visits coincided with covert calls that needed to be made with his trusted inner circle of contacts that he'd built up over the years.

He punched in a number from memory on his secure line.

Lingdao picked up the call immediately. 'Yes, sir!'

'Did everything go according to plan?'

'Yes it did, sir. Tang, Jin and I were able to leave the oil tanker undetected before the Special Forces arrived. According to all reports here in the UK, there were only five hijackers who were all killed when the ship was taken over by the military. The reports describe a group of Chinese dissidents seeking political asylum. I've already passed my report of reaction times by the British forces on to Peng Zheng in London.'

'And your getaway, were you all able to escape detection after leaving the ship?'

'Yes, sir. My two assistants were picked up as arranged by the two British men in their speedboat and made it back to Bembridge harbour on the Isle of Wight. I escaped on the jet ski that was brought out to the ship by the second British man in the speed boat. These two men will not be talking to anyone. They were taken care of immediately we returned to land.'

'Excellent! Now, for the time being, your two assistants are to stay undercover in England. From there, they are to organize a kidnapping of James Macrae's children. I will arrange for details to be passed on to them as to where and when.' Shen paused.

'As for you, you are to go to Birmingham where you will be contacted by a man who will give you further instructions on your next assignment. I will let you know the time and place where he will make contact with you. This assignment will not happen overnight since it needs to be meticulously planned and executed. Understood?'

'Yes, sir.'

General Shen sat back and compared the report he'd just heard from Lingdao with the intelligence report he had from the MSS. They matched. His three operatives had managed to make the hijacking of the Macrae oil tanker look like an attempt of asylum by five dissidents. He now had the strategy and reaction times of the British Forces in dealing with this type of incident and he had three agents safely planted in England to further his own agenda.

James let out a wide yawn. Despite having his usual run early in the morning, he was having difficulty waking up. He'd driven to the office on autopilot, scarcely registering anything around him. His mind was bursting with the wonderful time he'd had with the children. The only thing that spoiled it was Sarah wasn't with them. He snapped himself out of his reverie when the phone rang.

'James, DI Stella Hudson is here to see you.'

'Oh yes, please send her up.'

As the office door opened, James stood up and came around his desk to meet his visitor. She looked as slim and fit as ever, her eyes quickly absorbing everything around her. As a detective inspector, she would have been the last person you could have imagined fitted the role. It was her diligence and inquisitive mind that had tipped the balance and finally led to the capture of Britain's two most-wanted men, Hugh Stanfield and Dan Nash, both of whom were now dead.

CHAPTER 19

'Good morning, Mr Macrae, it's been a while since we last met. How have you been?'

'I've been well, thanks. Unfortunately, the recent hijacking episode broke the illusion that we were in for a period of plain sailing after Stanfield and Nash were taken care of.'

'Yes. That's why I'm here. As your local police force, we've been working closely with MI6. I'm also aware you're a signatory to the Official Secrets Act. I need you to look at the photographs of two men and one artist's impression of a third man. These three men were the ones involved in the hijacking of your ship and are also wanted for first degree murder.'

She spread out the photos on the desk. James peered carefully at each of them. 'No, I don't recognize any of these men.'

Stella looked straight at James. 'Please memorize their faces. These men are still at large, we believe they could still be in the UK. It's possible they might make a move against you personally after all the events of these past two years.'

James sat down. 'When's this ever going to end? Just when you think you're in the clear, another threat crops up out of nowhere.'

———————————

'Thank you so much, everyone. You've all been very kind.'

Wilf Stevens put down the framed oil painting that he'd just been given of the Bullring and St Martin's Church. He stood in front of all the Birmingham Municipal office employees flicking his retirement card in his hand. He swallowed hard and, with tears in his eyes, continued,

'Today is bittersweet for me. On the one hand I'm sorry to leave and to be honest, I never thought I would get old, that is old enough to reach retirement age. It truly has been a great pleasure working with you all. You've been more like a family to me rather than work colleagues.'

He reached into his suit pocket, pulled out a handkerchief and dabbed his eyes. 'On the other hand, I need to be home to support my wife. She needs me now more than ever.' His words trailed off and then he focused on Nick.

'But I leave you in good hands! Over the past three months, you've all got to know Nick working alongside me in this office. He's more than qualified for the job. 'So again, thank you for all your love, kindness and support over the years. This painting that you've given me today will always remind me of you all. Thank you!'

As the others left, Nick held out his hand to Wilf. 'Thank you to you too, Wilf. I wish you and your wife all the best for the future. Please let me know if there is anything I can do for you.'

'Thanks, Nick. You'll do a good job, I know. Just make sure everything goes smoothly for the G8.'

―――――――――――――――

The Cathay Pacific Airlines Boeing 777 flight from London Heathrow to Manila had one stop over in Hong Kong. On the first leg of his twelve-and-a-half-hour flight, James Macrae woke up from his nap and flicked on the overhead light. Stretching his neck, he pulled out his tray table and took a sip of water. He felt good about the decision he and Chris had made about buying into the Halifax terminal. He knew they were pushing the boundaries of their finances, but he was sure they find the necessary cash before the crunch came. Once they were over the hump, it would lead to much greater income and profit for the company. It had also given them the opportunity to be part of and have input into the Asia-Pacific Economic Cooperation (APEC) organization.

He opened the APEC binder he'd brought with him. It was his first involvement with the eighteen-member organization, and he needed to learn as much as he could before meeting with his particular business group: The Business Advisory Council. It was their job to advise insights and counsel for the APEC Economic Leaders. In short, they were subject matter experts.

He smiled when he read the executive summary:

With a combined annual income of over $13 trillion, the eighteen member economies of the Asia-Pacific Economic Cooperation accounted for approximately 55 percent of total world income and 40 percent of global trade in 1995. According to World Bank estimates, growth in the East Asian economies is estimated to average 8 percent per year over the next decade, and overall growth in APEC is expected to expand as well.

That's a lot of business for our ships and terminals.

As he read on, he realized things could only get better, since the member countries wanted to speed up customs and trade procedures between them. It was a subject he knew inside out. As an expert, he would be able to help them achieve an integrated economy and, because of this, his own shipping turnaround times could only improve.

Having transferred flights in Hong Kong, the second leg

of his flight was only just over two hours into Ninoy Aquino International. Descending over the Philippines was like looking down at a giant jigsaw puzzle that still needed piecing together, with its multitude of islands strewn randomly in the blue ocean thousands of feet below him.

Once through customs, James took a cab from the airport to the Manila Hotel through a maze of Spanish style and modern buildings all squeezed in together. As one of the most densely populated cities in the world, people jammed the sidewalks, while heavy thick exhaust fumes draped over them. Tightly packed cars, motorcycles and buses, all fought each other for every square inch of tarmac. It seemed that all the accelerator pedals fitted on every vehicle were directly wired to the horn. James would have been better off coming with the main group from Canada, as they would have had open roads with a police escort. That had not been possible, however, since he'd found it necessary to attend a meeting with the company's bankers, MidCom Commercial, in Birmingham to extend their credit lines. An answer to which they would have to wait for. Sadly, the former chairman and friend of James and his father Richard had passed away. Without that personal connection, there did not seem to be the same warm relationship. He would just have to be patient.

Arriving at the hotel he was pleasantly surprised. The five-star hotel overlooked the port of Manila, making him feel even more at home. In contrast to his frantic journey from the airport, as he entered the lobby, he was struck by the majestic opulence of the hotel. A series of high white decorative arches and pillars supported an attractive wooden ceiling adorned with ornate gold chandeliers. Across the polished marble floor, a pianist tinkled the keys of a grand piano adding to the calm

CHAPTER 19

and relaxing atmosphere.

In readiness for his private meeting with the Canadian contingent, he took a shower and then made his way to the hotel meeting room. He approached the registration desk and gave his name. To his surprise, he was given a name badge by the name of Angus MacNiel.

'We're sorry, Mr Macrae, with the late change there was no time to change the badge to your name.'

James nodded. 'Thanks, no problem. I understand.'

As he turned around from the registration desk, he was met by a smart middle-aged lady in a dark-blue skirt suit. 'Mr Macrae. Good to meet you. I'm the private secretary to our prime minister, Jean Chretien. He'll be leaving for the separate Economic Leaders' summit in Sumac Bay shortly, but I know he wanted to meet you before he goes. Please follow me.'

James was led to the other side of the room. 'Prime minister. It's a pleasure to meet you.'

Jean Chretien's face immediately lit up when he was introduced to James. 'Ah, Mr Macrae. It's a pleasure for me to meet you too. Welcome to our Canadian APEC delegation. I understand you are making a substantial investment in our country and expanding the Halifax port terminal. According to my ministers you will be able to substantially handle more grain and LPG exports?'

'That is certainly our objective, Mr Chretien.'

'Good! We're a political party that wants to diversify our exports. Even though we have excellent neighbours to our south, we want to make sure our trade is global. I've been made aware that my trade minister will be contacting you soon to discuss federal grants you may be eligible for. These are the applications that Mr MacNiel recently made.'

'That would be most appreciated. I look forward to working with you. Canada is a completely new venture for us, and I believe this will be the first investment of many.'

'Excellent, Mr Macrae. Now, as a subject matter expert on the APEC Business Advisory Council, I also understand you bring with you intricate knowledge of import and export procedures?'

'I do. Having been brought up in the international shipping and transportation business, I understand how to streamline trade practices that will lead to more open economies within the group. As you know, there is far too much red tape holding back business and economies.'

'I do indeed. That is one of APEC's main goals. Now, if you will forgive me, I have to leave to join the other leaders.'

'Thank you, prime minister.'

Shortly after the prime minister left, the Canadian group gathered to leave for the Philippine International Convention Center where a welcome reception would be held for all the supporting APEC ministers and business leaders. Transport from the hotel was made easier by police escorts.

Inside the ultra-modern Convention Center, set back from the road within expansive lawns and palm trees, different groups of delegates from all the member countries were scattered amongst high standalone tables serving hors d'oeuvres in the main reception hall. The atmosphere was loud with chatter and full of pre-conference anticipation. Several bars were set up on the mezzanine level, while servers dressed in black, served red and white wine on the main floor. No stranger to working a room, James introduced himself to several of the other attendees. While chatting with another representative from his business advisory group, he caught sight of what he thought was a familiar face out of the corner of his eye.

Who the hell is that? He asked himself. *I know that face.*

Still engaged in conversation, it hit him like a freight train. *Oh my god, it's General Shen, now the Chinese Minister of Trade and Development.* Not only had James seen his face in the press, but he'd also seen his photo in the MI6 headquarters after Hugh Stanfield and Dan Nash had been arrested. James felt his fists clench. *You're the bastard behind Euro-Asian Freight Services and Hugh Stanfield sabotaging and killing my employees.* James looked down and saw a knife on the table beside him. For a fleeting second, he had in mind to attack him. *Not a good idea!* James pulled himself together. *It may take me a while, but I'll find the right opportunity, don't you worry.*

James carried on the conversation with his small group and then excused himself to go up to the bar on the mezzanine for a gin and tonic. It would give him a good vantage point to view his adversary. As he stood waiting to be served, a very attractive lady dressed in a revealing black chiffon cocktail dress came and stood next in line to him. He turned and smiled. 'Hello.'

The stunningly attractive lady smiled back. 'Hello.' She paused while she read James's lapel badge, 'Mr MacNeil.'

James was just about to say, 'That's not my name,' but quickly realized who had come to stand beside him. It was no coincidence. James knew exactly who she was and what's more she knew exactly who he was. Her name was Meili Shabani. He recognized the photograph that his private detective had found on the *Mercantile News* journalist Greg Driver the previous year. Driver had been blackmailed by being set up by this very lady at a press conference in Shanghai.

James also knew it was highly likely she was an accomplice of General Shen.

'Ms Shabani. It's a pleasure to meet you. Which delegation are you with?'

'I'm with the Chinese delegation and act as an interpreter. With so many languages present here, it's a challenge for some of the delegates.'

'I'm sure it is. Can I get you a drink?'

'Yes. That would be nice. I'll have a white wine please.'

As they returned to the main floor and stood next to one of the scattered high tables, Meili turned her deep-hazel eyes on James. This wasn't a glance. It was an invitation. She raised her glass and took a slow drink, keeping her eyes focused on him the whole time. He noted her long manicured fingernails and felt his body heat rising. A hint of her perfume managed to magnetize his senses and started to sexually arouse him. He couldn't help but be attracted to this beautiful, tall and slim woman. After all he'd been separated from Sarah for some time.

'So, you're from Canada. I've always wanted to visit there. Perhaps, once this reception is over, Mr MacNeil, you could tell me more about it.'

Chapter 20

The Chinese ambassador to the UK, Jiang Enzhu, straightened his tie in the rear seat of his stretch silver BMW diplomatic vehicle. He was being driven west through London on Whitehall past the Cenotaph. The grand Portland stone buildings of the British government stood proudly either side of the road. Oozing with power and tradition, they could be intimidating for some. Not so for Ambassador Enzhu. He'd always had good relations with his British counterparts and was confident his meeting that he'd been summoned to, would reflect the usual cordial relations. As a seasoned diplomat from the Chinese Ministry of Foreign Affairs, as well as a member of the Hong Kong Preparatory Committee, he was well versed in political protocol. He was also familiar with the proposed transfer of the leased territory of Hong Kong back to China next year taking place on first July 1997, since he was a member of a working group with the British to ensure a smooth handover.

His car arrived promptly at the UK Foreign office on King Charles Street. As he ascended the grand marble staircase covered in a deep red plush carpet, he looked up admiringly at the vaulted ceiling and central dome. It was a time capsule of Britain's history and prominent position in the world. Led by his guide, he was taken into the foreign secretary's private office. Light from the floor-to-ceiling windows was subdued by net and the tied-back heavy brocade curtains.

Ambassador Enzhu strode, smiling, across the oak floor covered with a large grey oriental rug towards the foreign secretary, Jonathan Fernsby.

'Minister Fernsby, it's a pleasure to see you again.'

The foreign secretary stood tall behind his desk. He made no attempt to shake hands with his visitor or to smile. His face remained impassive.

'You can remain standing, Ambassador Enzhu. This is not a social call.'

The Chinese ambassador swallowed hard.

Fernsby's voice became louder but in a firm and calculated tone. 'Information has come to our attention of the gravest circumstances. We have evidence of Chinese involvement in the hijacking of the British ship *Constellation II* in British territorial waters. This hijacking was a clear act of aggression in British territory by known agents of your country. At the moment, I am managing to restrain the prime minister from declaring this an act of war!'

Ambassador Enzhu gave a faint smile, momentarily spreading his hands either side of him. Then, realizing this was not a joke, he froze.

'I don't know what to say, minister. Neither I nor my government has any knowledge of such an action. Indeed, why would we do such a thing? We have excellent relations with your country and look forward to a close future together.'

CHAPTER 20

'That is the question we want answering from you! We already know of your former unsuccessful efforts to take over the international shipping terminals of Macrae-Claybourne Logistics and now you continue to harass and commit heinous crimes against this company and its personnel. Let me remind you, ambassador, in the strictest terms, you have violated international law!'

Enzhu hastily gathered his thoughts to stand his ground. 'Sir, I can assure you the Chinese government strenuously denies any such wrongdoing. All necessary remedial actions were taken after the former events with Macrae-Claybourne Logistics. The individuals concerned in those matters are either dead or are imprisoned in Qincheng Prison. They were operating as individual criminals and had no ties whatsoever to the Chinese government. As for this hijacking, my understanding is that it was the act of five dissidents operating without any knowledge of our government. On behalf of my government, I dismiss this recent groundless allegation with the utmost exception.'

'Sir, that is for you to say, however I strongly suggest you take this message back personally and confidentially back to President Zemin. We have the names and descriptions of your three foreign agents that carried out this hijacking. Moreover, these agents are still on UK soil and are being hunted for both hijacking and first-degree murder.'

'Foreign secretary, on behalf of my government, I refuse to accept these false allegations, but I will certainly convey your message. This will undoubtedly affect the relationship between our two countries.'

Fernsby nodded his head firmly straight at his visitor. 'Is that so? Well, you can tell your president that unless he gets his house in order, the return of Hong Kong is off the table.'

Before the ambassador could respond, Fernsby abruptly ended the meeting.

'Good day, ambassador.'

———————————————

'Can you two stop arguing!'

Sitting in the back seat, Mason gave Mia another push.

'Stop bugging me, Mason!' Mia shouted back.

'Look, you two, I've had just about enough! You're both grounded next weekend.'

'Am I grounded too, Mom?' asked Olivia, looking up from the front seat; it being her turn to sit there.

'No you're not. Just Mason and Mia. They have to stop this constant niggling of each other.'

As Sarah drove her Land Rover along the narrow, winding coastal road towards Caernarfon on the way to school, a dark-coloured Rover pulled out behind her just after the church in the village of Trefor. A sixth sense alerted her. *That's strange, I'm sure that happened yesterday as well.* She continued up the hill but instead of turning left on the A499 main road, she quickly decided to turn right. She waited for a gap in the oncoming traffic and then joined in a line of moving vehicles going the other way. The gap in the line was too small for the Rover to follow her. As she looked in her rear-view mirror, she saw the Rover still stuck at the junction.

Sarah monitored her rear-view mirror constantly over the next couple of miles, but then retraced her steps using the Caernarfon bypass to reach the school that way. She did not see the Rover car again and safely dropped the children off at school.

———————————————

'So, Mr MacNeil, tell me more about Canada.'

'What is it that you would like to know?' James replied, looking deep into Meili Shabani's mesmerizing hazel eyes. The words being spoken didn't really matter. It was all part of a pre-mating game. He knew it and she knew it. The alure of her perfume, moist lips and the proximity of her warm body heightened his sexual desire.

Sitting closely on two high bar stools back in the hotel, James ordered a chardonnay for Meili Shabani and a scotch for himself. Underneath the overhang of the bar, he felt a long fingernail move up and down the top of his trouser leg. He drew in a quick breath as a strong electrical impulse shot straight to his groin. He was about to take her hand and lead her straight back to his room when a 'Breaking News' announcement on the TV behind the bar caught his eye.

Financial Crisis Spreads Across Asia

Within seconds, people gathered around them gazing hard at the TV. Someone shouted, 'Turn up the volume!' The barman did so.

The world is on the brink of a financial crisis tonight. Events are rapidly taking shape around the globe that could potentially affect the international banking system like a malignant bacteria. With a population of around seventy million people, Thailand has been an APEC member since 1989 but due to a lack of foreign reserves, Thailand has devalued its currency relative to the US dollar. This financial crisis has quickly spread to other Asian countries, causing other currency devaluations and vast flights of capital. Indonesia's currency value has plunged by eighty percent, while South Korea and Malaysia have seen catastrophic valuation falls of fifty percent. Panic is gripping the financial markets as it has now spread to the Russian and Brazilian economies. Stand by for further bulletins on this developing story.

James grimaced. 'Oh shit! I'd better make sure my own company's finances are safe and get back in touch with my group.'

Meili answered, 'I need to get back to my group too. Raincheck?'

'Yes, raincheck!' James answered and Meili was gone. Back in his hotel room, James called Laura. It was 10:30pm in Manila and 3:30pm that same afternoon in Birmingham.

'Have you seen the news, Laura?'

'Yes, James, we're on it. We're chasing all our receivables, although there are two Asian accounts that I'm starting to get concerned about. The Bank of England is also standing by to prop up the pound if we are affected.'

'Okay, Laura, I'll leave it with you. I'll be back in a few days. Call me if you need me.'

James loosened his tie and flopped back on the bed. He was full of conflicting emotions. He desperately wanted to make love with Meili and had almost fallen under her spell. Like a Venus fly trap, she was incredibly irresistible, but once in her clutches he knew it would be the end for him, his marriage and his business. The sudden financial crisis had saved him. It was now that he fully understood how Greg Driver had fallen from grace and how it had led to *Mercantile News* printing all the adverse stories of Macrae-Claybourne Logistics. After missing

CHAPTER 20

for some weeks, Driver had eventually been found washed up in the river Thames.

For the duration of the APEC conference, James deliberately avoided any contact with her or General Shen. He would just have to be patient for the right opportunity to seek revenge.

James returned from Manila to Ottawa with his Canadian group of delegates. He transferred flights from Ottawa to Halifax to follow up with his new partner, Angus. On reaching the terminal, Angus was out on the wharf discussing the construction expansion with one of the tendering contractors. Angus excused himself from the contractor and they went back into the offices.

James shivered. 'Wow, what a difference in temperature between here and Manila!'

'That's for sure, James. Come on, let's grab a coffee. So how did it go over there?'

'Better than I thought. I managed to speak with Jean Chretien, and, I have to say, I was impressed. He sure is export-orientated and what's more, he knew about our application for federal funding for the expansion of the grain and LPG terminals.'

'Well, that's good news! How about the rest of the business with the advisory panel?'

'Got to say that went well too. Since all the member states want to simplify trade between them by streamlining export and import procedures, I was able to make a lot of suggestions. They certainly want us to contribute more.'

'Good job, James! So, how's the financing coming from your end for the additions we agreed on?'

'Frankly, no problem. I'll give you a shout when I'm back in the office.'

'I think that's close. Just widen the eyes ever so slightly.'

Huang Genjo stood back and studied the picture some more. He was still in the safe house spending further time with the police graphics artist. She was trying to refine the face of Lingdao after the first attempt had been shown to Captain Moretti and his two officers that were on the bridge that day.

The artist did so. 'Does that look about right?'

'Yes. It's good.'

'Okay, now let me see if I can remove the beard and shorten the hair. Fugitives frequently follow this action thinking they can outsmart us. Tell me if you think we're on the right track.'

Huang looked at the second image, constantly moving his eyes between the one with the beard and the one without.

'I guess that would be realistic. His head always looked to me as though it was chiselled out of stone. Something like those US presidents on Mount Rushmore. He never seemed to have any emotion in his face.'

'Okay, now did you remember any other characteristics that you think could help identify this man? Any at all?'

Huang pinched his lips. 'I've been thinking about that every day and maybe there is one thing. When Lingdao walks, his right shoulder drops ever so slightly, more than the left.'

The artist made a note and underlined it several times. 'Thanks, Huang. It's a small detail, but it might be important in finally identifying him.'

'Still no sign of the hijackers anywhere,' Jack Fox said as he

CHAPTER 20

paced behind his desk.

Stella Hudson remained sitting. 'Nothing, sir. Despite circulating all these descriptions to all police forces and feeding them into the face recognition software on the security cameras at the airports, ports and rail stations, we don't have a bite anywhere. My belief is they're still in the country.'

DI Stella Hudson, being divorced, was throwing as many working hours into a week as she could. Now that she'd been temporarily brought in to work alongside MI6, this was now even more important.

'Well, the pressure is on from the prime minister down to get a result. Where are you at with your inquiries with the Italian port authorities?'

Finally, some progress. Your call to your opposite number in Europol, the EU law enforcement agency, after I was stonewalled by the Italian Coast Guard Police helped. I'm catching the first flight tomorrow morning to the National Police Headquarters in Rome to try to understand how the hijackers transferred from their freighter in Livorno and smuggled themselves aboard *Constellation II*. I'm hoping we can get hold of their security footage.'

'Good. We need to identify this Lingdao!'

―――――――――

Stella Hudson landed at Leonardo Da Vinci International Airport and immediately took a cab to Via Tuscolana, a forty-minute drive away on the south-east side of the city centre. She exited the cab and entered the glass-fronted office building of the Italian central anti-crime directorate. Everything inside the building was clinically clean.

'DI Hudson. Welcome, please come this way. The deputy chief of police is expecting you.'

She was led into a large office on the top floor adjoining a corner office and was met by a tall smiling man in an immaculate blue suit, white shirt and matching silk tie. He couldn't help casting an appreciative eye over his tall and attractive visitor.

'Ah, good morning, DI Hudson. The chief apologises for his absence this morning; however, he was called away at short notice last night to Sicily where we were able to arrest Giovanni Brusca, a top mafia boss who's been on the run for the last six years.'

'Good morning, Deputy Chief Lombardi. My congratulations, I know what it feels like to eventually arrest fugitives after so long! You must be overjoyed!'

'Thank you, we are. It's a big victory for us! Please have a seat.' Lombardi's smile quickly dissipated. 'Now let's get down to business. I understand that you've had difficulty obtaining cooperation from one of our branches, the Guardia Costiera?'

Stella sat forward. 'Yes, that is correct.'

He compressed his lips, seemingly to give himself time to think about the choice of his next few words, then, looking her straight in the eye, he continued, 'Honestly, if it wasn't for your persistence through Europol, we would not have found out what really happened that night when the Chinese freighter docked in Livorno and the hijackers transferred to your oil tanker, *Constellation II*.'

He let his words hang. Stella remained silent.

Lombardi adjusted his seating position. 'After an in-depth investigation, we were able to uncover a number of criminals within harbour security that were taking bribes to look the other way when illegal goods or people were being transported by ship. These individuals are now all behind bars, awaiting trial.'

Stella bowed her head. 'Well, at least that explains how these men were able to freely enter Europe and easily transfer ships. So, as I explained on the phone, I need two things from you. Firstly, I need to see the security video from that night and, secondly, to find out where the money came from to bribe the security staff to look the other way.'

Deputy Lombardi replied immediately. 'I have the security video here. Fortunately, we have a back-up copy after the port security personnel somehow "lost" the original copy.'

He turned on his computer and double-clicked his mouse to bring up the video. Stella sat wide-eyed, staring at the eight men and how easily they moved about the port even using a minibus. She leaned forward and peered at the faces of each of the men. After she'd seen the whole video, she sat back and looked at Lombardi.

'Can you play that one more time please and then freeze it when I tell you?'

Lombardi did so.

'Stop!' Stella moved closer to the monitor, carefully studying the faces of the eight men. 'I understand I can have a copy of this?'

'Yes, I have it here.'

'Excellent. Thank you. Now how about the money trail?'

Lombardi chuckled. 'That's something us Italians are good at, tracking money. With the mafia, we need to have sophisticated methods to keep tabs on their illegal movements and laundering of money. There's also a large black economy in this country too.'

Stella sat silently, hoping for the answer she needed. She wasn't disappointed.

'So, DI Hudson, there was a trail of money that passed through a maze of several international banks, the last one being through Andorra.'

'And the origin of the money?'

'It came from a shell company in China. It seems this company no longer exists.'

'Where's Mason?'

Mia and Olivia looked up at Sarah. 'Oh, he had rugby practice today and he hasn't come back up from the playing fields yet. I think he must still be in the changing rooms at the club house.'

'Oh, that boy. Honestly, he's always late these days.'

Sarah waited patiently with the girls while all the other parents and schoolchildren gradually went off home.

'Come on, let's go and find him.' They made their way out back to go down to the playing fields.

'I can't see him, Mom,' said Mia.

'Neither can I. Let's go to the club house.'

As they got there, Mr Evans was locking up.

'Oh hello, Mrs Macrae, can I help you?'

'Have you seen Mason?'

'He must have gone already. There's no one left here.'

Sarah started to feel uncomfortable and felt herself tremble. 'Come on, girls, let's check again!'

Mr Evans followed her up to the school where more teachers helped look for Mason. Finally, after scouring the school

CHAPTER 20

building and grounds, Mr Evans came back to her. 'I'm sorry, Mrs Macrae, he's not here.'

Chapter 21

'What's so important that needed my immediate attention on my return from Manila?'

Jiang Enzhu, the Chinese ambassador to the UK, stood rigid in front of President Zemin's desk.

'Mr President, I find it necessary to report to you in person, man to man, so to speak.'

'You'd better sit down.'

As Enzhu sat down, his right eyelid started to twitch. 'I was afraid of passing this information onto you through the normal channels.'

Zemin adjusted his glasses, but remained stone-faced and silent.

'After a face-to-face meeting with the British foreign secretary, he formally threatened the transfer of Hong Kong back to China is in jeopardy.' He paused. 'I was informed by Foreign Secretary Fernsby that they have irrefutable evidence that three Chinese agents were directly responsible for the hijacking of their oil tanker, *Constellation II.* Their prime minister is just short of calling this an act of war within British territorial waters.'

Zemin leaned forward and crossed his arms on his desk. 'That's impossible. There were five Chinese on that ship, but they were all individual dissidents. Nothing to do with us!'

'Of course I vehemently denied any such involvement or wrongdoing by China.'

'So, what's the problem?'

'I think you need to hear the rest. The British have evidence there were, in fact, eight Chinese nationals on the ship that day. The three agents escaped before the Special Forces took over the ship. They have descriptions of these men. Not only that, but they also allege the three agents killed the five dissidents before the Special Forces boarded the ship.'

'All of this is nonsense! Why would China do such a thing, especially just before the return of Hong Kong.'

'That's exactly what I stated in the meeting.'

'So, why all the fuss and why demand a one-on-one meeting with me?'

'Sir, this is why.' Enzhu took in a deep breath. 'Their prime minister believes there are two foreign affairs agendas being carried out by China. One is your agenda but there is another secret agenda being carried out by others in our government. They link the secret agenda to the attempts to take over Macrae-Claybourne Logistics' terminals, attacks on Macrae's family and now the hijacking of their ship.'

Enzhu carried on. 'I've been told to tell you, and I quote, "unless you get your house in order, the transfer of Hong Kong will not take place".'

Zemin sat quietly for a moment. 'What's your opinion of their foreign secretary?'

'Sir, I've known Jonathan Fernsby for many years. I believe he will have had all these facts verified before he spoke to me. I have a similar opinion of their prime minister.'

Zemin nodded. 'I see. Thank you for being so frank.' As an afterthought, 'Who else knows the reason why you're here?'

'No one, sir. When I considered what the British said about two secret agendas, it suggested to me that there may be other members of the party that are working against you.'

'Does Peng Zheng, our London head of security, know about this?'

'No, sir. I came straight to you, simply saying it was our regular bi-annual face-to-face meeting.'

'Good. Thank you. I'll be back in touch with you for our response to the British.'

Zemin sat alone, mulling over what he'd just heard. *Can there really be another agenda that I don't know about and, if so, who's behind it? An idea started to germinate.*

'James, you have to come here now!'

'Listen, Sarah, I can't just leave everything here and come to Wales at the drop of a hat. I've only just got back from the Philippines and Canada!'

Sarah broke down in tears. 'Mason's gone!'

'What do you mean, Mason's gone?'

She tried to stop sobbing. 'He hasn't come home from school and he's nowhere to be found. I'm at my wits' end. Please come!'

'Have you checked all his friends?'

CHAPTER 21

'Yes, he's not with any of them!'

'What about the girls?'

'They're here with me and my parents.'

James stood stunned for a minute then jerked himself back to reality. 'I'm on my way!' He ran out of the office, jumped in his car and spun his wheels out of the transport yard, arriving at the Welsh house three hours later. Darkness was beginning to fall.

Sarah's father opened the door. 'So glad you're here, James. We're all worried sick.'

Sarah ran a hand through her unkempt hair. 'I don't know what else to do. I've got everyone I know looking for him and the local police say it's too soon to call him a missing person!'

'What! They better! I'll get straight on it!' He picked up his phone.

James came back to Sarah, shaking his head. 'All I got was they're short of manpower but they will do what they can, given our family history.'

Sarah sank down onto the sofa. 'It's not like Mason to do this.'

'No, it's not. Was there anything out of the ordinary you noticed before today?'

Sarah closed her eyes for a few seconds. 'I did get the feeling I was being followed yesterday and this morning, but nothing came of it. It's possible I was mistaken.'

James's eyes widened. 'Oh god, please, no!'

'What?'

'I'm thinking Mason may have been taken!'

Sarah went pale and burst into tears.

James sat next to her and put his arm around her. 'Come on, we can get through this. Let's try to think this through. Did you notice what kind of car followed you?'

Sarah dried her eyes. 'I think, I think it was a Rover, definitely dark blue.'

Okay, anything else?'

'There were two people in the car, but that's all.'

James was quiet for a moment. He picked up his cell phone and scrolled through his contacts.

'DI Hudson?'

'Speaking.'

'James Macrae. Listen. I'm in Wales at my house. You asked me to call you directly if there was anything suspicious happening after the hijacking. Seems Sarah was followed for the past two days by a dark blue Rover car with two people inside and now my son Mason is missing. I believe he may have been kidnapped!'

'I hear you. Do you have a registration number?'

'No, we don't.'

'Alright. I'll get a nationwide bulletin out straight away. Stand by. I'll be back in touch.'

———————————

In heavy rain, the police car sat back in the shadows of a driveway at the intersection of the A4084 and the A5 at Capel Curig. A streetlight attempted to illuminate the junction set amongst barren fields and grey stone walls. It was 3:00am. A set of car headlights pierced the darkness and moisture from their right-hand side.

'Hey, Rhys. Look, there's a car coming from Plas y Brenin. Looks like it's in a hurry, especially in these conditions.'

'Alright, let's see what we've got when it gets to the junction.'

CHAPTER 21

Within seconds, the car came by them, failing to stop at the junction with the main road.

'It's a dark-coloured Rover. I wonder if that's the car we're after?'

'Light 'em up! Let's go get him and radio ahead for a roadblock at Betws-y-Coed!'

Rhys stepped on it to catch up the car while the Rover's driver tried to outrun them by straightening out the bends on the narrow two-lane road cutting from apex to apex. It fishtailed frequently, aquaplaning across the pools of water lying on the road. 'This is going to have a bad ending if he doesn't slow down!'

As they entered Betws-y-Coed, both cars sent high rooster tails of spray up against the stone cottages built close to the road until a barrier of flashing lights and vehicles brought the Rover to a broadside skid and stop outside the Royal Oak Pub. The car was immediately surrounded by armed police.

'Step outside the car with your hands up!'

Two men slowly got out of the car and stood with their hands high in the air. Other officers checked the car and the boot. There was no one else in the vehicle.

22

Chapter 22

President Zemin called in his own trusted agent, Kevin Tan, one of several that Zemin kept quiet about. Tan was one of the 'Shanghai clique' dating back to the time when Zemin was Mayor of Shanghai. Zemin's tight group operated independently under the radar outside the government, the army and the MSS and had tentacles spread across the globe. Deng Xiaoping had operated this way and when Zemin came to power, he continued the practice. Being a president was a lonely job. He needed to make sure he had a tight grip on power. With only a closed circle of advisors, you never really knew who was telling you the truth or who was trying to manipulate you. As time progressed, it was necessary to purge political enemies and shut down any internal unrest. Not only that, but Zemin needed to fight extensive corruption in his own party. Operating with his own undercover network of agents helped him do that.

'So, Kevin, tell me what you've discovered about the hijacking of the British oil tanker. Were there five hijackers or eight?'

CHAPTER 22

'Sir, there were eight. Five of the hijackers were Chinese dissidents. They were all dead before the ship was stormed by the British Special Forces. The other three were all ex-Chinese military men who were able to escape the ship.'

Zemin took in a deep breath. 'Are you absolutely sure?'

'I am.'

'Do we know the identities of these three men?'

'The British police have descriptions circulating of three *persons of interest* they are looking for. They are described as being armed and dangerous. We've managed to identify these individuals as being Chinese ex-military men.'

'Thank you. That will be all.'

Zemin sat back, alone. After a while, he picked up his internal phone.

'Shen. I need you.'

As Shen entered the president's office, he noticed Zemin push his chair back from his desk and stand up.

'Sit down, general.'

Zemin remained standing and glared down at Shen.

'Tell me again about this hijacking of the British tanker. Is this anything to do with China?'

'No, sir. Absolutely nothing.'

'General, is this the MSS official answer?'

'It is, President Zemin.'

'And can you tell me again how many hijackers there were on the ship that day?'

Shen looked up directly into the eyes of Zemin. 'There were five Chinese dissidents who were all killed by the British Special Forces.'

'So, where does your information come from?'

'Peng Zheng, our London embassy head of security. He has

sources inside the British authorities.'

'So, Shen, would it surprise you that the British say they have hard evidence that there were three more hijackers on board that day who were known Chinese military men?'

'It would. That would be ridiculous. These are nothing but lies from an imperial power.'

'Well, the return of Hong Kong is now slipping away. So, here's what you are going to do. With immediate effect, Peng Zheng is to be relieved of his post. He must be arrested and returned here, where you will personally throw him inside Qincheng Prison.'

'But, President Zemin—'

'No buts, Shen. Do it!'

Shen rose from his chair, desperately trying to remain calm. He walked silently out of the office. *How could the British know there were eight hijackers and how could they know they were ex-military men?* Something had gone wildly wrong with his plan and now with his ally, Peng Zheng, out of the picture, his plans for Birmingham had been compromised. Shen went back to his office, trying to control his breathing. He just needed to leave Peng Zheng where he was, at least for another day. He felt, at least for the time being, his own integrity had remained untarnished.

President Zemin sat down sneering. He knew Shen was lying, but he needed him to remain where he was for the time being. He would now have to systematically root out the rest of Shen's private network, but the imprisonment of Peng Zheng might just be enough to prevent the British from stopping the return of Hong Kong.

———————

CHAPTER 22

DI Stella Hudson rushed to the police station in Betws-y-Coed once she heard two Chinese males had been apprehended in a blue Rover. She arrived just as the first light of day appeared. It was still raining hard.

She opened the door to the interview room and stared directly into the face of one of the men she so desperately wanted to find since the hijacking of the *Constellation II*. Without removing her stare from his face, she joined the other detective already there.

'So, Tang, or should I call you by your real name and rank in the Chinese military?' Tang remained impassive.

She continued, 'Captain Yu, that's your name, isn't it?' She didn't wait for an answer. 'Where is the boy you kidnapped yesterday in Caernarfon?'

Tang sat motionless.

'Okay, I'll do the talking. For starters, you are being charged under the Terrorism Act with five counts of first-degree murder, hijacking and now kidnapping. You are looking at life imprisonment several times over.'

Tang smiled back at Hudson. 'I'm a simple businessman visiting your country. That's all.' After half an hour of getting nowhere, Stella ordered Tang to be locked back in his cell. He had not budged from claiming innocence.

She moved to the second interview room and briskly confronted Jin. 'So, First Lieutenant Shao, let's get down to it, shall we?' Jin sat up once he'd been addressed by his real name and rank. 'We now know from your colleague Tang, or Captain Yu by his real name, that it was you who killed all of the five student dissidents on *Constellation II*.'

Jin's eyes widened.

Stella continued, 'We also know you kidnapped Mason

Macrae yesterday. Where is he?'

Jin moved his handcuffed hands onto the table and started to wring them. He remained silent.

Stella tightened her fishing line of questioning. 'All told, you are being charged under the Terrorism Act for hijacking, five first degree murders, forcible confinement and now kidnapping. It's likely you will receive at least six or seven life sentences, and if you think Qincheng Prison is bad, we can better that. You will not be popular with your cellmates, especially those that don't appreciate the abuse of children.' She lowered her voice to a venomous whisper and leaned across the table. 'Your life, First Lieutenant Shao, will be hell on earth.'

Jin burst out. 'I didn't kill those men! Lingdao and Tang did that. I was just taking orders. They were both my superiors.'

'Maybe I can help you if you help me. Where's Mason Macrae?'

Jin started to sweat. 'He's tied up in a cave somewhere. We were keeping him there until James Macrae agreed to the ransom terms.'

'Where's the cave?'

'I don't know exactly. Tang sorted that out.'

Stella banged her fist hard on the table. 'You must know where it is!'

Jin jolted. 'It's somewhere between Caernarfon and here. That's all I know.'

'So why were you driving away from the area so fast? Wouldn't you go back to the cave to ensure your prisoner was okay to be handed over safely, once James Macrae gave you what you wanted?'

Jin looked down, shaking his head. 'We panicked. The cave

CHAPTER 22

became flooded. With the rising water, we were frightened we would be trapped. There wasn't enough time to go back deep inside the cave and get the kid.'

Stella stood up and went straight back to Tang's cell. 'Where's the cave you left Mason Macrae in?'

'I don't know what you're talking about!'

'Where's the bloody cave, you murdering bastard?'

Tang just smiled.

Chapter 23

The long grey metal box housing a large camera, one of several, hung suspended peering down on the main concourse in London's Euston Station. Several hundred travellers anxiously stared up at the forever changing LED boards checking their departure times and platform numbers. Like a silent stalker, the camera swept the area quietly from side-to-side. It stopped suddenly and unseen to the naked eye, zeroed in on one face. The camera locked in on the person and then followed the figure across the concourse to the entrance of platforms 8 to 11. Unknown to anyone except the security services, this camera was the first of an Internet Protocol design, enabling it to communicate via the internet to anywhere in the world. Several miles away, a monitor flashed an alarm in Thames House, the MI5 Headquarters on the north bank of the River Thames, close to Lambeth Bridge. Another camera on the same network tracked the person boarding the InterCity Express to Birmingham on Platform 10.

Lingdao pretended to look nonchalantly out of the carriage

CHAPTER 23

window as his London train pulled slowly into Birmingham's New Street Station. He scanned the platform, looking for anything suspicious. He was to make his way to a pub within a short walking distance in the city centre where he would be contacted by another man. He did not know who this person was or what he looked like, but he would be carrying a *National Geographic* magazine in his left hand.

Lingdao walked slowly out of the station into Stephenson Place by the HSBC Bank, trying to get his bearings. He checked the reflection in the shop windows for anyone trying to tail him. So far so good. For anyone who had known him in the past, he believed it would have been difficult for them to recognize him. His long black hair, moustache and goatee beard were gone. Now short-haired, clean-shaven and dressed in pressed black pants, blue open neck shirt and black quilted jacket, he looked as though he was taking a lunch break from any of the offices nearby.

He looked around the wide paved area leading to Corporation Street and then walked confidently straight ahead on the wide pavements filled with shoppers and early lunchtime office workers. He passed by a couple of landscaping contractors pulling out some drooping autumn flowers from the decorative large pots alongside the street and dropping them into a wheelbarrow. What he didn't see was one of the workers talk down into his orange work jacket after he'd passed by.

As instructed, he turned left into a narrow alleyway by the name of Cherry Street running between the Victorian office buildings on his left and a more modern department store on his right. He ducked into the store and quickly did a tour of the cosmetics counters. The air was heavy, almost choking, with the intensity of perfume fragrances. Spotting another entrance, he exited into a large church yard and walked directly through it, turning right on Colmore Row and then left at Barclays Bank and down Livery Street alongside Snow Hill Station. As with most cities, there was a blend of old and new buildings all mixed in together. Within a short walking distance, he spotted his meeting place, a Victorian four-story, red-brick public house on the corner of Edmund Street named The Old Contemptibles, named after the heroes of the British Expeditionary Force in World War One.

He pretended to take stock of the old building, while carefully studying that the pub was not under surveillance. Satisfied, he entered a dimly lit lounge on the left-hand side of the building. The air inside was dense with the smell of stale beer and smoke. Being just before lunchtime, the lounge was quiet. A dark walnut bar with a well-scuffed brass kick rail and several old-style beer pumps dominated the tired carpeted lounge scattered with a few round oak tables and chairs. He saw a sign for the toilets and went straight there, noticing an exit door to the side of them. Satisfied he had an escape route if he needed it, he went back to the bar.

In perfect English, he ordered a pint of bitter from an elderly grey-haired barman, grabbed a menu and made his way to an unoccupied booth on the far wall of the lounge. Holding up the menu in front of him, he studied the people starting to come into the lounge, wondering who would make contact with him.

———————————————

Nick Northrop stood back after taking his time surveying the new Birmingham municipal workshop.

CHAPTER 23

'You're doing a great job here, Colin. I'm very pleased.'

'Glad you think so, Nick, mind you, I'm only following in your footsteps. You set the bar high when you were running this place! By the way, how are you settling into your new job now Wilf Stevens has retired?'

'I like it! Gotta say, Wilf really helped me a lot. He certainly gave me a head start with the new responsibilities I've got now. As we get closer to the G8, I'm going to need a lot of help from you though.'

'No problem. Just let me know what you need, and I'll be there.'

'Good. Listen, I need to borrow a Transit tipper truck at lunchtime. I've got some rubbish I need to pick up at home.'

'Take that one over by the fence. It's just been serviced.'

Nick left his car in the yard and drove the municipal tipper, painted and lettered in the works department livery, out of the yard. Instead of heading for his home, however, he drove straight into the centre of Birmingham and made his way along Edmund Street from the west towards the Old Contemptibles pub. He drove slowly along the street, looking for anything suspicious. With all the trouble that had been taken for him to become a sleeper agent, he did not want to take any undue risks. He had a description of the man he was to meet and saw him approach the pub from the east side. The man, whoever he was, seemed cautious too.

Nick parked his vehicle in a no-waiting section of the road on double yellow lines. He turned on the amber warning lights on the light bridge on top of the cab and placed orange safety cones behind and in front of his vehicle. He got back in the cab and waited a few more minutes as the lunchtime crowd made their way into the pub. An unmarked van drew slowly up on a side street, but no one got out. Then another dark-coloured car parked at the junction of Livery Street and Edmund Street. His body stiffened. Straight ahead of him he just caught a glimpse of something shiny on the roof of the multi-story car park at the station. As a trained soldier and mercenary, he knew immediately the reflection of a telescopic lens.

Wearing an orange reflective safety vest and hard hat, he immediately got out of the truck and went to the drain at the side of the road, taking out a long metal handle to lift the grate. He carefully scanned the road behind him and saw another van parked on Edmund Street that had not been there when he pulled up a few minutes ago. He peered down into the drain. Apparently satisfied, he replaced the grating, picked up the traffic cones and hopped back into the truck. He turned off the hazard lights and drove off via the side street on his left.

Lingdao checked his watch. He'd waited ten minutes already, but no one had tried to make contact with him. He gave it another five minutes and then decided to leave. He finished his beer and rather than leave by the front door, he went to the exit door at the side of the toilets. He opened the door and stepped out into the alleyway only to face two armed police officers.

'Easy now. Put your hands up against the wall.'

Lingdao felt a pair of hands expertly frisk him for any weapons, then his wrists were tightly clamped in handcuffs behind him. The officer spun him around. 'You're under arrest.'

———————————-

James felt himself slip sideways. His eyes flicked open as he

CHAPTER 23

jerked his head upwards when the phone rang. He was still sitting on his lounge sofa. A police officer sitting at the other end of the room answered the phone.

'It's DI Hudson for you, sir.' James got up and picked up the phone.

'Hello.'

'Mr Macrae, we have some news.' James took in a deep breath but remained silent. Stella continued. 'We've got an all-out search going on for Mason as we speak. We can confirm that he was kidnapped by two men who have since been arrested. Mason is being held captive in a cave somewhere between Caernarfon and Capel Curig. We're combing the area as fast as we can.'

James looked over at Sarah who had just come into the room. He put the call on the speaker and spoke, 'There must be dozens of caves in that area. Most of them are old slate mines.'

'Yes there are. The problem we're up against is that the information we have is not specific enough to zero in on any particular mine. We're also concerned about the amount of rain and rising water levels.'

'Is there anything, I mean anything, else you can do?'

'No there isn't. We're working flat out. I'll be back in touch as soon as I have further news.'

'Thank you, DI Hudson.'

Sarah covered her face. 'I'm scared, James. Mason's all alone in a cave?'

James clenched his jaw. 'Yes, he is!' He paced around. 'I can't just sit here. I know some of those caves. God knows, I've spent years climbing and walking in that area. I'm going out to look for him! Call me if you get any updates from the police.'

James put on his waterproofs and threw some of his mountaineering gear into his Range Rover. With the windshield wipers working on fast speed, he drove out to where he thought would be the most likely spot to hide a hostage. He passed numerous police cars but went straight to the one cave he thought would be the most obvious. His four-wheel drive enabled him to get close to the cave entrance. He wore a cycling head lamp on his head and entered the cave. Slipping and sliding, he moved further into the cave, looking for any clues that might help him. There were none. After half an hour and shouting Mason's name out loudly, he gave up. Threading his way back down the mountain track, he checked another cave but still nothing. James wracked his brains. 'Where are you, Mason? Come on, talk to me.'

He pushed on further into the mist-covered mountains. As he peered hard through the murky atmosphere, he continued to mutter to himself. 'I'll try the Idwal Slabs next, that's a good spot.' White caps on Ogwen Lake roughed up the surface as the driving rain raced to meet him head on. He shivered as he parked his vehicle well off the road and took out his mountaineering gear. As he scrambled up the steep, grassy bank, he clutched onto the wet and slippery, rocky outcrops. Within minutes he'd lost sight of his Range Rover but could hear police sirens in the distance. He stood still for a minute catching his breath and, looking down, he saw scuff marks in the mud. His heart began to race. 'Could this cave be the one?' He found renewed strength and pushed on up to the mouth of the cave, carefully scouring the ground in front of him. And then he saw it. He leaned down and picked up a muddy cloth. It was a rugby shirt with the number 8 on the back. James looked up to the sky. 8 was Mason's number.

CHAPTER 23

Shrouded in mist, James thrust himself forward to where he thought the cave entrance was. He found it, turned on his headlight and climbed down inside the cave. The noise of gushing water got louder and louder the deeper he went, until finally he was met with a lake of inky black water. He could go no farther.

James sank down on his knees trying desperately not to panic. He'd climbed Ogwen slabs multiple times on all the routes from easy to hard. Somewhere he knew there was a fissure that led deep inside the mountain. He climbed back out of the cave. Covered in mud, he let the rain wash his face and hands. 'Okay, come on. Try to imagine where you are on a clear day.' He knelt down and rested his hand on a rocky outcrop covered in sodden lichen. Looking upwards he made his best guess and struck out at an angle of about thirty degrees. He climbed steadily upwards, always keeping a three-point hold onto the rock face. Reaching a ledge, he felt confident he knew where he was. *I think I'm about ten feet below the crack.* He ascended higher, losing his footing a couple of times but then, eventually, he found it.

Wasting no time, he attached a sling around a rock and used it as an anchor to abseil down into the fissure. The opening was very narrow at the top so he had to squeeze himself hard to lower himself down. Once past this obstacle, he lowered his headlight down into the cavern below him. The thin beam of light disappeared into the black void. He slowly abseiled down the steep face until it started to level out. He detached himself from the rope and scrambled further down inside the mountain. 'Mason! Mason! Mason!' He stopped and listened intently. There was nothing but the sound of running water. He squeezed himself through another constricted area and

then he saw him.
'Mason! Mason!'

24

Chapter 24

Nick Northrop drove the Transit tipper back to the works yard, dropped his copy of *National Geographic* in a bin and then left in his own car to drive back to his office in the Council House. It was exactly 2pm. He sat at his desk, pondering what had just happened. Clearly, the man who he was supposed to meet had been identified well before he'd entered the rendezvous pub. He took out his burner phone and called a number from memory.

A female voice responded. 'Central Painting.'

Northrop simply answered, 'Painting appointment cancelled today. Your contractor was otherwise engaged.'

He shut the phone off and wondered what would happen next. Whatever it would be, he felt safe in his position, and it wouldn't be long now before the G8 would take place. Once his mission was over, he would have enough money to retire and disappear into obscurity.

On the other side of the world, it was just after 9 pm on a cool evening in Beijing. General Shen was at home on his sofa studying his daily MSS confidential papers when he felt his burner phone vibrate. Knowing there were no listening devices in his apartment, he took the call.

Peng Zheng didn't wait for a response from Shen and said in a low, monotone voice, 'Lingdao has been apprehended. Also, Tang and Jin have been arrested by the British authorities. Northrop awaiting further instructions.'

Shen was quiet for a brief moment. 'Instruct Northrop to organize the first terror attack on his own. Transfer the money into his account and plan it one day ahead of the second attack.' He shut the phone off immediately. He had not mentioned anything about Peng's impending arrest and forceable return to Beijing. Shen knew he couldn't afford for Peng to be arrested in case he talked. Qincheng Prison would see to that. The order had already been given by himself to shut down that possibility.

Shen closed his files and turned out the light. The darkness helped him to focus his mind on the position he now found himself in. It was a position that had shifted dramatically in the last twenty-four hours. The British had identified and arrested all of his hijack team members and Zemin had ordered him to arrest Peng Zheng. It was clear that Peng Zheng, operating without knowledge of the Zemin's government, would be used as a scapegoat for Zemin to explain the hijacking to the British authorities. Zemin would hope that it would be enough to keep the return of Hong Kong back on schedule.

Shen's plans for Birmingham would need to be changed. Northrop would now have to do the work of two men. He would have to carry out the two separate terrorist attacks himself.

CHAPTER 24

———————————————-

In the narrow beam of light from his head lamp, James moved closer to the huddled body. He turned Mason over. Mason slowly opened his eyes. 'Mason, Mason. You're safe. I've got you.'

'Dad, is that you?' he mumbled.

'Yes. I'm here. Can you move?'

Mason slowly uncurled his body.

'Okay, now try to lift your legs up one by one and move your arms. Can you do that?'

'Yes.'

'Alright, good. Now, I'm going to attach you to me and I want you to try to walk as best as you can. I'll carry you when I have to.'

Step by step, James and Mason managed to inch themselves higher up the fissure. Using all his strength, James climbed the rope with Mason attached to his back. At the top he manoeuvred Mason through the narrow opening and onto the rocky outcrop. James heard voices below them. He sighed with relief and hugged Mason tightly to him.

'You hear that, Mason? You're safe. Everything's going to be alright.'

——————————

As the last rays of the sun disappeared behind the nearby offices on Weymouth Street, adjoining the Chinese embassy in London, Peng Zheng turned on his desk light and looked up at his ever-attentive and efficient male secretary. 'Ah, a coffee, just what I need right now to keep me going. It's going to be a long night.'

'You're welcome, sir. Is there anything that you want me to do before I leave for the evening?'

Peng smiled. 'Just make sure you shred those documents we went over this afternoon.'

'Will do. See you tomorrow.'

After his secretary left, Peng sat back in his brown leather office chair and considered what he had learned through his intelligence network since yesterday. Two of his agents had been arrested in Wales and now his third agent, Lingdao, had apparently been detained in Birmingham. All three were being held in custody under the Terrorism Act. It had been a disastrous series of events and would endanger Shen's plans for the G8 in Birmingham. Knowing this, he'd risked calling Shen immediately. Shen had been clear; Northrop would have to take care of both bombings at the G8.

He closed his eyes, trying to visualize how this could have happened. He surmised there must have been a survivor from the five dissidents on the tanker that day, who had given descriptions and relayed the whole story to the Brits. It had to be, since none of the crew had ever seen the eight men together and even then, only briefly, at least, according to the reports from his three agents. He knew what he must do. He would have to monitor all the British safe houses that he was aware of. Whoever spilled the beans would have to be taken care of by MI6 and hidden in a safe house.

He picked up his coffee and drank it. He would need to check out his theory of a surviving dissident. As he took hold of his pen, he felt a huge stab of pain in his chest. He jolted in agony, his head falling straight onto the desk. As his body twitched, foam trickled from his mouth.

CHAPTER 24

―――――――――――――-

'Mr and Mrs Macrae. You can see Mason now. Apart from cuts and bruises, he's recovering from hypothermia. He was not harmed in any other way except he has injuries to his wrists and ankles where he was tied up. It was fortunate you found him in time. We'll keep him here in the hospital for a day or so to monitor him.'

'Thank you, doctor.'

Sarah leaned down and kissed Mason on his forehead. 'Thank God you're safe.'

Mason looked up at them both. 'I thought I was going to die.'

James took hold of Mason's hand. 'Well, it sounds like you saved yourself. Rubbing and cutting your hand ties on the rocks and freeing yourself meant you could climb above the rising water.'

Mason gave him a weak smile. 'Did you find my rugby kit?'

'I did. That was a smart move.'

Mason's eyelids closed as he drifted off back to sleep.

Outside the hospital James turned to Sarah. 'Are you alright?'

'No! I'm not alright. You need to fix this! I can't do this anymore!'

James recoiled. 'Look, we're safe now and they've caught the two kidnappers.'

She snarled, 'For God's sake, James, you're not listening to me! You need to fix this, once and for all! You'd better get your priorities straight. Is your bloody company worth more to you than your own children?'

James winced. 'What?'

Sarah let out another infuriated gasp. 'We nearly lost our son yesterday and who's it going to be the next time? Mia, Olivia?'

James stabbed a finger at Sarah. 'Look, it's sorted out now!'

Sarah's face reddened. 'Yes, until the next time and there probably will be a next time! They'll just keep coming and coming for us.'

James stood back. 'I'm sick of this! Everything I do these days seems to be wrong! Listen, Sarah, I know it doesn't seem like it right now, but you and the children are everything to me.'

Sarah lowered her voice. 'I'm going to stay here with the children. The house is as secure as it gets and with my parents staying here, it's a big help.'

James looked down. 'I see. Nothing I do is good enough, is it!'

Sarah just shook her head and continued. 'The children are also better off in this school after the fiasco in the last one and DI Hudson has promised continued police support.'

James's body drooped in resignation. 'Is there anything I can do?'

'Apart from fixing this situation once and for all, yes, there is. I want our own.' She hesitated. 'I hate to use the term, but I want our own bodyguard. At least until I can be sure this nightmare is over.'

James inclined his head. 'Okay. I'll see to it immediately. Now I'm back, I'll concentrate on bringing this whole China business to a close. Perhaps then we can get back to living a normal life together.'

Sarah remained silent.

CHAPTER 24

James drove back to Birmingham feeling empty and alone. He turned on the radio hoping to lighten his mood, but instead the song 'We Had It All' by Willie Nelson came on. Every single word felt like a bayonet in his gut.

James snapped the radio off and clenched the steering wheel. He needed to face up to some home truths. Chris had spelled out clearly he'd been slipping badly at work and he'd criticised his drinking. He'd nearly ruined everything with Meili Shabani and he blamed himself for Mason's kidnapping. The final nail in the coffin was Sarah's ultimatum: *fix it!'*

Come on, Macrae! Pull yourself together! It's now or never.

He took in a deep breath and phoned Scott Farmer, the private investigator he'd used in the past to help him defend himself against his enemies.

'Hey Scott, James.'

'Hello, how are you?'

'Not great, to tell you the truth. That's why I'm calling. Can you arrange for round-the-clock protection for Sarah and the children? They will be staying in Wales for the foreseeable future.'

'Leave it to me. I'll make the necessary arrangements.'

Next, he phoned Jeremy Hirons. Sarah's ultimatum had triggered a turning point. She was right. He needed to fix the situation and he would need to plan his moves ahead, rather than wait like a sitting duck for his enemies to strike again. Maybe it was better Sarah, and the children were out of the way after all. It would enable him to keep odd hours and change tactics quickly 24/7 to zero in on the one man he believed was responsible for the repeated attacks on his family and business over the past several years.

'Hi Jeremy, it's James. How are you?'

'Not great right now. I've been side-lined for a while and am taking a break from work for a few months.'

'Oh, I'm sorry to hear that. Is there anything I can do to help?'

'Not really, but thanks anyway. What can I do for you?'

James sighed. 'Do you think we could have a chat off the record?'

'That's okay, but let me call you on a secure line later today.'

James finished the call and carefully mapped out in his mind his next set of moves.

Chapter 25

James left his Worcestershire home for work after a lonely and restless night thinking how he could outsmart his enemy. As he closed the door it sounded hollow and empty. The damp mist swallowed and swirled around his Range Rover, fogging up the windows and mirrors. The half-light was tinged with an eerie shade of yellow as the low angle of the sun struggled to penetrate the low clouds to reflect off the autumn leaves.

As he wended his way through the narrow country lanes, he kept the radio off. He needed to think about his meeting with Laura Wesley, his CFO, Martin Farley, his director of Legal Affairs and Chris. It was likely to be a difficult meeting since he presumed he would not get favourable responses to his questions. Thinking of Laura, she'd been with the company for over twenty-five years and had worked her way up in accounting. An absolute rock, she had been instrumental in identifying his old CFO, Hal Spencer, as being a traitor within the company. Martin had been a wonderful support as well. He would need to retain his cool.

No sooner had he entered his office than Chris stormed in. 'Where the bloody hell have you been? You charge out of here without saying a word to anyone and then just disappear off the radar. I warned you before, things are sliding. This can't go on!'

'Chris. I can explain.'

'You'd better because I'm not putting up with this anymore!'

'It's complicated.'

'Well there isn't time right now, we've got a crucial meeting starting.'

Laura entered the boardroom with her laptop and Martin followed with an arm full of files. They all exchanged greetings, but it wasn't the normal light-hearted banter.

'Okay, Laura. Let's get an update of our financial position.'

Laura moved her laptop to one side and leaned forward on the table lacing her fingers. 'I'll get straight to the bottom line. I can't release the stage payment for our acquisition of the Halifax terminal.'

James looked over at Chris. Chris scowled back.

'Why not, Laura, you knew the stage payment was coming up, right?'

'Yes, of course I knew the payment was due this week, but I warned you before that we would be short of cash, since we are up against the limits of our credit lines.'

Chris jumped in. 'I checked our sales and profit performance this morning and it's never been better. We must have more cash coming in!'

Laura nodded and frowned all at once. 'You're right of course, Chris, but you have to remember with the upsurge of business it meant the addition of more employees. Recruiting the right employees and then further costs to train them adds

CHAPTER 25

up quickly. Also, the costs of new equipment, including the two new mega container vessels has increased dramatically.'

James felt his shirt collar tighten. 'God, Laura, you have to find the money!'

'James, you and I have known each other for a very long time and if I say we can't make the payment, then I mean it.'

James looked at Chris. 'Angus will be furious. After all, there was no point in him partnering with us if we couldn't fund the expansion of the Halifax terminal. That was the whole idea, to expand the grain as well as the LNG and CNG terminals and take advantage of the increasing world demand!'

Chris straightened himself up in the chair. 'Agreed! Laura, we have to make that payment.'

Laura tilted her head down and opened up her laptop. She went straight to her cash-flow analysis, flexed her fingers briefly and quickly worked the keyboard.

James, Chris and Martin sat silently.

Laura looked up. 'This is what's going to happen. We will be over ninety days due on most of our payables, something both of you have always insisted we would never do. In addition, we won't make payroll next month, as we will have to pay out the quarterly government VAT tax.'

James rubbed both of his reddening cheeks.

Laura continued. 'Once it gets out that we are in financial trouble, you know what happens then. The banks will demand repayments of their loans and we'll go down faster than the *Titanic*.'

Chris gave a half smile. 'Oh come on, Laura, it can't be as bad as that. Surely?'

'You better believe it, Chris! Both of you also forget that our profit from Istanbul has been falling due to the severe competition we are facing from Ambarli.'

There was a marked silence, then Laura lifted her head up higher and swallowed hard. 'Look, I didn't want to say this, but I warned you both at the last meeting this would happen. You both kept moving the goalposts away from me and I don't have a magic wand to produce ready cash whenever we need it!'

James spoke quietly. 'Okay, let's step back for a minute. Before I left for the Philippines, you and I had a meeting with MidCom Bank to extend our credit lines. They promised they would do that.'

'No, James. They said they would consider it, but they did not agree to increase the limits at the meeting. I'm afraid this will not be an option for us at this stage. Yesterday I got a call back from them to say they would not be extending our credit lines. I had to beg them to keep our existing lines open, that is, without reducing them!'

'What! Why wasn't I told? And why wasn't Chris told?'

'I'm telling you now. You weren't available yesterday and Chris wasn't either, as he was in Immingham.'

James clenched his right fist. 'This doesn't make sense. We showed them how healthy our sales are. I'll call them immediately!'

Laura gently ran her hand over her hair. 'James, you can do that, but understand what happened while you were away at the APEC meeting.' Laura paused. 'Surely you remember the conversation we had when you called me from Manila?'

'Yes, of course.'

Laura continued. 'The onslaught of the Asian financial crisis has shocked the entire world. The Far Eastern countries have been pouring in billions of their foreign reserves to shore up

CHAPTER 25

their currencies. It's likely there could be a worldwide financial meltdown as a result of this. Interest rates this morning are already rising, which means our cash flow will be squeezed even harder. I also see world stock markets are in freefall and it's just flashed up on my screen that one of Japan's top banks has just collapsed under a pile of bad loans.'

'Bloody hell! I didn't see things deteriorating so fast. This is a disaster.' James bit his thumb nail. 'Hang on, Martin. We have the option of bringing in money from Macrae Holdings, since my parents left me all the shares in the company.'

Martin, who had remained quiet in the meeting, took off his suit jacket and rolled up his sleeves. He pulled out the files in front of him.

'James, you're not going to like what I have to say but here it is anyway. Your father and mother, as you know, appointed me to be the executor of their will since I have been their company and private lawyer for over twenty-five years. You are the major beneficiary of their assets with smaller equal shares being divided between your three children when they become of age. Apart from your parents' personal assets, such as their house and other belongings, Macrae Holdings LLC is a corporation that owns all of our port terminals. The corporation obviously needs to be continued as a going concern. So, after Richard and Mary's death, the company needed to continue to meet its obligations including paying its employees and taxes. Your inheritance of your parent's estate carries significant tax and valuation implications.'

James started to fidget. 'I know all that, Martin.'

'Yes, it's standard practice, however, we have to get signed-off valuations of each property from Spain, France, Italy, Greece and Turkey, plus a valuation of the worth of the forty-nine percent ownership of the Yanbu Terminal in Saudi Arabia. Until we have received these certified valuations, the banks will not lend against these assets. The current Asian financial crisis has only made the banks even more jittery. No one knows how deep the financial chasm is going to be, so doors are closing, and hatches are being battened down.'

Chris nodded in agreement. 'That's the same story I got from my father when he tried to borrow against Claybourne Holdings. Sure, the banks can guess at a valuation and then throw a low percentage of lending against it, but each of the banks don't want to unsettle their shareholders during this fragile world financial market.'

James rubbed his eyes. 'But, Martin, as executor of my parents' will, you could authorise a payment from the estate as a loan to Macrae-Claybourne Logistics, right?'

'I can and I will, but the amount of liquid cash at this time will not be enough to cover the stage payment for the Halifax purchase.'

'Okay, let's do this. Let Laura have access to this loan and let's suspend the monthly rent owing to both Macrae Holdings and Claybourne Holdings, that is if you and your father agree, Chris?'

'I'm sure he will agree. No one knows better than he does that cash becomes short very quickly when you expand a business.'

James turned to Laura. 'So, Laura, will that get us off the hook for the time being?'

'That's a question I won't know until I know how much money Martin can move over from Macrae Holdings. Also, with interest rates rising so fast, it will push up our expenses very quickly. One more question from me, do you think you will get the Canadian government grant to help expand Halifax terminal?'

James looked up at the ceiling. 'I don't know, I just don't know.'

———————-

Chris followed James back into his office and closed the door.

'Okay, let's have it. What's the excuse this time?'

'You'd better sit down, Chris.'

Chris sat down in a huff and waited for James to speak. James came and sat opposite him in front of his desk.

'I get that you are upset but there's good reason. I left here in a rush because Mason went missing. Turns out he was kidnapped by two of the hijackers from *Constellation II* who had been following Sarah and the children for two days. After some time, we got word the police had arrested these two, but Mason was not with them. It's a long story but I was able to rescue Mason myself. He nearly died and is now in hospital recovering.'

Chris put his hand to his mouth. 'Oh god, James, I'm so sorry.'

'I didn't have time to call you. Honestly, I was just focused on getting Mason back.'

'Of course. I understand. Sorry for my outburst!'

'No, I needed that and for the ones before. You and Sarah have brought me to my senses. I'm going to get my life back together and, somehow, I'm going to put a stop to the man who's behind all our troubles.'

Chapter 26

'James, you know I shouldn't be discussing something like this with you!'

'Yes, but you also know I'm a signatory to the Official Secrets Act! Do you also remember you told me once that Jack Fox liked to use you because he knew you played outside the rules from time to time?'

Jeremy sat back on his dining room chair, stretched out his legs and twizzled the stem of his red wine glass around. He'd put on some weight since James had last seen him and the former lines on his face seemed to have dissipated. A small scar on his left temple was new. Jeremy smiled back at James. 'You know I'm glad I came here to visit with you. We could never have this conversation over the phone, and I needed to get out of London for a break. Time off work doesn't agree with me. I need to get back into shape and back on the job.'

'Never thought I'd see you so relaxed.'

'Neither did I.' Jeremy shrugged as he looked appreciatively around the dining room. 'You have a beautiful country home,

James.'

James blew out his cheeks. 'I have Sarah to thank for that. It was once, now it's just an empty shell. A house is never a home without a family.' He sat up and quickly changed the subject. 'What happened to you after your visit with Jusuf in Istanbul?'

'Not going there, James. I told you, it's off limits. Anyway, that was a bloody good dinner. Didn't know you were such a good cook.'

'Huh! I'd like to claim credit for it, but my home help has stepped up since Sarah's gone and she cooks for me once in a while.'

'Well, her spaghetti Bolognese was excellent. Good job I'm not driving back to London tonight.

'Come on, let's get a coffee and a scotch and sit in the lounge and I can tell you my plan and why I called you.'

Jeremy sank into an armchair and took a sip of his Dewars twelve-year-old blend and nodded acquiescently as he warmed nicely inside. The crackling log fire roaring in the inglenook fireplace, throwing out a warm glow, added to his relaxed state.

James came and sat opposite him in the other armchair and let out a satisfied sigh.

'Cheers!' They sat in silence for a while.

Jeremy put down his scotch glass. 'Alright, James, let's have it. What's on your mind?'

James leaned forward. 'Basically, mate, I'm sick of being hunted. It's time for me to turn the tables and become the hunter and I believe you can help me.'

Jeremy opened up his hands either side of himself but said nothing.

'Way I see it, this guy Shen has a whole load of shit to answer for. We know he was the man pulling the strings on Stanfield and Nash, as well as Meili Shabani and what happened to Greg Driver. I also believe he was behind my parents' murder, and the attacks on my wife and children. Now we have a hijacking, a kidnapping and whatever else is going on in Turkey.'

'Okay, keep going.'

James put down his scotch on the side table. 'I know I can't get near to this guy in China or any other APEC meeting for that matter, since he's always surrounded by security, but what if I was to meet him on my own ground?'

'How do you intend to lure him to you?'

'Here's the thing. The G8 meeting is coming to Birmingham very soon. My understanding is that China will be invited to attend as a guest country, same as Russia was before they were admitted to the group. Chances are, Shen will be there as Minister of Trade and Development accompanying President Zemin.'

'Okay, I follow you, but how to get to Shen?'

'Easy, he knows my base is here and the Macrae Holdings office is next to the International Convention Centre on Gas Street. What if you leak through your channels that I've got hard evidence that he's responsible for the attacks on my family and business and am going public?'

'You mean you will set yourself up as bait and hope he comes to get even with you once and for all?'

'I do.'

'They all know each other! Look at their eyes.'

CHAPTER 26

Lingdao had just been unhandcuffed and led into the holding cell in Belmarsh Prison. It was the newest and most secure prison in Europe specifically constructed to house terrorists and other 'Category A Exceptional Risk' prisoners. As the steel door slammed behind him, he turned around to face outwards into the corridor looking through the jail bars. His head jolted backwards as he saw his former comrades, Tang and Jin staring back at him in their respective holding cells. He quickly turned his back on them, knowing it was no coincidence they were facing each other. He hoped no one had noticed his slight tremor.

Jack Fox stared back at Stella Hudson from the remote TV monitor they were viewing in the MI6 headquarters. 'No doubt about it! The body language from all three of them shows clear recognition. We've enough evidence to charge them right now. At least they won't be back on the street after the seventy-two-hour maximum limit.'

Stella sighed. 'That's another stupid law these politicians have, only being able to hold suspects under the Terrorism Act for a maximum of seventy-two hours without charging them.'

'Tell me about it! Okay, Stella, let's bring in Huang Genjo from the safe house and the crew of *Constellation II* and get these guys in a line-up as soon as possible.'

'Will do, Jack. I'll also get the forensic reports from the hijacking and compare them to their fingerprints and DNA. We should also lean on this Lingdao character and try to find out who he was meeting that day in Birmingham.'

'Agreed. Any luck on any other suspect sightings that day around the pub?'

'None as yet. We've got clips from street cameras that we're going over again but nothing unusual sticks out at this stage.'

'Okay, I've got Jeremy coming in any minute now.'

'Oh, I thought Jeremy was off on extended leave for the time being.'

'He is, but he went up to Birmingham last night and had a meeting with James Macrae, off the record. He called me this morning and wants to meet. I think you should be in on whatever it is he wants to share.'

Stella popped out to the ladies and when she came back, Jeremy was with Jack.

'Hi, Jeremy, good to see you!' Stella stood back and took stock of him. 'You look good, younger than ever! Whatever it is you're taking, I want some of it.'

Jeremy laughed. 'Nonsense, you're looking good yourself. As fit and trim as ever.'

Jack beckoned them to his round conference table. 'That's enough of the self-admiration talk for one day. Now, Jeremy, what's so important to get you to drive up to Birmingham to see James Macrae and then come here to tell us about it?'

Jeremy sat down and clapped his hands together. 'Fundamentally, James wants to set himself up as bait to get at the Chinese and General Shen specifically.'

Fox remained expressionless. Stella also showed no emotion.

Jeremy didn't wait for an answer. 'In essence, James Macrae has had more than he can take. His wife and children have left him, and he blames Shen for being the master of the attacks on his family and business. No matter what James does, or has done, he remains in the crosshairs of Shen, at least in his mind.'

Jeremy got up from his chair and stretched. 'Sorry, some-

CHAPTER 26

times I can't sit for very long before beginning to feel uncomfortable.' He put his hands on his hips, pushed his shoulders forward alternately and continued.

'He says he has enough evidence to point the finger at Shen. Apart from what he knows through his involvement with us, his own private detective, Scott Farmer, has evidence of Shen's involvement. Just recently, he's had to deal with the hijacking, and the kidnapping of his son and even this woman, Meili Shabani, who we know is an accomplice of Shen's, tried to pick him up at an APEC meeting in Manila. He knows he can't get near him in China, but he thinks Shen will be attending the G8 meeting coming up in Birmingham.'

Jack Fox put his hands together and rested his chin on the pyramid. 'James Macrae's a smart man. He's not wrong and yet he doesn't even know half of what we know. I'm going to need to think about this.'

Stella jumped in. 'How does he propose to set himself up as bait?'

Jeremy sat down again. 'He wants us to leak his plans to set up a one-on-one interview with *Mercantile News*, the international magazine that covers the shipping industry. He knows the Chinese read this magazine and even try to influence it. In the interview he plans to cover what has happened to his company in the last two years and state he has concrete evidence as to who was behind it. Even if we don't leak it, he will still go ahead with the interview. He's also sure the newswire and daily press will pick up the story and amplify it even more.'

Jack patted his mouth with his fingers. 'Hmmm, maybe this could work in our favour. Thinking about it, on the evidence we have so far on Shen, while we all know he's behind all these crimes, it would be difficult to find him guilty in a British court of law. There are too many loopholes he could crawl through. So if we can set him up in an attempt to kill Macrae, then we would have him for sure.' He bit his thumb for a second. 'The PM, including us, is wondering who's really running China. This might flush out the pecking order.'

Stella sat forward. 'We could shadow Macrae and his family while this is going on.'

'That's true, but let's just take a moment to analyse who's running China. We've got Jiang Zemin, who's both the general secretary of the Chinese Communist Party central committee as well as president. Then there's Li Peng who is premier of China and Deng Xiaoping is still an influential leader behind the scenes. But, if I had to bet money on the person who's hiding in the cobwebs, it's General Wu Shen. Pound to a pinch of snuff, he's the one with the hidden agenda and is strengthening his position to take over from Zemin.'

Jeremy nodded. 'That would be my guess too.'

Fox continued. 'Okay then, let's help Macrae set himself up as bait and maybe we can give Zemin a helping hand as well as ourselves, get our two countries more aligned and get this guy off Macrae's back once and for all.'

Jeremy added, more as an afterthought, 'On the other hand, if anything was to happen to Macrae, there would be hell to pay.'

'The prime minister will see you in his office now, sir.'

Anthony Bloxham, the chancellor of the exchequer, got up from his office desk and walked through the interconnecting

CHAPTER 26

door between number 11 and number 10 Downing Street. As he entered the main reception area of the prime minister's residence, he walked across the distinctive black and white floor tiles and turned to climb the grand staircase to the first floor. With his mind entirely focused on the Asian financial crisis, he totally ignored the ornate black wrought-iron balusters and handrail, the yellow-painted walls above the white wainscoting and the pictures of every prime minister that had governed the country.

'Come on in, Tony.'

'You're not going to like this, prime minister, but this Asian financial crisis is deepening by the day. Apart from Thailand, Malaysia, Indonesia and the Philippines devaluing their currencies, the contagious effects are now spreading to South Korea. The IMF is pouring billions of dollars into these currencies to help shore up their strength. Stock markets around the world are in freefall and Brazil and Russia's economies are now being affected as well.'

Geoffrey Lumley blew out his cheeks. 'So, you're saying that what began as a regional financial crisis is now rapidly becoming a serious financial threat to the whole world?'

'I am.'

'You better sit down.'

Bloxham grabbed the chair and sat facing his boss.

The PM continued, 'Okay, what can we do to contain this crisis and help stop the freefall of these economies before we all get sucked in.'

Bloxham coughed. 'In my mind, the one country that can help stem this worsening panic is China. God knows, if they follow suit and devalue their currency, the whole global financial system would be at risk of collapsing. If we can persuade China not to devalue its Renminbi and maybe contribute several billion dollars of their own money to their neighbours in aid, it could provide just enough economic stability to the whole region to restore world confidence.'

The PM rested his forehead on his hand. 'I see what you're saying. It's a lot to ask.'

'We need to do this, Geoffrey. After all, we're only just starting to see economic growth after the last recession. We're still in a fragile state.'

'Got it! I'll get a call booked with President Zemin. If he wants Hong Kong back in line with our original agreement, he will have to comply. Let me see what I can do, Tony, and let's hope you're right!'

Chapter 27

'You will now have to take care of the first G8 bombing yourself. Is that understood?'

'Understood.'

Nick Northrop pocketed his burner phone and contemplated his additional assignment. As a professional soldier and mercenary, he would need to be organized and well prepared since security would be at the highest level possible to protect the world leaders.

In his sparsely furnished apartment, he sat back in his only chair, ate his Subway sandwich, sipped his beer, and carefully considered the situation. It was a Saturday afternoon. Northrop wasn't a mercenary that simply relied on muscle and raw energy, instead he relied on his wits and technology. He knew if he was at the forefront of technological development, he would have an advantage over his adversaries. In short, he was a 'techy'.

When he first arrived in Birmingham, he'd rented his apartment in a twenty-storey high-rise block close to the city centre on Hagley Road at the junction of Fiveways. The tower block provided him with easy access to his office, as well as proximity to the central works department yard. This was necessary since emergency calls could occur at any time. Works vehicles might be required for road closures, diversions, or waste clean-up. The building also provided him with anonymity amongst his neighbours, underground parking for his car and ready access to five main roads radiating in all directions, giving him a choice of escape routes either by foot, car or bus. Three railway stations were also within a mile of his base.

As a mercenary soldier fighting mostly in Africa after he'd left the British Army, Northrop had built up a stock of the very latest tools of his trade. His cache of body armour, weapons, ammunition, explosives, and communication equipment were hidden in two lock-up garages, one to the south-east and one to the north of the city. He'd chosen lock-up garages, rather than self-storage warehouses since the warehouses always had security cameras and recorded entry and exit times. Lock-up garages could be entered at any time with no record of comings and goings. In each of the garages, he'd reinforced the metal door catches and locks, but made sure they looked grubby and neglected on the outside. He even left the graffiti that had been randomly sprayed over them. Security cameras and silent alarm systems were installed inside the garages and linked to his phone. These were some of the first Internet Protocol cameras ever released.

Having no police record, he made sure he stayed out of trouble. He'd even come in and out of the UK several times, completely undetected, using a private plane flying between Wales and Southern Ireland. One of those visits included the murder of Richard and Mary Macrae.

Northrop finished his lunch and hopped on the number 60 bus in the city centre that would take him to his lock-up garage in the district of Sheldon. He wore a blue Birmingham City Football Club hat. The journey would take about forty-five minutes and pass the football club ground. Nothing like blending in with local supporters in this part of the city. The block of ten garages was located just off the Coventry road, behind a row of shops.

With no one around, he quickly entered his garage. Inside was a dark-blue VW Caddy van. Except this was no ordinary van. Under the apparently standard skin of the works van was a highly tuned Golf GTI engine, beefed-up brakes and suspension, roll cage and strengthened front and rear bumpers. A trickle battery charger made sure the battery was always fully charged. Northrop unlocked the van and carefully checked its contents. He opened a metal military box that had been bolted to the floor and extracted a large, sealed polythene bag. The heavy bag contained what appeared to be dirty white putty.

Northrop smiled. *There's enough C-4 plastic explosive for me to use in the first attack.* C-4 was his favourite explosive. Like a malleable plastic, it was easy to mould into different shapes not only to hide it, but if moulded correctly it could produce a fierce cutting reaction through metal structures causing extensive demolition with a blast of 26,400 feet per second. With an indefinite shelf life, what was there not to like about this choice of explosive? He checked his M37 demolition charge assembly. All good.

He would check his second garage tomorrow. Now all he had to do was wait for the opportunity to plant the explosive.

'President Zemin. Always a pleasure to speak with you.'

'Likewise, Prime Minister Lumley. You pre-empted my call. I owe you an answer to the question your foreign secretary put to my ambassador. That is, was my country behind the hijacking of your tanker, *Constellation II*, sailing under a British flag? To that I can answer, categorically, no. However, the reason for my delay in answering you is simple. We carried out an extensive internal investigation into the matter and did find evidence of, let us say, a splinter group of dissidents acting completely independently outside of my government. It was this group of criminals that were responsible for the attack. I can now assure you that this matter has been dealt with and the leader concerned, once he knew of his impending arrest, committed suicide. The matter has now been closed.'

'President Zemin, with respect, how can we be sure our citizens will not be attacked again by these criminals?'

'I give you my word. My government has put this matter completely to rest. Now, can I take it there will be no more, if I can use your word, "hiccups" in our way to returning Hong Kong on July first?'

Geoffrey Lumley cleared his throat. 'I would like to answer yes to that but I, together with my government, are not yet fully convinced there will not be any further interferences from your country on the citizens and property of the United Kingdom.'

There was a period of silence until finally Zemin responded. 'What is it that you want?'

'President Zemin. We need your help and cooperation...'

'Oh?'

CHAPTER 27

'The Asian financial crisis is now spreading around the world like a malignant cancer. With foreign capital pouring out of these markets, and currency devaluations, global investor and consumer confidence is about to take a freefall. We need you to guarantee that you will not devalue your currency and, in addition, prop up your Far Eastern neighbours with substantial injections of Chinese capital. In short, we believe you can stabilize this crisis.'

'I see.' Zemin went quiet again... 'And if we do this, you can give us your assurance there will be no more roadblocks to the return of Hong Kong.'

'I can.'

―――――――――――――――――――

'You didn't have to call ahead to come here.'

Sarah looked up at James. 'I know, but it felt like the right thing to do.'

James smiled back. As he looked at Sarah, he felt the jolt of electricity in his body that he always felt when he saw her, especially if he hadn't seen her for a while. 'Come on in. You know you could have just come in and picked up those things you wanted. You have a key and it's still your house as much as mine.'

Sarah bent down on the entrance hall floor and took off her muddy boots. 'I wasn't sure if you'd changed the locks and maybe the security code.'

James shook his head. 'As far as I'm concerned, nothing's changed. We're still married and what's mine is yours. I'm still hoping we can get back together.'

Sarah remained quiet.

James pierced the uneasy silence. 'So, you're on your way home from Highclere Castle? Are you driving back to Wales tonight? You look tired.'

Sarah replied stiffly. 'Yes, I was down there working on the project for a couple of days. Mum and Dad have been looking after the children.'

'Look I'm just in the middle of preparing dinner for myself. Why don't you come into the kitchen, and you can tell me how they are.'

Sarah followed him into the kitchen and took stock of everything around her. 'Something smells good.'

'Yes, it's shepherd's pie.' He turned to face her and noticed her jeans and turtleneck sweater were muddy. 'Look, why don't you go and have a shower while I prepare dinner for us both. You've still got plenty of clean clothes to change into upstairs.'

'Oh, I don't know.'

'Well, it's a three-hour drive and you look like you need a rest and something to eat before you hit the road again.'

Sarah frowned. 'I guess I could.'

'Go on. I'll have it ready for you when you've showered.'

By the time Sarah had showered, the pie was ready and James had added some more carrots and broccoli. He set it up on the kitchen table.

Sarah came down in a fresh pair of jeans, a light-blue blouse and dark-blue crew-neck sweater. Her hair was tousled and wet.

'Come on, sit down and let's tuck in.'

'Thank you.'

'So how are our kids?'

CHAPTER 27

Sarah finished chewing. 'Actually, they're doing well. Mason has recovered well and somehow seems to have shrugged off what happened to him. I think it's a male thing.'

'That's good! What about the girls?'

'They seem to have settled into the new school and all three are making new friends. Mason is following in your footsteps by taking outward bound courses outside school hours. Mia is wanting to know more about my field of historical architecture while Olivia is, well, Olivia.'

'Well, that's good news. I'm glad they're all happy.'

Sarah took a drink of water. She was quiet and looked over at James.

'You know they miss you terribly.'

James took a deep breath. 'I miss them too. I miss you.'

Sarah looked down and started to eat again.

'So, changing the subject, what's happening at Highclere Castle?'

'Well, it's keeping me busy. The project is finally going well. The two ceilings are taking shape nicely and are completely in accordance with my drawings. Lord and Lady Carnarvon have now asked me to provide plans for the restoration of one of the larger run-down farmhouses on the estate. They want to make it into a holiday cottage but retain the exterior of the original structure.'

James laughed. 'That's good! I wondered what you'd been up to, covered in mud. I see the Land Rover needs a good wash too!'

'That vehicle is amazing. After all the wet weather we've been having, it was a godsend in all that mire. Come on, I'll help you clean up before I go.'

James was about to tell her not to bother, but instead said,

'Okay, I'll wash, you can dry. I don't use the dishwasher these days. No point with just me.'

They stood side by side in front of the kitchen sink. James turned to her and joked, 'I don't know why I don't use cardboard plates; it would be much quicker!'

They turned to each other, their eyes locking together. Sarah reached up and put her arms around his neck. James took his wet hands out of the sink, magnetised by her hazel eyes and pulled her body tightly to him. They kissed gently but as their breathing quickened, the kiss got deeper and longer.

Sarah came up for breath. 'Phew! What now?'

James dried his hands, took her hand and silently led her upstairs.

They made love passionately for some time and then lay back exhausted, both feeling contented and happy.

'Oh god, James. What are we going to do? I can't live with you, and I can't live without you!'

'All I know is, I love you, Sarah Macrae. I think about you and the children all the time.'

Sarah blew out a long sigh. 'I'd better call my parents and tell them I won't be home tonight. Let's get up, go downstairs, light the fire and talk things through over a drink.'

As the yellow and orange flames engulfed the rough-hewn logs above the glowing embers, sparks spat and danced their way up the large chimney and out into the cold night air. Sarah and James sat close together on the sofa, transfixed by the hypnotic effects of the flickering flames. With the occasional table lights turned off, a warm, blurring glow radiated around them.

James took a sip of his red wine, 'I've been thinking about us, Sarah. You were right to be angry with me. I did get caught up with the business and left everything to you.'

'So, what's your plan now?'

'Honestly? Well, I'm not out of the woods yet when it comes to Canada. There have been setbacks with raising the money for the merger, which we've overcome temporarily, but we desperately need an injection of cash. I'm afraid both Chris and I got carried away with the expansion of the company and its left us short.'

'Can't you borrow against Macrae Holdings?'

'We can, but the banks won't commit until they've received the latest valuations of the ports. Martin thinks it won't be long, but of course this Asian financial crisis has everyone on edge right now.'

'Yes, I've been following that as well. It's a right mess!'

'So, to answer your question, I still need more time to sort all this out.' He didn't mention getting even with Shen.

Sarah held up her wine in front of the fire. She swirled the wine around the glass and studied the legs. 'Why don't we just leave things as they are for the time being. We both need time to let things settle.'

James nodded quietly. He put his drink down on the side table and leaned over and kissed Sarah. He slipped his hand inside her bathrobe. Sarah put down her drink and they slowly slid down onto the rug in front of the fire.

Sarah whispered, 'I love you, James.'

'General Shen, you owe me!'

'How so, General Gulnaz?'

'Oh, the ever-innocent General Wu Shen! Which are you

today? General or Minister of Trade and Development?

'What would you like me to be?'

'You can start off by being a general.'

They sat down in General Gulnaz's office. Shen had come to Ankara to check up on the progress of the renewed silk road initiative.

'So why do I owe you?'

Gulnaz leaned forward on his desk and crossed his arms tightly.

'The short-range and long-range air missiles we purchased from you were not the latest technology. I was clear in my instructions, was I not?

'General Gulnaz, I gave precise instructions on what you needed.'

'Sorry, try again. We've tested them. They are nowhere near the capabilities of what you have now!' Gulnaz slammed the desk hard with his fist. You must take me for a fool!'

Shen kept his voice down. 'I certainly do not take you for a fool, sir.'

'Let me be clear, Shen. I want your latest technology. I kept my word in exchanging the latest Patriot PAC-1 System that we have. You must know that!'

Shen sat silent, trying to sum up a response. He was about to attempt an explanation when Gulnaz cut him off.

'Don't underestimate me, Shen! I have many friends in both the east and the west, which is more than you've got! Now either you send me your latest technology missiles, or your silk road initiative is off, including Ambarli port.' Gulnaz's angry glare sliced straight into Shen's eyes, and he stabbed his forefinger at him. 'And don't think you can take away your financial support from our country either. I told you before, as the link between the east and west, many countries want to invest here.'

Shen sat upright. 'General Gulnaz, the missile system you received was the latest at the time. Our new system had not been completely tested, but I can tell you now that this system can now be available to you. Let us remain good friends. We have to trust each other.'

Gulnaz got up from his desk. 'I'll trust you when I have that system installed here. I want it yesterday. Got it?'

'Got it!'

Shen left General Gulnaz's office. Normally he would have made sure he was not spoken down to, but, in this case, he needed to acquiesce. Turkey was too important for China to lose as a friend. It would be their bridgehead into the west. Not only would they continue to be a useful source of intelligence for what the West was up to, but China could get their hands on the latest Western technology. Technology could always be copied and enhanced. It could also be inspected for weaknesses that could be exploited at some point in the future.

Shen desperately wanted to share his ambition to be the Chinese leader with Gulnaz for accelerating China's expansion because Gulnaz could be a strong ally. He was a strong leader who could easily be bribed. All the essential qualities of a world leader, as Shen viewed it. He'd also shied away from asking why Gulnaz hadn't followed through on taking over the Macrae-Claybourne Haydarpasa port terminal, although he already knew the answer to that one. To have done that during the Asian financial crisis would have had catastrophic consequences for the Turkish economy. James Macrae didn't know how lucky he was.

Chapter 28

In the pouring rain, at exactly 8:30pm Hong Kong time, on Monday 30th June 1997, Prime Minister Tony Blair entered the Chinese delegation headquarters at the Harbour Plaza hotel in Hunghom, a district of Hong Kong. He ducked from under the umbrella that was being held for him and walked across the foyer to meet his counterpart.

'President Zemin, it's an honour to meet you, especially on such a historic occasion as this!' Blair shook hands with Zemin at their private summit before the handover ceremony of Hong Kong back to China.

'Prime Minister Blair, it is also an honour for me to meet you too. Indeed, it is a momentous occasion to have our territory returned to us after 156 years! Let us go and sit down one to one.'

As they sat in a private room, Zemin gave a wide smile and continued, 'Congratulations again on your recent election victory. As you know, we had a close working relationship with your predecessor, Geoffrey Lumley.'

CHAPTER 28

'So I understand. On his handover to me, he asked me to personally thank you for your firm stance on not devaluing your currency and foreign assistance to those economies in trouble during the Asian financial crisis. We thank you for helping to stabilize the world currency markets.'

Zemin wondered if Blair knew they would never have done this if Lumley hadn't threatened not to return the British colony back to China, at least on the agreed date. He smiled widely. 'We are pleased we could help. On that front, I look forward to working with you in the future, especially to develop increased trade between our two countries.'

'We also look forward to that. My understanding is that you will be attending the G8 summit coming up in Birmingham as an observer. This will be a good opportunity to bring us all closer together, not only politically but economically.'

'Yes, we agree. It would be a step forward for the world to eventually have a G9 group! Now, I believe we have a long night ahead of us. Let us join the cocktail reception at the Hong Kong convention centre. I'm looking forward to meet Prince Charles and Margaret Thatcher. I know Deng Xiaoping and her had an excellent relationship.'

'They certainly did. We wish to carry on this excellent association.'

Blair and Zemin arrived some time later at the convention centre in Wan Chai and joined the many dignitaries and guests for the handover ceremony and party. After live performances and fireworks, Prince Charles addressed the assembly and read the farewell speech on behalf of Queen Elizabeth II. 'I should like to pay tribute to the people of Hong Kong themselves for all that they have achieved in the last century and a half. The triumphant success of Hong Kong demands – and deserves –

to be maintained.'

Just before midnight, the Union Jack was lowered. After a few moments the flag of the People's Republic of China was raised. President Zemin stepped forward. 'On this grand occasion we welcome the transfer of sovereignty of Hong Kong from the United Kingdom back to the People's Republic of China. We are optimistic for the future of the territory as we introduce one country, two systems.'

Once the Chinese national anthem had been played, Prince Charles and the rest of the British delegation dissolved away, returning to the United Kingdom. At the same time, just after midnight in the pitch-black pouring rain, Chinese border guards at the Wen Jingdu border post opened the barricades into Hong Kong. Four thousand members of the People's Liberation Army streamed into the ex-British colony in armoured vehicles. Another strategic military port had now been added to the growing number of international bases.

———————————————-

Nick Northrop looked out of his office window across to the town hall. Designed like a grand Roman temple, it stood proudly reflecting the bright rays of sunshine from its majestic white limestone pillars onto the grey stone slabs in Victoria Square. It was an unseasonably warm autumn day with people starting to shed their coats and warmer apparel as the temperature started to climb into the high teens. Had she not been a statue, perhaps Queen Victoria might have taken off her heavy ceremonial robe and sighed in relief. For Northrop, however, he had other ideas in mind. It was a perfect day for reconnaissance.

CHAPTER 28

Northrop left his jacket in the office and went out just after midday for his lunch. He ambled down Colmore Row and picked up a roast beef sandwich, a Belgian bun and a Costa Rican coffee from the delicatessen shop on Temple Row overlooking the church yard of St Philip's cathedral. He picked an unoccupied bench on one of the paths radiating out from the entrance of the cathedral facing the Grand Hotel. It was a perfect observation post. Seemingly looking up into the sky as if to soak up the warmth on his face, he gently took a bite out of his sandwich. Several pigeons landed around him, cooing enthusiastically in expectation of some crumbs. On the perimeter of the churchyard, the last remnants of yellow and orange autumn leaves from the maple trees twisted and twizzled down in the warm, gentle breeze to the grass below. With bare trees, Northrop had an excellent view of the exterior façade of the hotel. Slowly he moved his head from side to side like a sunflower would follow the sun. His eyes acted like a sponge; recording the salient details he needed to know.

Over one hundred years old, the hotel was an impressive Victorian building faced with decorative brick and stone. He counted six storeys in all. Three separate prominent towers faced the street with roofs that resembled the French Renaissance style. A multitude of glass windows also faced the street. Once the bomb was detonated, this glass, together with jagged bricks, metal and mortar would end up in the very churchyard he was now sitting.

Northrop took a drink of his coffee and continued to look at the building as he drew his head back to drink out of the polystyrene cup. He decided the bomb would need to be planted inside the building for maximum explosive effect. An exterior bomb would also be difficult to conceal due to the intense security arrangements. The streets around the hotel would be sealed off and it was highly likely there would be large crowd barriers erected between the church yard and the street. He knew that on Saturday 16th May, next year, there would be mass demonstrations planned by an organization known as Jubilee 2000. This was a coalition of seventy different agencies calling for the cancellation of unrepayable developing world debt by the year 2000. Thousands were expected to attend the demonstration from all over the UK and abroad. However many turned up, it would provide a good diversion for the security personnel and possibly a motive for terrorism, especially on the scale Northrop was being paid to create.

Having studied the building plans and development applications for the hotel in the council archives, he knew that the Grosvenor ballroom on the second floor was thirty metres long and ten metres wide and had been constructed using strong steel girders and cross beams. He would need to design the shape of the C4 plastic explosive to cut through these steel I-beams. If he could achieve that, he could rain carnage on the restaurant, café, bar and reception rooms below. It would be a masterly design and create a blast so big there would be very little left of the hotel by the time the dust had settled. A thing of beauty to which any self-respecting demolition expert would be proud. He hesitated to call himself a terrorist. They simply created chaos for some ideology or other, whereas he was a professional soldier; an expert mercenary, and a businessman.

Feeling satisfied with his assessment, he finished his sandwich and bun, took a last swig of coffee and made his way to the front entrance of the hotel, dropping his rubbish in a convenient bin just outside the churchyard. Two large square stone planters full of red and white geraniums adorned

CHAPTER 28

the front entrance as he entered the main reception. He strode confidently past the front desk across the polished marble floor and ascended the grand staircase to the first floor. The heavily carpeted stairs, with wrought-iron balustrades, wrapped themselves around the tall cluster of interior marble pillars in the vast hallway.

A set of tall double doors stood open on the landing giving him a full view of the empty Grosvenor ballroom. As he entered, he couldn't help but be impressed by the ten-metre ceiling height, his brain assessing in milliseconds that with high ceilings you could gain more velocity for the heavy debris pouring downwards from the roof. He didn't dwell on the ornate pillars at the side of the great ballroom or the decorative ceiling and cornices. He exited the ballroom and ascended the four floors above. The first three contained standard-sized bedrooms but the top ones contained the private suites. Northrop quickly decided it would be a waste of time to plant the bomb in one of the suites. Not only would UK security staff sweep these rooms several times, but each of the G8 premiers would have their own security staff inspect them as well. Likewise all the rooms in the hotel, but with perhaps a little less scrutiny.

The blast would need to be strong enough to cut straight down through the floors and bring the whole structure down with all the people inside from the floors above. Anyone below in the ballroom, meeting rooms, bar, restaurant, and cafeteria would be flattened. The bomb needed to cause a massive death toll with total destruction to cover up the one person he needed to kill. That man was President Zemin. He didn't know who had commissioned the hit, only that it needed to be carried out professionally. To simply kill Zemin alone would put whoever commissioned the hit under intense scrutiny. Being politically aware, he surmised that the one person who had the most to gain from this was General Shen.

Northrop descended the stairs and returned to the hotel reception area. He inspected the adjoining bar and lounge and then continued to the floor below where the restaurant and cafeteria was housed. Satisfied, he returned to the front desk and was about to leave when a concierge approached him. 'May I help you, sir?'

Northrop turned towards him and smiled. 'Actually, you can. I'm from the council and, as you know, we have the lord mayor's reception booked here where the new lord mayor takes on the responsibility for their one-year term. We also thank the outgoing mayor for their achievements and their service. As always, we have a block of guest rooms booked. Can you confirm which floor the block of rooms will be? Some of our guests like to retire early and need to have quiet rooms away from the festivities.'

The concierge nodded. 'Yes, I can tell you that.' He walked over to the computer terminal on his antique mahogany desk and typed on the keyboard. 'Looks like there's a group of rooms booked on the third and fourth floors.'

'Excellent, and can you tell me if all the rooms are away from the elevators?'

The concierge looked back at his screen. 'Yes, that was a specific request.'

'Splendid! I look forward to seeing you then.'

Northrop walked back to his office. He knew he would need to arrive early for the lord mayor's reception and gala dinner to get a room on the fourth floor, mid-way between the lift shafts. In his terms, the 'sweet spot'.

CHAPTER 28

Satisfied he'd formulated his plans for the first bomb, he sat in his office to consider the second one. In his mind there was no need for a second explosion, but his employer had insisted there should be two. He wasn't sure if they wanted to replicate the IRA Birmingham pub bombings from 1974 when bombs were simultaneously planted in two public houses, The Tavern in the Town and The Mulberry Bush, or they really wanted to add additional suspicion that it was a terrorist bombing campaign that would cover up the assassination of one man. Whatever, he was being paid handsomely for his expertise and was enjoying a bumper payday since he now had to prepare two bombs. It certainly was becoming an easier life than sweating it out in the hot, humid, mosquito-ridden African climate.

He left his office and went down to the archives in the basement where he located the CAD architectural plans for the International Convention Centre. He took them back to his office and spread them out across his conference table. After scanning the first series of drawings, he found the page he wanted. A devious plan was already forming in his masterly criminal mind. *You want an explosion; I'll show you one!*

Chapter 29

Late in the afternoon, James and Laura pored over papers in the boardroom of Macrae Holdings. Dusk was already setting in across the misty canal network in Gas Street Basin.

'How long do you think it will be now before the banks extend our lines of credit, Laura?'

'I spoke with the chairman of MidCom yesterday. They are just waiting for completion of the Istanbul terminal valuation.'

'Hmm. Why the delay on that one?

'Seems that the notice of compulsory purchase from the Turkish government, which we quickly fought against and shot down, was the reason.'

'Yes, that was a loser from the word go. One word from us to the international press about that and they would have seen a massive outflow of foreign capital. Turkey knew they would have been the next to fall in the Asian financial crisis.'

'Okay, James. Let's come to the sticky part. We will be short of cash again in two months. If we are to get an injection of capital sooner, you and Chris will need to give personal

CHAPTER 29

guarantees for additional borrowings. Are you in agreement with that?'

'Yes, we've discussed it already. Sarah and Jenny are not really happy about it, but they know it might be necessary. Being able to complete the deal with Canada will be a huge step forward for us and our percentage of profit is healthy. If we can just get over this hump, we'll be well on our way.'

'Okay, James, I'll get the PGs drawn up straight away.'

There was a knock on the boardroom door. James's admin manager entered. 'Excuse me, James, DI Hudson is here to see you.'

'Ah yes, I'm expecting her. Laura and I are just finishing up.'

'Come on in, inspector. Can I get you a coffee?'

'Thanks, that would be great. Milk, no sugar.'

As Laura left, James grabbed himself and his visitor a coffee. When he returned, Stella Hudson had her back turned to him and was looking out of the window across Gas Street Basin.

James put the coffee down on the boardroom table and went to stand beside her. 'It's a great view on a nice day. Can't see much right now.'

Stella kept looking out of the window. 'I didn't realize you were so high up here. Even in the haze you can see down the canal and over to the International Convention Centre.'

'Yes, the office has a great view. These warehouses have all been extensively refurbished since my great grandfather first started the business. This was the hub for the distribution of industrial goods to the outside world when Birmingham and the Black Country was at the centre of the Industrial Revolution. Stuart Macrae started the business from his house nearby but eventually opened the warehouse and office here so he could see all the network of waterways beneath him and keep an eye on his barges. With these binoculars, you can see all the way down to the Old Turn junction where the Birmingham canal splits both eastward and westward. Down here to our left is the canal that goes south-west to Worcester which links to the River Severn and allowed goods to be exported from Bristol all over the world.'

'Fascinating. Your company certainly has a great history.' She turned around and they both sat down.

'Thank you. By the way, you can call me James. After all we've been through together, I figure it's okay to use first names.'

'Why not?' Stella cupped both her hands around the coffee mug. 'James, we need to discuss your plan to lure Shen out into the open. Unofficially, Jack Fox has told us to go ahead. Officially, he knows nothing about this.'

James tilted his head. 'When you say "us", who do you mean?'

'Jeremy and I. I know Jeremy isn't available right now, but he will be back at work quite soon. But here's the thing, even if you can get Shen to come after you and we can intercede, then we can't lay a finger on him because of his diplomatic immunity.'

'Which means he can do what he likes and walk free?'

'Yes.'

James shook his head and gritted his teeth. 'I know diplomatic immunity provides foreign government representatives protection from criminal or civil prosecution under the laws of the host country, but it shouldn't allow them to be able to get away with murder!'

'You're quite right, of course, but there could be circum-

CHAPTER 29

stances where diplomatic immunity could be waived.'

'Oh?'

'Yes, diplomatic immunity can be waived only by the official's home country government. There have been a few instances when an official commits a serious crime that is not related to their diplomatic responsibility.'

'So are you saying China might waive Shen's immunity?'

'Don't know at this stage, but...' Stella paused.

'But what?'

'James, before I go on, I need to remind you again of your oath to the Official Secrets Act.'

'You have my oath and my signature. I'm well aware of the penalties if I was to ever break silence on these matters. I don't fancy going to jail for a long period of time.'

'Alright then. We have reason to believe Shen is trying to seize power for himself, perhaps even to dislodge President Zemin. There have been several things that lead us to think this may be a possibility.'

James gazed back at her. 'Interesting.'

'Firstly, China was behaving itself well before the return of Hong Kong, but we think that the hijacking of your ship was an act that Shen committed independently. Meetings between our foreign secretary and their ambassador seem to point to that. In addition, the three lead hijackers were all military men under Shen's command at one time or another. We also believe the murder of your parents was the result of Shen working through their London head of security who appears to have recently had a heart attack. It was through this man that the mercenary, William Brocklehurst, was recruited to commit the murder. There's other evidence we have, but it's enough for us to believe we can convince China, or more specifically

Zemin, to waive Shen's immunity.'

'Speaking of this mercenary, Brocklehurst, did you ever pick up the scent on him?'

'No, he's gone off the radar for the time being, but we think he went back to a group of mercenaries called Sandline International operating in Sierra Leone.'

'What about the hijacker, Lingdao? According to Jeremy he was picked up in Birmingham. Do you think he was after me or could there be something more involved than that?'

'We're sure he was after you, but what worries us is that he was about to meet someone, but the actual meet never happened. Whoever it was must have smelled a rat. We couldn't afford to leave Lingdao free any longer.'

'Hmmm. Well, whatever, Shen is still responsible for all the sabotage, and murders of my parents and employees. If I can get him out of the convention centre down to this office, I'll have a chance to get at him myself. I need him to know that I have all the evidence locked in the safe in this office. Can you feed that information through your intelligence channels?'

'We can.' Hudson took stock of James for a second. 'Now we need to make sure that if worst comes to worst, you can defend yourself. We know you are a member of the Hereford and Worcester Shooting Club and have several firearms, but we want to assess your physical capabilities at the West Midlands police training centre.'

James smirked.

'This isn't funny, James. You need to take this seriously.'

'Sorry, but you realize I've been brought up with tough love from my father. I served my apprenticeship in some of the busiest ports around the world. They're surrounded by some of the dingiest and criminal-infested neighbourhoods you could ever find in the world. So yes, I've been involved in a few brawls in my time, but, in any case, I thought you were always going to shadow me.'

'We will, but don't underestimate Shen; he's a cold and ruthless killer.'

———————————-

Nick Northrop woke early on the day of the lord mayor's reception and gala dinner. It was a Saturday. He'd already visited his lock-up garage in Sheldon the evening before and brought back with him thirty pounds of C4 plastic explosive. It was tightly wrapped and sealed in plastic and stowed in a suitcase with wheels. He'd left it safely locked in his car, parked in the underground garage of his apartment block.

With the blinds still closed, he made himself a coffee, sat down at his kitchen table and went through a checklist in his mind of all his detailed plans. Next, he checked his backpack and pulled out the contents carefully onto the table. It wasn't as though this would be his inauguration in planting a bomb. On the contrary, he could have been considered a veteran. Nevertheless, he pushed himself to be meticulous. Familiarity was his enemy.

The rucksack contained a packet of latex gloves, flashlight, screwdrivers, scraper, Polyfilla, plasterboard cutter, a small tin of white and a small tin of off-white emulsion paint, paint brush, self-sealing plastic, small pry bar, a bag of dust taken from his own vacuum cleaner, sandpaper, extension cable and a hair dryer. Next, he checked his M37 demolition charge assembly, long-range timer and set of lithium-ion batteries. He repacked the bag.

Finishing his coffee, he got up and went into his bedroom and placed his best dark suit, white shirt and blue silk tie, another set of casual clothes and his toilet bag in another suitcase with wheels. After doing some grocery shopping and washing, it was early afternoon. He drove his car and parked it in the Grand Hotel's underground garage, took out his rucksack and the suitcase containing the C4. He checked in to the hotel at 2 pm.

He was given a room on the fourth floor which suited him perfectly, however he had to ask for a room midway between the lifts which were situated either side of the hotel. As he entered room number 414, he took the Do Not Disturb placard, placed it on the outside handle, closed the door and engaged the deadbolt. The room looked tired with the same nondescript layout as every other hotel in the world. A queen bed, bedside tables with reading lamps, chest of drawers opposite with TV, side armchair and foot stool all in a dark brown and cream colour scheme. Not so grand after all.

He saw an interconnecting door to the adjoining room. He opened his door and made sure the other one was locked, then closed his own door and locked it. Next, he went over to the window, carefully sliding the net curtains to one side and peeped out onto St Philip's cathedral. The room was perfectly placed since he assumed the visiting leaders of the G8 would be in suites above him and facing the churchyard. He smiled to himself. At least their body parts would end up sprayed all over the churchyard and maybe give them a head start to Heaven or Hell, depending on what people thought of them.

He rubbed his hands together. *Okay, let's get down to work!* He entered the bathroom and checked the layout. *Excellent, just as I thought.* He inspected the roll-top bath and, just like

CHAPTER 29

many other hotels, it had been panelled around the outside and painted white in an attempt to modernize the bathroom. Wearing his latex gloves, he opened his rucksack and extracted the screwdriver he needed. He carefully withdrew all the screws from the panel and gently eased it away from the bath. He smiled when he saw the metal Queen Anne cast-iron legs. They would give him a gap of approximately six inches underneath the bath to work with. Lying flat on the tiled floor he used his flashlight and ran the beam from right to left. Dust had built up over a period of time that he would have to replace after his work. The plasterboard wall on the other side of the bath was more of a cream colour or white that had faded over time. He gently tapped on the plasterboard from one end of the bath to the other. It sounded solid at one end but hollow at the other. Wasting no time, he used his plasterboard cutter to neatly open up the wall. It was only necessary to cut the two sides and the top since the bottom of the board was not attached to anything. He was able to open up a hole about eighteen inches long by six inches high. He gingerly took out the piece of plasterboard and placed it on the other side of the bathroom. He estimated the hollow section went much higher than the bath itself.

Northrop opened the suitcase and took out the C4 plastic explosive. The C4 came in the form of eleven-inch-long strips that could easily be handled safely. He laid it out on the bathroom floor and started to massage the putty-like substance into the shape he wanted. Suddenly he heard the click of a door handle. Someone was trying to open the interconnecting door to his room. He exited the bathroom quietly, closing the door behind him, and tip-toed over to the door to see the handle turn down.

Chapter 30

'Good morning, everyone, let me introduce you to Angus MacNeil, president of Halifax port terminal, Nova Scotia, Canada. As our new partner, we want to welcome Angus into our family.'

James, Chris and Angus put down their pens and shook hands after signing the partnership agreement in the company headquarters in Birmingham. The management group of Macrae-Claybourne Logistics clapped enthusiastically.

James continued. 'Halifax port terminal is now part of the Macrae-Claybourne Logistics Group. Together we are expanding the terminal and integrating their facilities with our expertise and logistics system. Janet, you and your team will need to plan a visit there to change their current systems over to ours. Rob, you will need to work with Angus, so we are completely seamless.'

Angus waited for James to finish. 'Thanks, James and Chris. It's an honour for me to be part of your company. I've admired your company and its progress now for a while and your timing in expansion could not have been better now the economy of both Europe and North America is turning around. I look forward to getting to know you all and working together with you. Thank you.'

After the meeting Martin Farley and Laura got together in Laura's office. 'What do you think, Laura?'

'Well, they've done it! I can't deny it's a great move for the company. I just hope the loan from Macrae Holdings comes in time – or the grant from the Canadian government, for that matter. Our cash reserves are perilously low.'

'Good morning, foreign secretary.'

'Good morning, Director Fox. It's a pleasure to meet you. I look forward to us working closely together. Having said that, I guess you are no stranger to this office.'

Jack Fox appraisingly looked across the desk at Russell Shaw who had just been appointed to the position by Tony Blair, the new prime minister. He wondered how he would handle Britain's foreign policy compared to his predecessor.

'No, I'm not. I'm looking forward to working with you too.'

'Now, I understand you wish to speak to me about Turkey?'

'Yes, that is correct, minister. I'll get straight to the point. MI6 is becoming increasingly concerned about this country. Frankly, their recent actions are becoming more contentious. As members of NATO, they also want to join the EEC and yet they are strengthening their relations with China. In our opinion, it's not possible for them to play on both sides of the street.'

Russell Shaw nodded. 'Can you be more explicit?'

Fox replied immediately. 'I can. As a member of NATO they have received a Patriot Missile Defence System, but now we have learned they also acquired a Chinese Missile System and installed it in the Köroglu Mountain region. What concerns us most is the possible exchange of these defence technologies. If we add that to the massive influx of Chinese capital being injected into the country to feed the Chinese expansion of their silk road, we may be losing a strategic partner to the east.'

Shaw leaned back in his office chair and fiddled with the pencil in his hands. 'I see, and where does Russia fit into this?'

'Since the breakup of the Soviet Union, they are less of a threat to Turkey, but we believe these two countries will now grow closer together from purely a trade point of view.'

Shaw nodded. 'So, are you saying we are in a tug of war with China over Turkey?'

'I am, minister.'

'What's your opinion on what we should do?'

'Well, I'm not a politician, but I don't think we can afford to just sit idly by and watch this happen. Why not help speed up Turkey's acceptance into the European market.' Fox said it more as a statement than a question.

'I hear you. This is something I'll have to discuss with the PM and our European partners. Is there anything else you think I should know?'

'There is, minister. We believe that China has two agendas. One is their official agenda, owned by President Zemin, and the other is a hidden agenda being carried out by a man who not only heads up the military, but also serves as Minister for Trade and Development.'

'Are you referring to Wu Shen?'

'I am and, what's more, we believe he wants to depose Zemin

CHAPTER 30

and take control as leader of the People's Republic of China.'

'Surely this has nothing to do with us. Why would we interfere?'

'Because this man's actions has caused the deaths of several British subjects on British soil and directly interfered with our commercial interests. I can send the file over for you to study.'

Shaw clenched his jaw. 'Please do. I will certainly need to review these actions. If these acts are as you say they are and I don't doubt it, director, what do you think we should do about it?'

'That will be for you and the prime minister to decide.'

Jack Fox left the meeting satisfied he'd come clean about the current danger of Shen and satisfied he could still do something about it. Unofficially, of course.

Northrop stood motionless behind the interconnecting door from the room next door. He positioned himself to grab the person around their neck should they enter his room. After several tries of the door, he heard a woman's voice say, 'It's okay. It's locked. We'll make sure our door is locked too. We don't want anyone coming into our room!'

Northrop let out a quiet sigh. The last thing he needed was to be caught in the act of planting a bomb. For the next hour he tightly packed the putty-like explosive in self-sealing plastic and pushed the contents up into the void. The plastic was essential to prevent the attention of sniffer dogs when the deep security sweep would take place. Satisfied he'd sealed everything tightly, he manoeuvred the long-range timer and detonator into place, installed the new lithium batteries and armed the system. The calculations for the timing of the blast had been made for exactly three am on the morning of Sunday 17th May. Northrop had even calculated the one-hour difference of daylight saving which would occur between the time he planted the device and when it was detonated. That would be the time when the hotel would be full, and all the guests would be in their rooms. Should there be any late or early birds in the meeting rooms or the twenty-four-hour cafe downstairs, they would be crushed anyway.

Northrop stood upright and arched his back after packing the wall full of explosives. He took a few minutes to loosen the stiffness he felt in his arms and shoulders. Once he felt supple again, he delicately placed the piece of plasterboard back into place and used Polyfilla to seal the gaps. After flattening out the joints with his scraper, he used the hairdryer and dried them off sufficiently until he could carefully smooth them off with the sandpaper he'd brought with him. He cleared the dust away as best as he could with a damp rag.

Satisfied with the replacement of the plasterboard, he mixed the paint he had and blended it with the rest of the wall. He used the hairdryer again to dry it off and then evenly distributed the dust he had brought with him under the bath. He replaced the panel around the bath and stood back to critique his work. All that was needed was a slight dab of paint on the heads of the screws, a good clean-up and the return of the suitcase and rucksack back to his car. He could then shower and get changed ready for the lord mayor's reception and gala dinner.

CHAPTER 30

DI Stella Hudson and another male counter terrorism officer of Chinese origin looked through the one-way glass into the main interview room in the recently opened Belmarsh Prison. The control room, like the rest of the prison, was brand new and contained all the latest recording and video equipment. On the other side of the glass Lingdao sat behind a fixed table, together with a duty solicitor that had been assigned to him for his right to legal advice.

'What do you think, Stella?'

'Not sure yet. This guy, "Lingdao", has so far refused to cooperate with us. He hasn't uttered a word since he was brought in here, not even to his former colleagues, Tang and Jin. He knows we're watching him around the clock. What he doesn't know is that we've now identified him as Colonel Liao Min, a former army officer under the command of General Shen. We also know the whereabouts of his family and his role in the Tiananmen Square massacre.'

The assistant chipped in, 'That should be enough to scare him.'

'I don't think so. This guy will be a hard nut to crack. I think we'll just have to keep layering on the evidence and squeeze him like a vice until he finally cracks under the pressure. Remember, he faces life imprisonment for first degree murder, several times over. And, under the Merchant Shipping and Maritime Security Act, he will face another life imprisonment sentence for piracy. He doesn't know we have a victim and a witness to murder up our sleeve either.'

'So, what's our priority?'

'We need to find out who he was supposed to meet in Birmingham and why. That's crucial.'

'Do you want to play the good guy, bad guy routine?'

'No, I think this guy's too smart for that. Let's just use this prison, being the most secure in the whole of Europe and the fact he will never see his family nor China ever again.'

DI Hudson strode confidently into the interview room and introduced herself and her assistant to Lingdao and his solicitor. Cameras and recorders were activated.

Hudson settled herself into her chair. She remained quiet for a few moments while she studied Lingdao with piercing scrutiny. Lingdao countered her back with an unrelenting stare.

'So, Lingdao, or should we call you Colonel Liao Min.' Hudson smiled. She thought she saw a hint of a flicker in his eyes when his name and rank was mentioned, but couldn't be sure. She hoped the cameras would pick it up. She continued, 'You are charged with first degree murder, attempted murder, and piracy. I must also warn you further charges of terrorism are also being prepared. Sentences for these crimes carry life sentences, so the reality is you will never see outside this prison again.'

Lingdao remained motionless. Hudson smiled again. 'Let me tell you a little bit about our prison. It's the most secure prison in Europe, perhaps the world for prisoners like you. Yes, we also have solitary confinement, something similar to what you have back home in Qincheng Prison. In fact this prison has been called Britain's Guantanamo Bay. Does that surprise you?'

Lingdao continued to stare fixedly back at her.

'So, Colonel Liao Min, you will not be better off than your friend from Qincheng Prison, Huang Genjo, will you? Do you remember him? He's a real nice guy once you get to know him.' There was no response from the prisoner.

CHAPTER 30

'Oh, I forgot to mention that Huang is very thankful for his release from Qincheng and is looking forward to a healthy and happy life. Of course he has told us of you murdering his friend on the deck of *Constellation II* and how you shot him in the chest and left him for dead.'

Lingdao laced his fingers together and continued to keep his eyes glued on his opponent.

Hudson smiled again. 'Oh, another fact I overlooked, the UN International Court of Justice in the Hague has footage of you back on that fateful day in Tiananmen Square committing atrocities against your own citizens. I'm sure there will be further convictions piling up on you.'

There was still no response.

Hudson decided to throw out a fishing line. 'Did I mention that Huang overheard you discussing your plans with your two assistants, Tang and Jin, to hijack the tanker and report the British response back to General Shen?'

Lingdao's lips parted momentarily as he took in a breath. Hudson caught the moment. She pushed on. 'Of course you already know Tang and Jin are imprisoned here as well, don't you?'

Still no response. 'Well I might as well tell you that they are also going down for life imprisonment for first degree murder as well as kidnapping. It's likely though that the judge will give them credit for telling us about General Shen and his plans for taking over several ports in Europe. If you like, we can help lessen the degree of punishment in your case, if you do the same. While it's likely your sentences will be high, it can make a huge difference as to how you are treated inside this prison. Let's just say you can earn yourself some privileges. Perhaps you might even be considered for a prisoner swap at some time or another. Who knows?'

Hudson shut up and looked at her fellow counter terrorism officer. She shrugged and sat back. There was silence. The solicitor leaned over and spoke quietly with Lingdao.

Lingdao sat up and with a poker face spoke for the first time. 'What do you want to know?'

Stella immediately sat forward. 'Who were you meeting In Birmingham that day when you were arrested?'

Lingdao's shoulders slumped. 'I don't know.'

'You don't know, or you really don't know?'

'I don't know. I was supposed to meet a man in the pub who would be carrying a copy of a *National Geographic* magazine. He never turned up.'

'Who gave you those instructions?'

Lingdao looked down but said nothing.

'Did those instructions come from General Shen?'

Lingdao took another deep breath. His solicitor spoke to Lingdao. 'You don't have to answer that.'

Lingdao looked up. 'No.'

'Then who?'

'London.'

'You mean your embassy in London?'

'Yes.'

'Why Birmingham?'

'I don't know. Some event or other.'

Hudson looked at her counterpart.

'This is all for now. We'll continue the interview later.'

Stella Hudson met up with Jack Fox back in the Belmarsh Prison control room.

'Good job, Stella. At last he's finally starting to talk. So, it's clear Birmingham is the target. Has to be the G8!'

'Has to be. So we obviously have at least one unknown man here in the city that is a threat to security. I can't help feeling that the pub he was to meet his contact in is almost opposite the Grand Hotel. Is that definitely the hotel the leaders of the G8 will be staying?'

'It is. We'll get a team and do a deep security check for both bugs and bombs even before the normal schedule of security checks start. Let's go over the security camera footage again for that day when this character was supposed to meet his contact. Maybe we've missed something.'

Stella frowned. 'Maybe there are two designated targets. The G8 meeting and Macrae.'

Chapter 31

'And lastly, I want to thank all of my fellow councillors and city employees for the wonderful support they have given me during this past year as lord mayor of this wonderful city. Thank you all so much!' Marion Arnott-Job stood back from the microphone and bowed. A loud burst of applause broke out amongst all the guests. The standing ovation eventually died away as she approached the mic again.

'It is now my pleasure to welcome our next lord mayor of Birmingham, Sybil Spence.' Another round of enthusiastic applause broke out.

Nick Northrop sat back with his group of ten people around one of the many round dinner tables set up in the Grosvenor ballroom in the Grand Hotel. His table, like many of the council workers attending the function, were some way away from the head table. He scanned the room, taking in all the local dignitaries that were attending. Amongst them sat James Macrae with his partner. He recognized them from all the local press coverage they had received recently. As he focused

CHAPTER 31

momentarily on them, Chris Claybourne just happened to look his way but swung his gaze away seemingly not registering anything.

'James, take a look at a guy sitting at the table in the corner. I've caught him several times looking over at us. Don't do it now. Leave it a few moments. He's sitting next to the woman in the blue dress.'

'Who is he?'

'I don't know but there's something odd about him. It's just a feeling I've got and it's not a good feeling.'

James waited a few minutes and then got up from the table to go to the gents. He scanned the guy carefully as he walked towards the ballroom doors. He was back a few minutes later.

'Nope, doesn't ring any bells with me.'

'Me neither.' James logged the man's image in his memory. Maybe, whoever it was, would slowly permeate from the deeper levels of his memory and rise to the surface sometime later.

———————-

Before Northrop left the hotel the next morning, he meticulously checked for any signs of his activities in the bathroom the previous day. There were none. He checked out before 7am as he did not wish to bump into any other guests from the gala dinner the night before.

He drove out of the underground car park knowing there was no more to be done in the hotel. With several months to go before the G8 meeting, the timing device would see to it all. He hoped that the bomb would not be discovered by the sniffer dogs the security forces would undoubtedly use. Job number one completed.

Instead of driving back to his apartment, he took a circuitous route to his second lock-up garage, located behind a block of shops on Rocky Lane in Hamstead to the north-west of the city. He parked and crossed the road to access the narrow lane to his garage. Being early on a Sunday morning, it was quiet. He opened his garage and checked the contents. He would need more C4 for the second bomb that he would plant in the International Convention Centre. Satisfied he had enough explosives and detonators, he also decided he would swap his car just before the G8 meeting and leave it out of sight in his other Sheldon lock-up garage. He would then use his VW van ready for his swift escape after the G8 meeting. From there, he would be well positioned to drive south-west to Haverfordwest in Wales and fly out in a small private plane, undetected, to Ireland.

James opened the tail gate of his Range Rover and heaved his heavy suitcase into the large cargo space behind the rear seats. He placed a second bag full of Christmas presents for Sarah, Mason, Mia, Olivia, and Sarah's parents in there as well. He felt happy and contented and looked forward to spending the holiday from Christmas Eve to New Year's day in Wales with his family. It would be the first time they would all be together for months.

He reversed out of his garage and signalled to the on-duty officer in the unmarked car in the driveway that he was on his way. He'd already given his itinerary to the police on his proposed whereabouts after Stella Hudson had informed him that a threat to both him and his family still existed since there was someone certainly lying low in Birmingham who should have contacted Lingdao. MI6 were working on the assumption that the Chinese, or perhaps more specifically Shen, were working on the IRA model of separate terrorist cells. Security for the G8 meeting as well as James and his family had been stepped up.

James turned on his radio and tuned into the BBC News on Radio Four. A correspondent noted that there had been a summit in Luxembourg earlier on in the month and the European Union had decided not to include Turkey as a candidate to join the European Union.

James sighed, knowing this would probably cause a rift between Ankara and the EU headquarters in Brussels. He further surmised that this would push Turkey closer to China and, in turn, cause further competition for their own Istanbul seaport at Haydarpasa. Whilst they were holding their own, their profitability had been badly squeezed by the competing port of Ambarli that was now being funded by the Chinese. No longer were they trying to hide behind front companies as a silent partner, they were now openly taking over ports in full view of the international community. It was a stark turnaround from their previous actions.

James turned down the volume on the radio and thought more about their financial position. Laura had managed somehow to keep the company afloat, but the transfer of funds from Macrae Holdings had still not materialized, neither had funds come through from the Canadian government in the form of a grant. 'It's coming,' was all he heard these days.

Stop it, James! he said to himself. *For God's sake, leave the business behind and focus on your family. If you bring all your worries with you, it will just cause more heartache and misery.* He turned the stereo back on and listened to one of his old favourite groups, Fleetwood Mac. Stevie Nicks' haunting and mesmerizing voice singing the song 'Sara' immersed him in his deep love for his wife and partner. How could he have let the business drive a wedge between the two of them? Not only was she beautiful, but she was also talented, intelligent and a great mother. He vowed he would get his business back on track and finally force an end to the evil mastermind behind all his troubles of the last few years.

Three hours later, in Wales, James closed the five-bar wooden gate after entering the long one-mile winding driveway connecting his house to the road. Before he got back in the Range Rover, he looked out to the west where a watery sun was just casting its last weak golden rays across the sea towards him. It felt as though there was frost in the air and yet he felt a warming glow of expectation relishing the fact the family would be reunited once again. He remembered the happy time when he and Sarah had first visited the house, a converted wool mill, and purchased it from friends of Sarah's parents.

As he pulled into the gravel driveway in front of the house, Mason, Mia and Olivia all came charging out to meet him.

'Welcome home, Dad! Merry Christmas!'

Beaming, James got out giving them all a big kiss and a squeeze. 'Oh, how I've missed you all, but now we can spend a whole week together.'

'Hurray! Hurry up, we've got lots of things to show you!'

Sarah stood back at the open front door beaming. A large holly wreath with red bows hung from the top of the door. James walked towards her and with searching eyes they just looked deeply at each other, finally ending in a tight hug.

James closed his eyes for a second and blew out a large breath. 'It's good to see you and be home together again!'

Sarah's eyes caressed him lovingly as she closed the door.

The atmosphere inside the old mill contrasted starkly to the cool breeze coming in off the ocean. Inside the reception hall with its high vaulted ceiling and sky lights stood a large, artificial Christmas tree resplendent with white lights and decorative ornaments. The white snow effect on the tree contrasted perfectly with the stone walls and stout timbers of the house. As James entered the large open-plan kitchen from the hallway, the enticing aroma of freshly baked bread and pastries greeted him. He could see that Sarah had been busy baking sausage rolls and mince pies. Judging by the flour all over the front of Mia and Olivia, it was clear they'd been helping.

Sarah dabbed her hands on her apron. 'We're up to our elbows here in flour, James, can you make us all a cuppa?'

'Sure can! Wow, that was some welcome!'

'Well they've been excited for us all to be together again ever since you and I sorted everything out in Bromsgrove. It's a weight off all our shoulders.'

James looked over from the kitchen into the family room where a log fire was burning in the inglenook fireplace. 'Where's Bryn and Catrin? I thought they were joining us for Christmas?'

'They are, but Mom and Dad left earlier to get ready for their big concert featuring the Caernarfon Mixed Choir in the castle this evening. We've got tickets, so once you've dropped your stuff upstairs, we can go and then afterwards we'll all come back here for our Christmas Eve dinner.'

James and Sarah walked holding hands down the quaint, narrow cobblestone streets of the town towards Caernarfon Castle, while Mason, Mia and Olivia all stayed close by, bundled up against the cool breeze. James was aware of a concealed police surveillance. Once inside the castle hold, several hundred people were gathered facing a raised platform set against the castle ramparts. As the choir broke into song, the full depth and breadth of their intermingled voices were neatly captured within the thick walls of the thirteenth-century stronghold. It was a magical setting. James looked up at the clear sky, enveloped by the battlements, and immersed in the hypnotic sounds of the choir. It was a spellbinding moment.

The week between Christmas and New Year passed quickly. They had played games, walked along the beach, chatted and relaxed. A true family gathering. By the time New Year's Day came around, James was ready to go back to Birmingham and get to work. There were just six more months before they all got back to living together there. He hoped he could keep his company afloat and end the terror that one man had caused.

Chapter 32

While James was on holiday with his family in North Wales over Christmas, Nick Northrop kept working. Now on the final straight of his mission, he needed to ensure his plans for the two bombings were watertight. He also needed to make sure his real identity was still secure, and his escape plans were all in place to disappear right after the G8.

Sitting in his office the day after Boxing Day, he opened his post. Of particular interest was a letter he'd written and addressed to himself three weeks ago. He hoped it would have arrived earlier, but it must have got caught up in the backlog of post prior to Christmas. It was a letter that he'd carefully crafted and forged. The letter was on a genuine Birmingham International Centre (ICC) letterhead addressed to the General Manager Public Works Dept.

Dear Mr Northrop,
The purpose of this letter is to inform you of a serious drainage problem with the ICC.

A number of exhibition organizers have complained about the noise caused by heavy rain draining from the flat roof during the recent intense rainstorms that we are now starting to experience. It seems the sound of the gushing water is so loud that it interferes with conferences and presentations that are being made inside the exhibition halls.

We understand the architects designed this central drainage system from the flat roof to feed straight down into the canal system below. They insist that the central drainage pipe has to be situated at the centre of the building to avoid load stress on the roof during rain, freezing and snow conditions.

Since the G8 meeting is coming up soon, we cannot afford to have this problem exist. We have contacted the construction company to rectify the problem, but they referred us back to the architects. In turn, they have advised us that the centre of the building, where the main drainpipe is located above the Birmingham canal system, is in fact on council property. We understand that it is only you who can authorize modifications to the drainage system to rectify the problem.

We respectfully ask that you treat this situation as a matter of urgency. As with all the other G8 preparations, we need Birmingham to re-establish itself as a world-class city.

If you have any further questions, please do not hesitate to contact me.

Yours faithfully,
Ian Trevellyan
Managing Director ICC
cc: WestMid Design Services
cc: SCY Construction Group

Northrop stamped the receipt date on the letter and sent

CHAPTER 32

another letter back acknowledging that the matter was being looked into. He did not post it, but placed a copy of the letter on file. The original reply was shredded. He picked up his phone. 'Hi, Colin, did you have a good Christmas?'

'I did thanks, Nick. Probably drank and ate too much!'

'Me too. Listen, I need your help. I'll be down to see you in about half an hour. Just want to make sure you'll be in, and that those new sixty-foot aerial lifts have been delivered.'

'They have.'

'Great. See you in a bit!'

Northrop strode into the central workshop amidst a cacophony of air wrenches, hammering and BBC Radio 1 all trying to compete with each other. 'Come on, Colin, let's go and talk in your office. You need to see the letter I've just received.'

Colin cleaned his hands and then sat down behind his desk. He picked up the letter Northrop had given him and read it. 'Well I'm not surprised in a way. Can't believe the amount of rainfall we've been getting lately. Probably global warming. Who knows. What do you want to do about it?'

'Well, I wanted your opinion. The ICC is correct in stating that we are responsible for the drainage, especially since the canal system underneath and around the convention centre is all listed and protected.'

Colin scoffed. 'Needs to be if you ask me! That canal system is real history on our doorstep. Birmingham should be proud of its industrial heritage. We were the centre of the world and the catalyst for development in every other country. Good job the history buffs protected these, otherwise they'd have been filled in long ago and forgotten.'

'My point of view too. Look, I've got the plans for the ICC

here. Let's take a look and see what we can do. Obviously we'll have to act quickly since the G8 meeting will be here in just over four months.'

Northrop unfolded the roof and elevation plans of the ICC. Colin stood over the drawings and pointed to the artificial eves in the structure. 'I see these valleys in between the eaves carry the rainwater out to the outer drainpipes?'

'Yes, that's correct. It's this area in the middle we're concerned with. All the water in this area drains down this central pipe. According to this, the diameter of that pipe is eighteen inches.' Northrop stood back with a deadpan face and looked at Colin. He already knew what he wanted but he needed Colin to come up with a solution, since it was possible the security services might question him on what modifications were being carried out prior to the G8.

Colin sat quietly for a few moments and then took a Water System and Maintenance Manual off a shelf behind him. He leafed through the pages until he found what he was looking for. He put on his reading glasses to study the small print. Running his forefinger down a sizing chart, he looked up at Northrop. 'This is what we need, Nick. Look, these PVC pipes that we are using to replace the old ductile iron freshwater pipes in all the municipalities could be used as an inner pipe creating a sort of noise barrier within the original pipe.'

Northrop leaned closer to the manual. 'Yes, we even have those in stock given all the replacements we are doing right now. So you think we could use those sixteen-inch diameter pipes?'

'Don't see why not?'

Northrop put his finger in the air. 'How about if we wrapped a flexible chimney liner insulation blanket around the inner

CHAPTER 32

PVC pipe. It could help fill the one-inch gap around the pipe and act as a further noise insulator?'

'How much would we need?' Colin asked.

'Forty feet.'

Colin thought for a second. 'So the PVC pipe comes in eight-foot sections. We need five of those and we can easily get the same length chimney insulation liner, join them all together on the roof and slide them down inside the existing drainpipe, secure it and bingo!'

'Brilliant. You're a bloody genius!'

Colin beamed as Northrop patted him on the shoulder.

'Okay, Colin, make out a workshop order and I'll sign it. Pipes we have in stock. Can you get the chimney liner organized?'

'Easy, there's a stainless-steel supplier just down the road. I believe they fabricate flexible liners and supply insulation blankets as well. I can call him now if you like.'

'Do it! I want to get this job done as soon as possible. I'll schedule a work crew once we've got all the necessary materials together. We'll need the new aerial lift as well to position all the materials on the roof of the ICC.'

'I've asked for this joint meeting of MI6, MI5 and the police Commissioner since we are becoming increasingly concerned about security for the upcoming G8 meeting.'

In the ops room, at MI6 headquarters, Jack Fox stood quietly, anchoring his steely grey eyes on the team in front of him. The group of attendees remained sullen faced and perfectly still.

'We have a number of serious concerns that need to be

addressed separately. Number one. The organization known as Jubilee 2000 now has a coalition of over seventy different agencies who are organizing a focused protest, to coincide with the G8 meeting. They are calling for the cancellation of unrepayable Third World debt by the year 2000. It is estimated there could be between forty to fifty thousand demonstrators attending the mass demonstration in Birmingham. These demonstrators will be coming from all over the UK and abroad. Whilst we believe the intent of the group is peaceful, and sincere, we need to be aware of right-wing fringe elements and known agitators penetrating their numbers to ignite violence. Jubilee's plans are for the demonstrators to circle Birmingham city centre linking hands in a show of solidarity with the Third World. That circle could be as much as seven miles in circumference.'

The room became restless, trying to imagine the sheer size and enormity of the task for police to control such a widespread mass of people.

Jack Fox continued. 'So, each department under your control needs to pre-empt this demonstration and be on the alert for known militants coming from here and abroad. In addition, I'm asking the treasury department to pay special attention on who and where funding is coming from to support Jubilee 2000.'

Fox turned and addressed the man sitting directly in front of him. 'Immigration needs to know who to look for prior to passengers arriving at passport control.' He then broadened his outlook to the rest of the group. 'Each of you have your own teams specializing in every aspect of security, so you need to brief everyone on how serious this demonstration will be. It goes without saying that the demonstration planned

CHAPTER 32

for Saturday May 16th will not end in the afternoon but carry on overnight in the city centre outside the Grand Hotel. Remember this hotel faces the large churchyard of St Philip's cathedral, a perfect spot for a mass demonstration. Above all, every team leader will need to plan for contingencies. Understood?'

There was a loud response. 'Yes, sir!'

Fox nodded in response. 'Our second concern is the specific threat of terrorism. I'm going to hand you over to DI Hudson of the West Midlands Police. She is also working in conjunction with MI6.'

Stella stood up and spoke in a commanding and firm tone. 'Good morning, everyone, we have hard evidence there is at least one foreign country planning a terrorist act in Birmingham. Arrests have been made of three Chinese males who not only hijacked a British vessel in British territorial waters but were later caught in further criminal acts being committed within our borders. We now know there is an imminent threat to the G8 meeting from an unknown person who was due to link up with one of the arrested men. We do not, as yet, have a description of this man but be aware we have a clandestine person planning some sort of terrorist act. You could say as Frederick Forsyth put it so succinctly, *we have a 'Jackal' on our hands.*' There are three million people residing in the West Midlands. It is our job to uncover this one person before it is too late.'

Stella waited for the low murmur in the group to subside. 'So, eyes and ears open for a person who may seem perfectly legitimate on the surface, but is a "sleeper". Of specific interest is the Chinese embassy in London. Their head of security, Peng Zheng, recently committed suicide, although we believe he was murdered to keep quiet. From acts committed last year we know he has an underground network of criminals working to undermine British interests and possibly his own government representatives. Special interest needs to be taken in a man named General Wu Shen who also acts as minister for Trade and Development for the Chinese government. Our belief, after extensive intelligence reports, indicate there may be an attempt to assassinate President Zemin of China.'

Jack Fox stood up as the noise in the room subsided, and in a grave voice spoke, 'So, there it is. We want maximum effort for security and well-conceived contingency plans from each of your specialist teams. Go to it!'

After the meeting, Stella Hudson joined Jeremy Hirons who had just been cleared to return to work. Together they studied the CCTV footage again of all the cameras around the locality of the Old Contemptibles Pub on the day Lingdao had been picked up and arrested. Nowhere was there any sign of anyone loitering or looking suspicious. It just didn't add up. Lingdao was clearly meeting someone, but that somebody was nowhere to be seen.

She ran the video again from the camera that was set up in Edmund Street. It clearly showed a Birmingham Municipal Works truck parking just before the supposed Lingdao rendezvous. It was hard to see the features of the workman since he had a white hard hat on as well as orange coveralls. There was nothing unusual about his appearance and she knew the council had already started to inspect all the drain and sewers in the vicinity prior to them being welded and sealed before the G8. Stella looked over at Jeremy. 'This is all we've got. It may be nothing, but I'll still have one of my team check this council worker out.'

CHAPTER 32

———————————————

'Hey, Nick. I've got all the insulation material we need for the convention centre drainpipes here in the workshop.'

'Good job, Colin! Okay, so I'll arrange for a work gang to install the inner pipe on Friday the second of January. We'll all be back at work then, but I expect it will be quiet both in the city and the ICC since most people will take this day off to make a longer break after New Year. Best time to install it!'

'Good thinking but my guys won't have time to wrap the insulation around the pipe before we leave at lunchtime on New Year's Eve.'

'No worries, Col. I'm not doing anything as my family is all up north so I can come in on New Year's day and do it. Shouldn't take long.'

'Are you sure?'

'Yep, I still like to work with my hands. Desk jobs are okay to a point, but I still like to be in a workshop!'

'I'd help you if I could but me and the wife will be in London staying with her brother and family. Boring bunch, if you ask me, but has to be done!'

'No, that's fine. Won't take me long.'

———————————————

'Good morning, President Zemin. I have all the information you requested.'

Zemin looked up from his desk at his own trusted special agent, Kevin Tan. He pushed his heavy black-framed glasses further up on the bridge of his nose. 'Please, sit down.'

Kevin rested his notes on his crossed legs and spoke directly.

'Peng Zheng was never notified by General Shen that he was being dismissed and returned to China. Instead he suffered a fatal heart attack caused by an ingestion of aconite and another stimulant. This was not an accident or suicide. It was a planned murder.'

'Is it your belief that Zheng was murdered to keep him quiet before he was brought back to Qincheng Prison?'

'It is. We have since uncovered a trail of information that points to Shen ordering Zheng to use his underground network of mercenaries to murder the parents of James Macrae.'

Zemin pressed his lips tightly together. 'An act that Shen strenuously denies!' Zemin was quiet for several seconds. 'And the hijacking of the British tanker, was that an act directed by Shen?'

'It was. The three hijackers who carried out the operation were former officers close to Shen. Two of these men then kidnapped the son of James Macrae but were subsequently arrested and the son was rescued. As for the third hijacker, it seems he was arrested by the British police on another operation. We do not know what this operation was.'

Zemin's face muscles tightened. 'Yet another lie by General Shen! Give me a reason why I shouldn't have Shen arrested right now!'

The agent looked down at the notes on his lap. 'Sir, if you want to completely remove your opposition and enemies, then we need more time to completely identify his inner circle that could always be a potential threat to you.'

'I'm getting impatient!'

'President Zemin, this man Shen is a skilled adversary with a well-organized network. We have noted that he visits his mother in a retirement home outside Beijing frequently.

CHAPTER 32

This is the time when he communicates mostly with his accomplices. We are also watching another close associate of his, Meili Shabani. We think she is more than an accomplice, maybe even a partner.'

Zemin rested his cheek on his left hand. 'Alright. Intercept these calls. I will give you until after the G8 summit. I can certainly use his knowledge and experience there. He's a fool. With so much talent, he didn't need to make an enemy out of me! Why couldn't he be patient in trying to rebuild trust with the Western leaders. Instead he wants to pursue "wolf warrior" diplomacy. It's just too fast, too soon.'

'There is one more thing, President Zemin. Since Peng Zheng has been murdered, we have no way of learning who his underground contacts are in the UK. He was the only link to them. It's possible they may still be carrying out clandestine activities ordered by Shen.'

―――――――――――――――――-

Nick Northrop drove out of his apartment building at Fiveways and drove north-west from the city centre towards Hamstead. Being early morning New Year's Day, the streets were deserted. Scattered litter left over from the revelries of the previous night danced around in circles caught up in the cool breeze tunnelling down the empty city streets. He took the road through what was known as the Jewellery Quarter and parked at Hamstead Railway Station half an hour later. Taking his empty rucksack, he locked his car, crossed over Rocky Lane and walked down the rutted passageway beside a pharmacy shop to access his lock-up garage. A dog barking in the distance was the only sign of life.

Once inside the garage, he quietly closed the door and

immediately proceeded to stash his other C4 explosive into his rucksack. He also took a quantity of Tannerite, a binary explosive to act as the detonator for the C4. Since Tannerite could only be activated by a high-velocity bullet, he would need to use his Remington M24 sniper rifle with telescopic sight from a safe distance away from the ICC. Being so far away from the explosion, it would ensure his safety and enable him to immediately make his escape and disappear into obscurity forever.

One hour later, Northrop arrived at the council central workshop in Digbeth. The industrial area was again empty of any activity. Once inside the yard, he locked the outer gate and then locked himself in the main workshop.

He stood back and scanned the still bays. It reminded him of the hollow seclusion he had felt nearly two years earlier after he had killed the former workshop supervisor in the old premises. The irony of the moment brought a caustic smile to his face.

Colin had placed the pipe sections together with the chimney liner close to the long work bench at the side of the shop. The chimney insulation came wrapped in single-sided aluminium foil, being waterproof, moisture-proof and corrosion-resistant.

Northrop placed his rucksack on the bench and proceeded to work quickly, moulding quantities of C4 explosive around each of the five eight-foot pipes. Satisfied the explosive was smooth and even, he tightly wrapped polythene sheeting around the C4 and then glued the chimney insulation liner into place on top of that. The result was a pipe of five sections that would be joined together and fit exactly inside the existing central drainpipe at the ICC. For the top section pipe, he cut away

CHAPTER 32

twelve inches of the insulation inside the outer aluminium foil. He then poured Tannerite into the hollowed section and sealed the top of it with a layer of fiberglass. Once the fiberglass had hardened, he smoothed the surface and painted it the same colour as the PVC pipe. To the naked eye, the top of the inner sleeve of the pipe and insulation liner looked solid. Satisfied the job was complete, he loaded the five sections of the pipe into a works van, locked it inside the workshop and left for the evening. He would return in the morning.

33

Chapter 33

'Mr Macrae?'

'Speaking.'

'Yes, good morning, Mr Macrae. My name is Isla Corbett, I am chair of the Board of Governors for Bromsgrove Academy. I'm calling to advise you of recent changes at the school.'

'I'm sorry, Ms Corbett, but I have no interest in your school after the events that took place there last year.'

'I understand and that is why I am calling you. On behalf of the Board of Governors we wanted to ask you if you would consider returning your children to school here.'

'And why would I do that?'

'Let me explain. In the case of Mason, his expulsion was wrong. I can tell you that the other boy is no longer with the school.'

'I repeat, Ms Corbett, you should have intervened at the time. That would have avoided the scandal and humiliation for my family. If I hadn't had my hands full at the time, I would have taken the matter further.'

CHAPTER 33

'Yes, you could have done that, however, I wanted to let you know we have a new headmaster starting in January when the new term begins, and the Board of Governors wanted me to let you know.'

'I see. Well I appreciate you letting me know. I will need to discuss this with my wife.'

'Thank you, Mr Macrae, and again please accept all of our apologies for the distress this whole matter has caused. I look forward to hearing back from you and your wife.'

James placed the receiver back in its cradle. He looked out of his office window at the constant movement of trucks and trailers below thinking about how Sarah might react. Now back at work after a wonderful holiday he missed his family terribly, but felt he needed to be alone until he could even the score with the man that had caused him so much misery and heartache.

The phone rang again, snapping James out of his thoughts.

'James, Karin Janssen is here to see you from *Mercantile News*.'

'Oh yes, we have an appointment.'

A lady with brown hair tied back in a ponytail, probably in her thirties, confidently entered the office and shook hands firmly with James. 'Mr Macrae. It's a pleasure to meet you. Thank you for the invitation to interview you.'

'You're welcome, Ms Janssen. I don't think we've ever met before?'

'No, we haven't. I was a journalist with the magazine a while back but then took time off having a family. Now I'm back and must say I'm enjoying getting back into the industry again. So much has changed!'

They both smiled at each other.

'Well, that's really what I wanted to speak to you about today. When we spoke on the phone, I originally was going to update you on the progress of our company, particularly with the amalgamation of Macrae Shipping and Claybourne Cartage, but so much more has happened since then.'

Karen smiled. 'Oh! This sounds like the basis of a good article! Are you okay if I record this interview?'

'Yes, that's perfectly fine.'

'Good! Let's get started then.' She pressed the record button on her machine and referred to her notes. 'So, Mr Macrae, can you give me an update on all the latest developments at Macrae-Claybourne Logistics?'

James leaned forward towards the recorder. 'Prior to the last two years, Macrae Shipping faced some very significant challenges but I'm happy to say that the partnership and creation of Macrae-Claybourne Logistics has substantially increased our market share, our customer satisfaction index and revolutionized the logistics industry.'

'Can you quantify that?'

'I can. Our door-to-door delivery times have shortened our customers supply and delivery pipelines by an average of seventeen percent. This means our customers are now seeing much healthier profits. Of course our proprietary software system has played a big part of that success.'

'That's impressive! But does this increased business end there with your software and integrated marine and land transportation system? In other words, will your recent growth now level off after the initial boost of these combined resources?'

James grinned. 'Good question. The short answer to that is no! Here's why. We have two new Post Panamax container

CHAPTER 33

ships operating at full capacity together with an expansion of our truck fleet and new cold store warehouses. Couple that to the fastest port turnaround times in the business means you will see continued growth and prosperity for both our customers and us.'

Karin looked up from her notes and replied, 'Is there anything else our readers should be interested in?'

'There certainly is. I'm excited to announce that Macrae-Claybourne has now expanded beyond our European bases and now has a presence in North America with a new terminal in Halifax, Canada. This has given us an entry into the North American Free Trade Area of Canada, Mexico and the United States. In addition we have become a member of the Advisory board of APEC giving us a window to the whole Pacific trade area.'

Karin nodded in appreciation. 'That is certainly important news for our readers to know, but I'm somewhat puzzled by your earlier comments, and I quote, "Prior to the last two years, Macrae Shipping faced some very significant challenges. What exactly did you mean by that?"'

James clenched his jaw and looked directly back at Karin. She noticed his face started to flush.

'For some time this company and its personnel have been victimised by the terrorist actions of one man.' Karen's eyes widened, but she remained silent. James continued, 'This particular person has been directly responsible for murder, grievous bodily harm and widespread sabotage against Macrae Shipping and now Macrae-Claybourne Logistics. This man directed the actions of Euro-Asian Freight and Pair-Tree Capital to specifically destroy this company with the sole purpose of taking over our international sea terminals in

Europe so they could be used at a later date for strategic naval bases.'

Karin started to scribble rapidly on her pad and was about to ask a question when James gritted his teeth. 'Through my own extensive investigations I can also prove that this man was responsible for the murder of my parents and one of your journalists, Greg Driver!'

Karin's eyes widened.

'Be under no illusions these are not, I repeat, not wild accusations. To this day this one person continues to mastermind and direct heinous crimes against my family, my company and the British people. Not only was a Macrae-Claybourne tanker recently hijacked, but five murders took place that day and now the kidnapping of one of my children was thwarted by swift action by the British police force.' James remained completely still.

Karin swallowed hard. 'Can you tell us who this man is?'

'I can. He is a Chinese general by the name of Wu Shen. He is also the minister for Trade and Development in the Zemin government. Ironically, he cowers behind diplomatic immunity.'

Karin blew out her cheeks. She was just beginning to realize she had a front-page blockbuster article. She switched off the recorder.

'Mr Macrae, I have to ask this to be fair to you. Is any of this *off the record?* I ask this as I know that will be the first question my editor asks and I'm aware of the past history between our two companies.'

'No, Ms Janssen. I stand behind every word I said. I have irrefutable evidence that I intend to use and take it to the next level.'

CHAPTER 33

As Karin Janssen left the office, James grinned. *With an explosive article like that and leaked information through MI6 that I have the evidence in the Macrae Holdings safe, we'll see if Shen likes to be called out, especially as a coward.*

Shen sat quietly alone in his secret apartment close to his mother's retirement home. He saw himself moving closer to his goal of becoming the supreme ruler and leader of China, however for the first time in his life, he was starting to feel insecure. After his recent meeting with President Zemin, when asked to relieve Peng Zheng from his post, he had felt a definite chill from Zemin. Later, Zemin seemed to accept that Zheng had suffered a heart attack, but in subsequent meetings, Zemin's body language had been difficult to read. On the one hand he seemed pleased with the rapid silk road expansion in Turkey but still, there was just something missing from Zemin's behaviour that he just couldn't put his finger on.

After skimming off over six million dollars from the failed collaboration of Pair-Tree Capital, he considered cutting and running on his own. His stash of money was safe in his secret offshore accounts, and he had several false identities he could use to disappear. He wrestled between finishing his plans with the assassination of Zemin or cutting ties with China. Escaping now would mean losing his chance of becoming supreme leader of China, his ultimate and life-long ambition. He focused on how far he had come. His position could still be considered strong. Even though he'd lost his main agent in the UK, the orders that Peng Zheng had passed on were already beyond the point of no return. They were like a tsunami wave that had been triggered but could not be stopped. The planned assassination of Zemin was set. He surmised he would have to tread even more carefully in the future, be patient and continue to hide in plain sight.

As he continued in his introspective mood, he decided he needed a win. Zemin had definitely appreciated what he'd accomplished in Turkey. Perhaps now was the time to capitalize on that. He decided to float the idea of a state visit to the country, marking the bilateral cooperation between the two countries. That would surely help him rebuilt trust with both Zemin and General Gulnaz of Turkey. It would also make the west sit up and realize that China was now a fully fledged world power and deserved respect.

Nick Northrop arrived back at the council yard the following morning to find all the technicians hard at work in the workshop.

'Morning, Colin. How was your New Year?'

'Oh, not bad but I'm sick of turkey and sitting around all the time. I needed to come back to work, eat a decent corn beef sandwich and recover from the holiday!'

'Yeah, I remember those family holidays filled with family friction. They used to drag on forever.'

'I see you prepared all the pipes. I'll drive the bucket lift if you want to drive the works van and we'll meet the crew outside the ICC.'

CHAPTER 33

They parked their vehicles at the rear of the ICC, just off Cambridge Street. It was the main goods receiving entrance for the exhibition halls. Nick jumped out of his van and immediately went to the security office.

He smiled widely at the duty officer. 'Good morning. Happy New Year!'

'Happy New Year to you too. What can I do for you? You know we're closed for the holiday?'

Nick smiled. 'I know. We actually don't need access to the interior of the halls, but we're carrying out a council work order for the ICC for modifications to the roof drainage system. Here's the paperwork.'

The security officer put on his reading glasses and studied the work order and the letter from the managing director of the ICC to the council about the drainage problem. He came outside his office and looked at the Birmingham City Council painted vehicles and the work crew in uniform. 'So, do you just need access to the roof?'

Nick pointed to the bucket lift truck. 'We do, but we don't need to access the roof from inside the building. We have a bucket lift.'

'Oh, that's good because I'm under strict instructions not to let anyone into the building until after the holiday.'

'That makes sense. Is there anything else you need from us?'

The watchman shook his head. 'No, everything's in order. Let me know if you need anything. Don't fall off, eh!'

Nick walked over to Colin and the work crew. 'Okay, boys, let's get to work.'

It took just over four hours to complete inserting the new sections of inner insulated pipe into the main drainpipe. After securing the inner pipe to the outer pipe, Nick made sure there was sufficient space around the drainage pipe for a high-velocity bullet to penetrate the asphalt roofing felt from an angle and enter the pipe to detonate the Tannerite and C4 explosive. As he supervised the group, he cast his eyes westward. There were a number of high-rise buildings that he would need to consider. With most people still on holiday and the city being quiet, they had completed the work unhindered. After the crew cleaned up afterwards, it was as though nothing had changed.

For a while Northrop had been considering the best position for him to take aim at the Tannerite detonator installed in the top of the central drainpipe. As a trained soldier and mercenary he knew he was an excellent sniper, based on his personal number of successful 'kills'. His own record of a kill at just over 2,000 metres had never been published, and nor would it be. He knew there would be military sharp shooters on all the elevations around the Grand Hotel, council buildings and convention centre so he needed to be well outside that circle. At first he considered the GPO telecommunications tower. At a height of 150 metres he would have an excellent trajectory to shoot down at the roof of the ICC, but to a military man it was an obvious choice to secure and station one of their own there. Not only that, but it would also have taken too long to come down the tower and escape undetected.

After spending days walking around the area, he decided the west of the city had a better choice of high-rises from where he could take a shot. He considered the Hampton Inn, a twenty-storey building 400 metres south-west of the ICC but as he returned to his own apartment block at Fiveways, it occurred to him that his own building might even be worthy of consideration .

He estimated his building was approximately 800 metres from the ICC, outside the circle of military protection and easy enough for him to hit the top of the drainpipe. It was also a building sixty-five metres high and had a clear trajectory to the roof of the ICC.

He picked up his sniper binoculars from his apartment and made his way to the roof. There, he scanned a full three hundred and sixty degrees around him. No other building looked down on the roof of his building. He went to the edge of the roof on the east side and crouched behind a large air-conditioning unit. Resting his elbows on the parapet, he focused his binoculars on the roof of the ICC and established he had a clear line of vision to his target. Without wasting any time, he used the binoculars to work out the exact distance and angle to the drainpipe. Once back in his apartment, he could finish his trajectory calculations using the manufacturer specifications of his Remington M24 rifle and the type of long-range cartridge he would use. All his other calculations of wind speed, direction, humidity, and temperature would need to be made on the actual day to be clinically precise for the time of the shot. He would only need to make one supersonic range shot. Once it had been fired, he could make his escape using his modified VW van, parked close by, and drive to the airfield in Wales.

―――――――――――――-

DI Stella Hudson and Jeremy Hirons stood on the top floor of the West Midlands Police Headquarters in Lloyd House. They looked through the office window in the direction of Colmore Row. In spite of the clear blue sky and sunshine, the cold February day outside reflected their mood.

'I don't like it, Jeremy. We're still no closer to identifying the person who was supposed to meet Lingdao that day, the *Jackal* as I call him and the open area opposite the Grand Hotel is an invitation for a mass riot. To have the G8 leaders stay there, and China's Zemin for that matter, is asking for trouble.'

'I agree, Stella. At least we have a contingency plan for housing the leaders when they come if we need to. There are only a few of us who know where that is. We're keeping it that way. As for the open area in St Philips's churchyard, that will certainly be an area where we can confine the demonstrators and keep them under control. The side streets can easily be sealed off and the area around the Grand Hotel will also be restricted.' Jeremy stood back from the window and steepled his hands in front of his chin. 'Tell me again about your enquiries into that council truck being close to the pub when Lingdao was arrested.'

'That truck was just one of many that has been consistently inspecting the drainage system around the city as a security precaution before the big meeting. Our team visited the Birmingham council public works manager, and he confirmed the inspection was legitimate. In fact, the manager himself is ex-army, REME in fact. Good to know we have an expert running that side of things! He will also be liaising with us and the military for security. Come on, let's grab a coffee.'

Jeremy took a drink from his cup. 'Did you see the article in this month's *Mercantile News*?'

'If you mean the interview with James Macrae, I did. It's

CHAPTER 33

explosive to say the least! Provocative, in fact.'

'Yeah, he really laid it on thick. We've managed to leak to Shen the evidence Macrae has. We've also relayed to him that the International Criminal Court is backed up with the sheer volume of work with war crimes of the former Yugoslavia to start inquiries at this stage. So, all in all, it may set the trap with James Macrae as bait. If Shen falls for it, then the Birmingham visit will be his opportunity to finish Macrae off once and for all.

Chapter 34

James and Chris sat down with Laura and Martin in the empty boardroom. Laura was smiling.

'So, Laura. Good news?' James queried.

'Yes, I do have good news. Makes a change, doesn't it?'

James laughed. He and Laura had worked together for a long time and shared the same sense of humour. 'Come on then, let's have it!'

'So, I didn't have to borrow against your personal guarantees that you and Chris gave. Once MidCom Bank found out that we were talking to other banks, they promptly stepped up and increased our credit lines. Can't say I like their new younger management style, though. They tend to focus too much on computer screens instead of real personal relationships.'

James sighed. 'I know what you mean. Nowadays people just want to communicate with a keyboard. Face-to-face meetings, conversation and handshakes are rapidly disappearing.' James snapped himself together. 'Anyway, does this mean we're out of the woods with the impending cash crunch?'

CHAPTER 34

'It does, but since our company has expanded so much in such a short time, I want us to consider splitting our banking services working with additional banks. Northern Merchant Bank are prepared to take over the leases on all of our equipment. I need you, Chris and Martin to review their terms and conditions before any agreement is finalised.'

Chris chirped up. 'Sounds promising and could help us in our expansion. Let's take a look.'

James joined in. 'Yes, and once our new investments start to return profits then we can reduce all our borrowings as soon as possible. Now, I also heard from Angus this morning that the Canadian government will be providing a grant for the expansion of the Halifax terminal, although we don't have any details or anything in writing yet. I don't think we can rely on this, however, since nothing is certain until we have written confirmation. So, I guess we're good for the time being, assuming that Northern Merchant Bank's terms are satisfactory.'

Chris looked over at James. 'One down, one to go. We just have to get the Chinese off our backs.'

After one hour they finished the meeting and gave Laura the go-ahead to bring Northern Merchant Bank on board. James returned to his office and called Sarah.

'Hi, my love. How are you?'

'I'm good but tired. Mason, Mia and Olivia are back at school and seem to be happy and I'm working flat out on the Highclere project.'

'Good. I'm glad all is well with the kids. I have some news on that front.' James took several minutes to explain about his conversation with the chair of the Board of Governors at Bromsgrove Academy. 'So what do you think?'

'Well. Like you said, it's a bit late, but at least it vindicates Mason and puts the school back on track.' She hesitated for a second. 'I don't think we should yank the kids out of this school now though. Since we're getting back together, it's logical for us to live near Birmingham, but I think we should also look at other schools too in the meantime.'

'Yep, that's my feeling too. Oh, by the way, we seem to have overcome the recent financial squeeze and we didn't need to use the personal guarantees!'

'That's a relief. I was worried about that.'

'Alright, give me a shout when you're going back to Highclere, you can spend some time here.'

'I'd like that!'

James finished the conversation feeling good about the decision they'd made. It would suit all of them.

———————————

Shen sifted through his incoming post on his office desk. It was 6:30am, his quiet time. As he thumbed through a number of letters, his eye caught the frontpage headline of *Mercantile News* that had been delivered at the same time. He sat up, jolted by the sudden shock.

Shipping CEO makes stunning accusation against Chinese Diplomat.

As he read the article, his neck veins started throbbing, his anger rising by the second. Just as he was trying to restore Zemin's confidence in him, Macrae had the nerve to torpedo him in full view of the world. He drew in deep breaths to compose himself and evaluated his options. Normally a person

CHAPTER 34

would issue a flat denial and immediately launch a lawsuit against the other party. He decided, however, that he would remain silent.

His phone rang. 'Come to my office, now!'

Inside the president's office, Zemin rose to his feet. There was no greeting. His fiery eyes strobed Shen, 'You've screwed up big time, Shen!' He waved a copy of *Mercantile News* in front of him. 'This personal attack on you reflects on the whole country, including me!' He wiped the spit from his mouth. 'Just as we're regaining trust with other countries after Tiananmen Square, you seem hellbent on wrecking it! It's lucky for you and for me that you have diplomatic immunity!'

Shen remained calm. 'Sir, these accusations are completely false.'

Zemin rubbed his face hard. 'Here's what's going to happen. China will immediately deny these accusations, stating they are completely without foundation. We will probably say something to the effect that the Chinese government will take retaliatory measures against anyone propagating these preposterous lies. We might also mention that Macrae's false allegations are being made by a man who is losing ground in an ever-competitive world.'

Zemin continued to stare at Shen. He kept his inner contempt hidden well. 'So, you need to keep a low profile from now on until our meeting with the G8 in Birmingham. I need you and your team at the ministry for Trade and Development to fine tune our restructuring proposals for joining the World Trade Organization (WTO) which will come up at the G8 meeting. The members will undoubtedly need us to amend our tariff policies before we are even considered to be a signatory to this organization. Now, get out!'

Once Shen left the office, Zemin picked up his phone and spoke with his own 'Shanghai clique' agents. 'Tighten the noose on Shen and make sure we can flush out his whole network by the time the G8 meeting starts.'

Shen calmly closed his office door and sat alone. Without Peng Zheng, his link to their UK underground network had been temporarily severed, which meant he would need to take matters into his own hands. Once Macrae was out of the way, he could still pursue his goal of taking over his marine terminals. He'd already received intelligence through MSS that Macrae had damning evidence on him gathered by his own private investigators. If he could destroy Macrae and the evidence all in one, that would be the ideal solution. From this point his path was clear. Once Zemin was assassinated, he could take over the leadership and reenergize the Chinese dragon.

———————————

The month of March arrived. Normally it would be cold and damp, but instead, it became unseasonably warm. Buds of crocuses, bluebells and daffodils started to sneak into the light, drawn out by the longer days and warmer sunshine. Even the grass began showing early signs of green. Gradually, the drab grey and black shades of winter receded, being replaced by the ever-increasing pastel shades of spring. It even smelled and felt like spring and seemed there was a direct correlation between the weather pattern and the mood of the country. People's optimism was rising in line with the barometer. Surprisingly enough, even strangers said 'hello' to each other

CHAPTER 34

when passing in the street.

Nick Northrop entered the West Midlands police headquarters in readiness for the G8 security committee meeting to which he'd been invited. Present would be representatives from the police, army, bomb disposal squad, MI5, and MI6. The chairman stood up. 'Good morning, everyone. I need everyone's full attention. Although we've been active during the past two months, we are now in the final nine weeks of security inspections before the G8. It is now time for our deep sweeps of all sewers, canals, roads, tunnels, bridges and buildings in our designated area. It seems we are fortunate with drier, warmer weather so we should start securing the sewer system early before the incessant rain showers of April set in. In conjunction with the city council, police divers will scour the entire canal system around the area of central Birmingham and the International Convention Centre. In addition, army bomb disposal experts will complete an in-depth sweep of the sewer system. Full breathing gear must be used. Now, let me pass you over to Nick Northrop, public works manager of the city.'

Nick Northrop stood up. 'As requested, I have brought with me copies of all the road, sewer, canal and infrastructure plans so that nothing can be missed in your security plans. I have on hand a team of council workers that can assist you in any way required. Please be advised that many of our workers will be employed cleaning and painting council property in the area. Each one of these workers will have photo identity and signed work orders stamped for that day.'

A member of the bomb squad raised his hand. 'Can you assure us that all rubbish bins and containers will be removed from the area during the meeting?'

Northrop nodded. 'Absolutely. There will be none.'

The chairman stood up again. 'Thank you, Mr Northrop. One final note. Once inspected, each drain and sewage cover will be welded up and sealed by the police.' As Northrop left the room, the group discussed in detail the security of the Council House, The Grand Hotel and the ICC.

Northrop walked back to his office. He knew he was taking a huge risk being part of the G8 security plans, but it afforded him inside knowledge that he could use to his advantage. He'd managed to keep his past hidden and no one knew where he lived. He decided the only object that could lead enquiries to him was his car. Parking in his underground car park or even near to his apartment was a giveaway. He decided to take out the VW van from his lock-up garage in Sheldon and swap it with his car.

Chapter 35

The council welder flipped his welding mask up off his face, wiped his brow and looked up at the police supervisor. 'That's the last of the drains welded up and sealed.'

'Good, that takes care of any underground bomb risks.' The supervisor radioed into the security central office. 'All clear on section twelve.'

By early morning on Friday 15th May, the security detail carried out their last checks of the G8 venues before the dignitaries arrived. The canal network had been cleared by security using police divers and all previous searches using sniffer dogs, bug detectors and hand-held X-ray devices had failed to detect any bomb threats in the area. This included room number 414 at the Grand Hotel or the central drainage pipe at the ICC. Strong crowd barriers had already been erected well away from the Grand Hotel and the ICC.

During the afternoon, the leaders arrived from Canada, France, Germany, Italy, Japan, Russia, UK, USA and the European Union, checking in at The Grand Hotel in time for the opening reception at the council buildings hosted by the lord mayor and Prime Minister Blair. After the reception the leaders had a working dinner to discuss their prime concerns and finalize the agenda for the main meeting to be held the following day.

As the sun rose on Saturday, busload upon busload of demonstrators began arriving in the city and started to form a circle around the centre. With the warm weather, their mood was jubilant as they chanted and waved protest banners calling for the cancellation of developing world debt. Unknown to the demonstrators, however, the G8 leaders had already left for an offsite meeting thirty-five miles north of the city at the secluded Weston Hall country estate.

Approaching midday, the Chinese government Boeing 700-500 descended slowly on its final approach over Coventry into Birmingham International Airport.

'Don't let me down, Shen! As guests of the G8, our combined purpose here is to instil confidence in the members that we are a politically and economically trustworthy state with common values and beliefs. Your job here is to prepare the ground for us to also join the World Trade Organisation. Stick to the script you and I have discussed and do not deviate from it! In turn, I will continue to convince the other leaders that we are ready to join the group and be a responsible partner. Hopefully, by this time next year, the group will be renamed the G9. This is the only way China can continue to expand both economically and politically.'

Shen looked across at his boss. 'I will not let you down, sir! My team and I are well prepared and ready to report on the progress of restructuring our economy in line with WTO guidelines. As we discussed, it's likely it will be at least two years before our tariff policies are aligned with those of the organisation, but we have real tangible progress to show.'

'Good. Now, once we get there, we will attend the main reception. Keep to your group and even though this is to be a social event, use it to influence the other members, while I mix with the other G8 leaders.'

Shen smiled. 'I believe there will also be other prominent business leaders and their partners attending this reception.'

Zemin nodded sternly at Shen. 'That is so, but I repeat, stay on script as Minister for Trade and Development.'

As President Zemin and Shen arrived at the Grand Hotel, the number of demonstrators in St Philip's churchyard had swelled considerably, chanting, 'No more debt! No more debt! No more debt!'

Side streets became tightly packed with protesters but, at least for the time being, the demonstration remained peaceful.

As Zemin entered the reception at the convention centre, subdued lighting reflected down from the tall ceiling on the dozens of delegates mingling amongst the scattered tables filled with appetizing hors d'oeuvres and drinks. The loud chatter in the room subsided abruptly as he was warmly received by all the other G8 leaders. He'd already met President Clinton the previous November on a state visit to the United States. He'd also met Tony Blair in Hong Kong and was a personal friend of Jean Chretien, the Canadian Prime minister. They shook hands firmly and were quickly joined by the other leaders appreciative of Zemin's open and warm diplomacy.

Shen looked on from a distance, keeping his inner contempt for his leader under control. How could Zemin be so buddy-buddy with everyone, when China should now be flexing its muscles after centuries of being exploited by foreign powers.

He swallowed hard. For now, Zemin's orders could not have been better, allowing him to separate from his boss. Shen took a glass of champagne from a waiter and while mixing with his WTO working group, he scoured the other guests until he finally found the one he was hoping to see. He was not disappointed. James Macrae stood in a circle with several other couples. He appeared to be on his own and kept glancing at his watch. As the reception continued, Shen kept within his own group but kept a surreptitious eye on Macrae. Finally, he saw Macrae give his empty glass to a waiter and shake hands with the circle of people he'd been talking to. Macrae left the reception hall and passed through the security personnel and left on the canal side of the building. Shen quickly made his apologies and went to the panoramic window overlooking the canal complex. He saw him walk south along the pathway to his own office building and enter it.

Once inside his own building, James passed by the security officer guarding the entrance and entered his office meeting Stella Hudson in the darkened boardroom. She was looking through the window at the towpath below that came from the convention centre. She turned to face James. 'Did he show any signs of trying to follow you?'

James frowned. 'No he didn't, although I believe he was watching me when I left. Do you think he will take the bait?'

'Hard to say. He definitely needs to shut you up and tonight would be his best opportunity. With a crowded reception and all the demonstrators milling about outside keeping the security team occupied, it would be the perfect time for him to just slip out and follow you. We just have to wait.'

James went to the window and stood next to Stella in the half light. 'Did you ever find out who Lingdao was supposed

CHAPTER 35

to be meeting that day?'

'No, we still don't know who he is. It's extremely worrying since we believe it's likely he could surface this weekend. We know we're looking for a man, we just don't have a description.'

'How can you be so sure?'

'It's the only explanation that ties in with what Lingdao has told us. Since Lingdao is a military man we're sure he's linked to Shen and it's possible that President Zemin could be Shen's target, that is, after he's dealt with you.'

'Hmm. It's a mess alright. You know, come to think of it, I had a weird feeling at the lord mayor's dinner that someone who was there looked familiar, but I haven't been able to place him.'

Stella turned towards James, squinting her eyes deep in thought. 'Are you sure?'

'Yes, my partner Chris mentioned that one of the guests had been looking over at us. I casually went to the washroom later so I could see for myself but even though he looked familiar I couldn't think who it might be.'

'That's funny, the council seems to keep popping up all over the place. When Lingdao was arrested, the only vehicle or person that was close by was a council truck inspecting a drain and we drew a blank on that one.'

James looked back at Stella. 'Interesting.' He hesitated. 'You know, since my family was in Wales, I came to work here on the Friday after New Year's day and I saw council workers carrying out some kind of repairs on the ICC roof.'

'Really!' Stella tapped her foot on the floor. 'Hmm, I guess with all the preparations, the council is bound to be at the centre of things. Could be our man is hiding in plain sight, I wonder.'

James didn't respond immediately. He repeated, 'Hiding in plain sight.' He paced back and forth. 'Oh my god! The person who was at that dinner reminds me now of the photo of that mercenary MI6 showed me at the time my parents were killed. I'm not sure it's him but it could be.'

Stella immediately reached down for her police radio mic. 'Agent Hirons, are you there?' She waited momentarily for an answer. 'Agent Jeremy Hirons, come in?' No reply came.

'Shit! Stay here, James. I'll be back! Don't let anyone in.'

Stella dashed to the street below on the front side of the warehouse. Situated some fifty metres away was a dark-blue Transit van parked at the side of the road in darkness. She tapped on the side of the van and the rear doors opened. Inside the van were two plain clothed officers monitoring tv screens of the surrounding area while Jeremy Hirons was monitoring his own MI6 network.

Stella closed the door behind her and stared at Jeremy. He broke off the conversation he was having over his own intercom.

'Jeremy! We've might have an ID on the man that was supposed to be meeting Lingdao that day. Macrae thinks he saw the mercenary who killed his parents at the Lord Mayor's dinner recently.'

Jeremy thought for a second. 'That's impossible! That was William Brocklehurst, the former officer of the Staffordshire Regiment who killed the Macrae's. He's dead. We received intelligence on that nearly two years ago.'

Stella shook her head. 'What if he's not dead? He could have been hired by the Chinese again and is in plain sight here. When I think back, the council seems to keep cropping up.

CHAPTER 35

First we had the council truck in the area when we arrested Lingdao. Then James thinks he's seen Brocklehurst at the Lord Mayor's dinner and he just told me he saw council workers on the roof of the convention centre after New Year.'

Jeremy rubbed his face hard. He looked over at the officer next to him. 'Pavan, pull up the files and photos of all the council people involved with the G8 meeting. Let's compare them to the last photo we have of Brocklehurst.'

Pavan's fingers clattered on his keyboard and within seconds his screen filled with a montage of faces and titles. Jeremy and Stella both leaned forward and examined the profiles in front of them. Like sponges, their eyes absorbed every small detail. They compared a shaven-headed Brocklehurst with a gallery of council workers.

Within seconds, Jeremy and Stella stared at each other, their eyes wide open. Jeremy was the first to speak. 'It's him, has to be!'

'Bloody hell! It is. Damn it, he's been right under our noses the whole time! Let's get an immediate arrest warrant out for Nick Northrop.' Stella moved to the rear doors of the van. 'Listen, I have to get back to James Macrae.'

———————

Standing at the convention centre window, Shen had watched Macrae enter the warehouse office complex where his company, Macrae Holdings, was located. He quickly turned around and scanned the reception guests. They were all occupied in enthusiastic chatter with one another.

As he walked towards the exit, he passed several tables of hors d'oeuvres at the side of the reception area. On one of the tables, a chef was carving a large prime rib of beef under a heat lamp. He had several sharp carving knives to the side of him. Shen picked up a plate, but it slipped from his hand. While the chef's attention was distracted, Shen dropped his napkin over one of the knives and quickly slipped it into his pocket. On his way out he entered the cloakroom and helped himself to a light raincoat and a trilby hat that he found close by. As he left the convention centre, he spoke deliberately to the security guard that he needed to get some fresh air and would be back shortly. Bending his back forward from the waist, he walked slowly along the towpath keeping his head down and opened the warehouse main entrance door. As he entered the foyer, he arched his head slowly upwards towards an approaching security guard.

Shen winced, trying to smile and croaked, 'Can you help me please.' When the guard was close enough, Shen sprung upright and quickly spun around behind him stabbing the knife into the side of his neck. As a military man it was his signature move which he'd perfected early on in his career. As the guard slumped backwards, Shen grabbed him under his arms and dragged the limp body, dumping it in a nearby utility room. He used the raincoat to mop up the blood as best as he could from the foyer floor leaving little trace of it to be discovered. Tossing the trilby hat to one side, he moved stealthily towards the stairwell, rather than the elevator, and made his way up to the Macrae Holdings top floor offices. Shen knew he had to move fast. This would be the only opportunity he could settle the score with Macrae and remove the last obstacle for taking over the strategic European ports that he needed for China to dominate the continent. If, by chance he was caught, the British authorities could never detain him because of his diplomatic immunity.

Shen had no idea that all the security personnel watching over James Macrae had been cursorily distracted with the discovery of the second threat, the jackal. Macrae would die.

———————————-

James continued to stand looking out of his boardroom window towards the convention centre. Dammit, surely after publishing such a defamatory article on Shen, he must have riled him to the point of revenge. Instead, all he had seen was an old man shuffling down the towpath towards his building.

Chapter 36

President Zemin finished off his conversation with the French president, Jacques Chirac, and the Russian president, Boris Yeltsin. 'Of course we will meet tomorrow morning again where we can continue our conversation for future political and economic cooperation between our countries. Thank you for allowing China this opportunity to speak with your group. We are grateful for your generosity of spirit.'

Zemin then moved to the side of the reception and spoke to his personal security guard. 'We'll be leaving shortly to return to the hotel in the limousine. The other leaders are also on the verge of leaving. What news of Shen?'

'He left by the canal entrance some time ago. According to our private network he followed James Macrae to his offices.'

Zemin smiled. 'As we predicted. It's a good job we have his network all identified.'

All the leaders arrived back at the Grand Hotel within the hour. They accessed the rear of the hotel from Edmund Street, which was sealed off well away from the demonstrators. They congregated in the main ballroom where the G8 security chief was waiting for them.

Raucous shouting from the ever-growing crowd at the front of the hotel was audible, even there.

'No more debt! No more debt! No more debt!'

'Gentlemen, the police have informed us that the number of demonstrators outside the hotel has swelled to an estimated seventy-five thousand. While the crowd is under control, we are weary of right-wing extremists infiltrating the group. These individuals are being extracted as best as we can, but we must now activate our secret contingency plan and move you to a safe location. Please have your staff gather your things so we can depart within the next half hour. There will be enough room for yourselves and wives of course, as well as a few senior members of your delegations.'

In less than an hour the convoy of cars arrived at the Swallow boutique hotel approximately seven kilometres away where the G8 leaders were shown to their private suites.

———————————————

Nick Northrop lay low on the roof of his apartment block. He looked through his night vision finder and located the central drainpipe on the roof of the convention centre. What a pity he couldn't take a shot and finish the job right now, knowing all the leaders were within the building. The trouble was the reception was in the symphony hall well away from exhibition halls three and four, where the leaders would meet the following day. The pipe bomb when it went off would totally destroy those halls and everyone in there. He smiled, relishing the idea of a well-earned retirement. Palm trees, women and alcohol.

Satisfied he'd prepared everything ready for the activation of the pipe bomb in the convention centre, he returned to his apartment below and waited for news of the explosion at the Grand Hotel. He smiled, thinking he would actually hear the explosion before the calamity even hit the newswire. His adrenaline level increased with the expectant excitement of two masterly created bombs within seven hours of each other. Even if his cover was blown with all the high-level security, no one knew where he lived. He would be long gone before they even got a smell of him.

The West Midlands police main control room was buzzing with action.

'Get SO19, the special operations team, to Northrop's home address now! Let's get another team to his office as well as the main council yard. Circulate his photo now, showing him with hair. It will be easier to spot him.'

Within half an hour SO19 had battered in the front door of a semi-detached house in Shard End, only to find a retired schoolteacher in bed with his wife. Raids on all the other locations where it was thought Northrop might be also drew a blank.

The commander smashed his fist on the desk in the control room. 'Get everyone out of bed that works with Northrop including all the HR people. Someone must know where he

CHAPTER 36

is!'

'Already on it, sir!' was the reply.

'Good. Set up roadblocks and seal off the city! We need to get this bastard now!'

In the subdued light, James stood patiently at the boardroom window. There was still no action on the towpath below him. As he shifted his weight from one leg to the other, he caught a fleeting glance of a shadow behind him reflected in the glass. Instinctively, he ducked down and moved swiftly to his left. The dark figure behind him stopped, his right hand in mid-air holding a knife as though he was aiming to cut James's throat. James threw a solid punch into the side of the dark figure, but the man managed to block it hard with his left forearm. The man then spun towards James. James stepped back as his attacker lowered his right arm and held the knife out in front of him.

James backed up quickly behind the boardroom table.

'You didn't think you could hide from me forever, did you, Macrae?'

Stalling for time, James answered. 'General Shen, you had my parents killed and have systematically terrorised my family and company. You will pay for this, even if I have to kill you myself.'

Shen laughed. 'Oh, you stupid man. What makes you think you could do that?'

Slowly James slid his right hand down to his side and felt for the heavy soapstone carving of the walrus sitting on the sideboard cabinet behind him. Shen moved forward slowly around the table holding the knife at waist height. As he moved closer to James, James took hold of the stone carving and threw it into the chest of Shen. Shen buckled momentarily but still came forward managing to stab James in his side. With limited space between the cabinet and the table, James kicked out his right leg. Shen tried to use his left hand to grab his leg but instead James quickly moved to his right, just enough to get inside Shen's right arm and grab it with both his hands. Using all his strength, he bashed Shen's knife hand onto the cabinet top. Shen grabbed James around his neck with his other arm. James felt Shen's tightening lock on his windpipe, but continued to bang Shen's hand onto the cabinet until he dropped the knife. Once James's hands were free he back-elbowed Shen in his face, but Shen kept the lock on his neck.

James pushed back hard, continuing to back-elbow Shen. As they careened backwards, they fell over, locked together, with James on top of Shen. James tried to get up, but as he did so, Shen lashed out with his right foot and caught James in the groin. James buckled, but as he fell he used his right elbow to fall onto Shen's stomach. Shen was winded momentarily. James came down on top of him. As he fell he felt the soapstone carving close to him. Using every ounce of strength he had left, he lifted up the heavy carving and smashed it directly on Shen's head.

Shen passed out, but in a frenzy James continued to hit him.

Somewhere in the distance, James thought he heard shouting. 'James! James!' He felt an arm go round his neck and then it became clear to him what was happening. A police officer was pulling him off Shen and Stella Hudson was screaming at him to stop.

CHAPTER 36

James tried to stand as the officer pulled him back off Shen. He looked back at Shen, his eyes cold and empty. As he dropped his left hand, it felt wet. He looked down and saw blood oozing from under his shirt. The officer gently sat James down on a chair. He felt dazed and disorientated.

'James, James, do you know who I am?' Stella looked at him straight in the face and then turned to the officer. 'Let's get him back on the floor and bind his wound until the ambulance gets here. They should be here any moment now.'

― ― ― ― ― ― ― ― ― ― ― ― ― ―

Wilfred Stevens, the former general manager of the public works department was woken up by loud banging on his front door. Grabbing his dressing gown, he immediately went and opened it.

'Mr Stevens?'

'Yes. What the hell's going on?'

'We need to come in and ask you some questions. It could be a matter of life and death.'

He led the two police officers into the lounge.

'I don't understand. How can I help you?'

'Sir, you hired a man by the name of Nick Northrop nearly two years ago?'

'Yes I did. Why? What's he done?'

'It's what he might do. We believe he's planning to assassinate one or several of the G8 leaders.'

Stevens' eyes widened. 'That's impossible. The man I hired is a former officer of the Royal Engineers. He came with impeccable references and worked hard, so much so, I promoted him into my position when I retired.'

'Do you know where he lives?'

Stevens rubbed his chin. 'If I remember correctly, he rented a house in Shard End.'

'No he doesn't. We've already been to the address listed in the council HR records. Please try to think where he might be based.'

Stevens shook his head. 'Honestly, I really don't know. I know he was single and worked long hours, in fact he was always at work early and left late. The only thing I can think of is, I went to the reference library on the way home one night and I thought I saw him drive past on Broad Street in a Ford Mondeo.'

'Thank you, Mr Stevens. If there's anything else you remember about him, please call this number.'

———————————-

Stella Hudson was back in the West Midlands control room, together with Jeremy Hirons and the G8 security team. She took a deep gulp of black coffee and stood up to address the group. Tired faces and red eyes stared back at her.

'Okay, here's what we know so far. According to DOT records, there is a Ford Mondeo registered to a Nathan Northrop. The trouble is the address given is the same one we drew a blank on in Shard End. So, circulate this registration number and let's scour the area for this car. If I was Northrop, I would want to live in an apartment, not a house. It's more anonymous. Let's follow up on Steven's comment that he saw Northrop driving west on Broad Street. Make sure you check out all the apartment underground carparks that way as well.'

CHAPTER 36

One female officer stood up. 'DI Hudson. We've checked the list of apartment renters in the surrounding area and there is no reference of a Nathan or Nicholas Northrop.'

'Okay. Understood. Nevertheless, let's go door to door with Northrop's photo. We are using the photo we found in his council HR file. It shows him with hair and without his former moustache. We also believe he has had the Staffordshire knot tattoo removed from his wrist. Be careful with this man. He will be armed and dangerous.'

Chapter 37

In the early hours of Sunday morning, the night manager of the Grand Hotel moved from his office behind the reception desk and went over to the front door. His footsteps on the marble floor echoed around the large entrance hall normally filled with guests. Several armed police officers were stationed there both inside and outside the hotel.

He stood alongside one of the officers. 'How's the situation outside now?'

The officer in charge arched his back and frowned. 'So far so good. The crowd has thinned quite a bit. People are getting tired.' He hooked both his thumbs inside his bulletproof vest. 'They probably can't speak anymore after all the shouting they've been doing! Let's hope we can keep it that way, at least for the next twelve hours or so.'

'Good to know. The G8 leaders would probably have been safe here after all. As for their delegations, they're still working flat out in the various meeting rooms. These people never seem to...'

CHAPTER 37

At that moment, inside the bathroom wall of room 414, the neatly packed timer silently completed an electrical circuit with the detonator attached to the thirty pounds of C4 plastic explosive. If Northrop could have witnessed a slow-motion film of the blast, he would have patted himself on the back in conjuring up such a masterly piece of art. Like lightening, the explosion cut a swath of destruction straight through the centre of the hotel, severing the thirty metres by ten metres wide steel girders and cross beams above the ballroom.

The duty officer at the front door was still in conversation with the night manager when the deep boom of the explosion immediately burst their eardrums. Clothes were shredded to pieces and ripped off as the group were savagely somersaulted through the glass-front doors and into the street outside. Strewn across the road, the officer managed to open his eyes. The incessant roaring sound in his ears seemed like he was standing next to a jet engine on full thrust, while the immense pain pounding inside his head felt like a monster migraine. Seemingly, in surreal slow motion, he witnessed all the hair on the bodies around him burning off into smoking ashes. Body parts lay everywhere, peppered with glass fragments and shards of hot iron.

Inside the hotel meeting rooms and cafes, people buried under the mass of butchered bricks, mortar, and steel, lay either completely still or groaning, their skin raw after being incinerated by the rabid explosion. Six floors worth of humanity and construction materials became an interlaced mixture of shrapnel punching its way directly to the ground and into the basement until it could go no farther.

— — — — — — — — — — — —

Seven kilometres away, the shock wave of the blast shook the windows of the Swallow Hotel. Lights flashed on all over the hotel. Several faces peered from behind bedroom curtains to see the flames, white and black smoke eerily erupting into the night sky from the city-centre. On-duty security staff immediately went from bedroom to bedroom issuing instructions for everyone to meet downstairs in the lobby.

Being a small boutique hotel it did not take long to gather the entire group of guests together. A motorcade of limousines, together with police cars stood outside ready to evacuate the hotel.

The head security officer took in a deep breath and addressed the group. 'Everyone, it is with the deepest regret that I have to inform you of an explosion at the Grand Hotel. All I can say at this stage is that it is serious. There have been a number of casualties, but we do not know the number of fatalities or injured people. All emergency services are currently focused on this area. It is too early to speculate if this is the work of terrorists.'

Helmut Kohl, the chancellor of Germany, spoke asking everyone's unspoken question. 'Are we safe here?'

The security chief stuttered slightly. 'I'm assured by all of our security personnel that we are safe here. If, by chance, we have to evacuate, there are vehicles at the ready to escort us away.'

President Clinton stood. 'What does the group feel about continuing with the meeting later this morning?'

Tony Blair responded gravely. 'All of us have at some time or another been threatened by violence by either terrorists or other individual parties. Intimidation is not new to us as politicians or statesmen. If we postpone or cancel the meeting,

CHAPTER 37

then we are showing we can be harassed and intimidated by these grotesque acts of violence. It is my view we should carry on and let the emergency and security forces deal with this grave situation.'

Clinton replied. 'I agree. We must show a defiant and united front not only to the world but to these faceless cowardly terrorists.'

Meanwhile reports of the growing number of deaths and injured people continued to rise. It became clear that these numbers would be in the hundreds since many of the demonstrators in St Philip's churchyard had also been injured by flying debris.

———————————————

Nick Northrop had been peering from behind his bedroom curtains waiting for the hotel bomb to detonate. Normally calm in this situation, he had bitten his one fingernail down to the quick. When, at last, he witnessed the explosion of flames, debris and smoke in the distance, he started to relax. One down, one to go. He wondered if the hotel bomb had succeeded in killing its intended target. For a brief moment he considered cutting and running before it was time to detonate the second one. Money, it always came back to money. With only a few hours to go he couldn't resist waiting for the hefty lump sum payment to be credited to his offshore bank account in Andorra.

He kept getting up and checking the roof of the convention centre for any sign of activity. He'd seen police activity on the roof before but, as yet it seemed none of the inspections had uncovered the pipe bomb. He felt his eyes close as the sound of emergency vehicle sirens faded away into obscurity. Sometime later he rolled over and felt a lump in his side. He woke up to find he was lying on top of his night vision scope.

He checked the travel clock on his bedside cabinet. It was 5:37 a.m., and the early fingers of daylight were already starting to grope their way across the city skyline. He rubbed his eyes and eased himself up from the bed. He checked the roof of the convention centre once more and to his dismay, he saw members of the bomb squad using a large tripod and carefully dismantling the top of the pipe. He kept his eyes focused there for several minutes, but there was no mistake, it had been discovered.

Without waiting any longer, he grabbed his rucksack that he had already prepared and headed for the door. He did not take his sniper rifle or scope. All was quiet on the landing outside his room, so he made his way to the service elevator, considering it to be safer than the main elevator. The stairs from the twentieth floor would take too long. He exited on level P1 in order to avoid the main lobby. Now all he had to do was exit up the stairs from the utility rooms out of the back of the apartment block. He had been unable to park his VW van in the underground car park due to its height, so it had been parked close by in a municipal car park.

Stella Hudson together with an army of security personnel had pursued every tiny detail and lead they had on William Brocklehurst aka Nick Northrop. Throughout the night, the team of police and army personnel had cloaked the entire city, getting anyone out of bed they needed to. Tracking of the Ford Mondeo had drawn a blank, but every apartment building security camera footage had been meticulously scrutinised,

CHAPTER 37

frame by frame until they eventually found him. In addition to the dragnet of personnel, army bomb disposal experts located the pipe bomb on the roof of the convention centre. Had it not been for James Macrae idly mentioning he thought he saw someone he recognized at the Lord Mayor's dinner and seeing council workers on the convention centre roof they might not have connected the dots between each piece of evidence.

Stella sat by the TV monitor in the undercover operations van around the corner from the main entrance of Northrop's apartment block. They had waited and watched his apartment from several rooftops not far from the apartment complex. Stella and her team were reluctant to storm his apartment just in case he had set up a booby trap bomb. They knew all too well what kind of adversary Northrop was. If he was going to die, he would not have cared how many innocent people went with him.

'DI Hudson, he's coming out of the underground car park now. He has a rucksack on.'

Stella swallowed hard. 'Can you see if there are any wires coming out of his cuffs to any kind of a pressure switch in his hand?'

'Not possible to see from where I am.'

'Anyone else see anything like a bomb on him?'

'Number five here. Looks like he could have a switch in his hand. He's crossing a yard with no one around right now. I've got a clean head shot. Even if he releases the switch, no danger to other persons.'

'Take the shot!'

Northrop's head exploded instantaneously. He fell straight to the ground. No explosion occurred as the remote key to his VW van fell down beside him.

When James came to, as his eyes flickered open, he tried to focus on the man standing over him. At the same time, his mind was trying to fathom out where he was and what had happened to him. The light coming through the window seemed to increase in intensity causing him to squint. He looked at the saline drip hanging on a chrome stand to his left-hand side and a digital blood pressure and heart monitor unit to his right. He tried to push down on both his hands on the bed to try to inch himself higher up. The man gently lifted his head and added another pillow underneath it and then moved to the bottom of the bed and studied a chart. He looked up at James and smiled.

'Welcome back, Mr Macrae. I'm Dr Varma and you are in the Queen Elizabeth Hospital. You suffered an abdominal trauma caused by a stab wound last night. Without getting into detail, we operated on you, repaired your organs and stitched you up. I'm happy to say there will be no long-lasting damage. Since you lost a lot of blood, we've given you a blood transfusion. You will be sore for several days but with the antibiotics you are receiving you should heal up quickly.'

James tried to speak but his mouth felt dry, his tongue was stiff, and he found it hard to swallow.

'Here, let me help you take a sip of water.'

James leaned forward and sucked a few drops of water through a straw from the glass held up in front of him.

'Thank you, doctor.' He lay back on his pillows and tried to piece back together the events that had led him here. As the doctor left he saw there was a police officer at the door. The

CHAPTER 37

officer turned and spoke.

'Don't mind me, Mr Macrae, I'm here to guard you. There is a visitor here to see you and the doctor has just given me the okay for him to see you.'

Jeremy Hirons came into the private ward and placed his hand on James's. 'How are you feeling, James?'

James grimaced and gave a weak smile. 'Sore. Feels like I've been in a giant spin-dryer all night.'

'Well, it sounds like you're going to make a full recovery. Sarah is on her way from Wales right now. She should be here soon.'

James smiled.

'Shen is here in the hospital as well. He has a concussion and a fractured skull. Right now he's in an induced coma and under careful supervision. Needless to say, he's heavily guarded.'

James tried to inch himself higher in the bed and winced. 'Do you think the Chinese will protect him because of his diplomatic immunity?'

'Hard to say at this stage. Normally the foreign secretary would summon the Chinese ambassador and demand that Shen should stand trial here and face up to the charges against him without diplomatic immunity. In this case, however, since President Zemin is here with Prime Minister Blair, we're expecting those two to speak directly to each other. If you're asking me, I would say the Chinese will protect Shen and demand him to be returned to them. I hope I'm wrong.'

James tried to shake his head but winced again instead.

'There's something else you should know, James. There was a bomb explosion in the Grand Hotel earlier this morning. Unfortunately fifty-seven people are dead and several hundred have been injured. The G8 leaders, including Zemin were all safe since they had been moved to another secret location earlier due to the Jubilee 2000 demonstrations.'

James closed his eyes. 'When does it end?' He lay still for a few moments and then asked, 'What about the jackal?'

Jeremy frowned. 'Thanks to you, we know who he is. Stella and the whole security team together with half of the British police force have been out combing for him. Looks like they have him.' He looked down again at James, but he'd already dropped off to sleep.

Zemin sat in his suite at the Swallow Hotel with his own private security detail. He spoke quietly, 'Let's get our embassy staff down here from London immediately and make the necessary arrangements for the dead and injured from our group that remained at the Grand Hotel last night. Words can't describe how sorry I am for the families and friends of our delegation.' He took in a deep breath and placed his hand on his heart. 'Is there any further news on what caused the explosion?'

Kevin Tan responded. 'So far as we know, there's no word yet. If it was a terrorist bomb, no one has claimed responsibility.'

Zemin got up from his chair. 'Hmm. After all we've discovered on Shen and what we've discussed before, I've a feeling Shen could be behind this. Now, what's the news on him?'

'He was taken to the Queen Elizabeth hospital not far from here. After he went after Macrae, we learned that there was a fight and both men were injured badly. Shen has a fractured

CHAPTER 37

skull and is in intensive care right now while Macrae has stab wounds.'

Zemin remained silent, pacing up and down the room.

Tan continued. 'Do you want to demand Shen's release on the grounds of diplomatic immunity, and we move him back to China by air ambulance?'

Zemin patted his forefinger repeatedly on his lips. 'Not sure right now. Let me think about it some more. In the meantime, round up every one of Shen's network and ship them to Qincheng jail. Oh, and make sure that girlfriend of his, Meili Shabani, is taken in as well. We'll decide what to do with them all later.'

Zemin sat alone in his hotel suite, deep in thought. He had an hour before the G8 meeting would resume at the convention centre. After some time he got up and as he was putting on his jacket and tie, his phone rang.

'Yes, send him up.'

Blair entered the suite. He looked tired and drawn. They shook hands and sat down.

'Prime Minister Blair. I wish I could say it's a pleasure to see you this morning, but the night's events have been tragic. It seems we have all lost people that we cared for very much.'

'Yes, for all of us, it has been an appalling attack on both humanity and democracy. I'm sorry for your loss. We are making every effort to find who was responsible for this heinous act of terrorism.'

Zemin raised his eyebrows. 'Terrorism?'

'Yes, the news has not been released yet but I can tell you this was a deliberate act of terrorism. All evidence points to a bomb hidden some time ago.' Blair remained silent, staring at Zemin. As if to summon up courage, he lifted his head higher and pressed his lips tightly together. 'President Zemin, I will come straight to the point.'

Zemin tilted his head to one side.

'According to our intelligence, we believe the bomb was an attempt to assassinate you, but made to look as though it was an attempt by a section of extremist Jubilee 2000 demonstrators to kill all the other G8 members as a statement against capitalism.'

'I see. What makes you believe that I was the intended target?'

Blair leaned forward towards Zemin. 'UK intelligence has good reason to believe this. The man we arrested and found guilty of the hijacking of the Macrae tanker, Lingdao, was working on direct instructions from your General Shen. Lingdao also told us of his involvement with your London head of the security Peng Zheng. We have evidence Zheng was working directly with Shen and that Zheng has an operative in Birmingham that Lingdao was due to link up with.'

'I still don't see how you see me as the intended target.'

'We believe this operative planted the bomb in the Grand Hotel some months ago specifically on instructions that came from Shen to Peng Zheng. Shen is a calculated killer and was definitely responsible for the attacks on the Macrae Shipping terminals in Europe and the attempted murder of James Macrae himself last night.'

Zemin took off his glasses and wound them around his thumb and forefinger. He looked directly into the eyes of Blair. 'You realize I could create a huge international incident out of these accusations!'

Blair stared directly back at Zemin. 'I do, but I don't believe you will.'

CHAPTER 37

'I see and why is that, Mr Blair?'

'Because I don't believe you were behind Shen's actions. On the contrary, you are here in Birmingham to hope to become a responsible member of the G8. You also demonstrated that China was a responsible global power when you intervened in the Asian financial crisis and your personal diplomacy and leadership style is already reflecting itself in economic development prosperity for your people. Further, you are making genuine strides to join the World Trade Association. These are not the actions of a leader that wants a war with the rest of the world. No, Shen's actions are that of a military man planning a takeover of other countries by force, corruption and murder. In short, Shen was trying to assassinate you last night while trying to remove the last obstacle to take over all the Macrae terminals that could be used for future military bases.'

'You don't mince your words, do you, Mr Blair.'

'I don't when I believe them to be true. Tell me I'm not wrong, after all you've had your own agents shadowing Shen.' He paused. 'Haven't you?'

Zemin gave a hint of a smile. 'What would you like me to do?'

'Lift diplomatic immunity from Shen and let us prosecute him here in the UK with all the charges brought against him. That way you will move a huge obstacle out of your way to join the G8 and the WTO.'

Zemin nodded. 'I see.'

Blair continued. 'You and I could be great friends personally and our countries have much to learn from each other.'

Zemin stood up and put his glasses back on. He reached out his hand towards Blair. They shook hands.

Immediately Blair had left, Zemin summoned his own personal security agent, Kevin Tan.

'We have a job to do, and you will have to do it fast. Blair wants us to lift Shen's diplomatic immunity so they can prosecute him for all the crimes he's committed against the UK. If we did this, it would show good faith to the rest of the world that we are a friendly country who wants to work with the west. It would give us a huge boost, however, giving Shen up could lead to an intelligence leak of untold proportions. He knows too much, and it would make me look weak at home. So, you will need to get to Shen. It's time to terminate him.'

'What about Macrae? Should we finish him off as well?'

'God, no! That would set our progress back years. Let him be. We will continue our expansion by our *lend and bend* programme to foreign countries until they break.'

Chapter 38

James Macrae eased himself back on his pillows as Sarah came into his room. She leaned over and kissed him gently on his forehead and then sat down keeping his hand between hers. She caressed it lightly.

James's eyes brightened as he tried to smile.

'Thank God you're okay! I just spoke with the doctor, and he confirmed you will make a one hundred percent recovery.'

'Yes, I was lucky.' He tried to make light of the situation by saying, 'you should see the other guy,' but it fell on flat ears. Sarah just shook her head.

Sarah stared at him for several seconds. 'Listen, James, I love you more than you could ever imagine but are we ever to be free of this monkey on our back?'

James took in a deep breath. 'Honestly. Yes.'

'Then tell me why I should believe that?'

James lightly squeezed her hand. 'The architect of the plan to take over our terminals and attack our family is no longer a factor. General Shen was the man behind Hugh Stanfield and Euro-Asian Freight, Pair-Tree Capital and the mercenaries that killed Mom and Dad. Right now he's in intensive care fighting for his life after attacking me. The British authorities believe that he can be brought to justice if the Chinese are willing to waive his diplomatic immunity status. According to Jeremy Hirons, Tony Blair will be talking directly with Zemin. He's a president that wants to become part of a G9 organisation. Giving up Shen would pave the way for that to happen.'

'I hope you're right! After the turmoil of this year, it would be good to get back to normal. We're nearly at the end of the summer term so this means we can all be together again as a family. The children love and miss you so much.'

James felt his eyes watering up. 'I love and miss you all too. What happened this weekend puts a closure to this horrible chapter in our lives.'

Sarah stood up and kissed him on his lips, caressing his forehead. 'I can't wait for things to go back as they used to be.'

'They will. I promise you.'

———————————————

Tony Blair addressed the final press conference of the G8 meeting.

With both hands on the lectern, he spoke with unwavering conviction. 'Let us take a moment of silence to remember our friends and colleagues that lost their lives last night together with the many that were injured. We pray for them.'

He struggled to keep his emotions in check.

'On behalf of the other G8 leaders and I also include President Zemin of China, we condemn this evil act of terrorism.

CHAPTER 38

Our unanimous message is that we will never be intimidated by terrorism in any form. Never underestimate our resolve to hunt you down and bring you to justice, no matter how long it will take.'

He then took time to summarise all the political, economic, and social agreements that had been agreed during the meeting and in turn, each leader gave a speech summarizing their views and conclusions of the meeting.

The meeting had been a success and held the promise that with the inclusion of Russia in the group and the likely admission of China at some time in the future, it would herald a new era in world affairs. Unfortunately the optimism of the meeting had been dwarfed by the hotel bombing.

The Queen Elizabeth Hospital or QE as it was known, together with all the other district hospitals, were overflowing with the multitude of patients injured from the blast at the Grand Hotel. Pressed for space, the wards and surrounding corridors were full of stretchers. The QE emergency department had drafted in as many extra doctors and nurses as possible from outside the surrounding region. They moved amongst the stretchers loaded with the stricken victims crying and moaning in pain. Makeshift dressings on the casualties were coated in blood as they waited for attention. It was a chaotic scenario of unequalled proportions.

Kevin Tan pulled the cloth cap down on his head and wrapped his raincoat tightly around him in the damp blustery morning. He carried a briefcase and made straight for the hospital administration office. A sea of pale faces and red eyes greeted him as the admin staff looked up from their desks.

'Hello, I'm Dr Chen from University Hospital, Coventry. After receiving the regional alert asking for help, I came as quickly as I could. Put me wherever you need me.'

A secretary adjusted the elastic band on her ponytail. 'I can help you, Dr Chen. Thank you for responding. Let me check your credentials and we can get you started.'

He produced copies of his certifications from the UK General Medical Council (GMC) and his ID from University Hospital, Coventry. The documents had hastily been put together by his team who based them on a real doctor that was named Chen and did work at that hospital.

The secretary checked his credentials but also made sure to check his GMC number on the UK Central Register to see his registration status, certifications, and training. It all checked out. She made out a temporary ID dated for today and slid it across the desk to him.

'Dr Chen, you can change into a set of scrubs from the stock room just along the corridor. You will need your ID to enter. Check in with Emerge then. That's where you will be needed the most.'

'Thank you.'

Kevin Tan changed into a set of green scrubs in the changing room and hung on his ID tag. Instead of going to the emergency department, he immediately followed the signs to the oncology department where he filled out a requisition and gave it to the internal hospital pharmacist to fill. He drew out a wrapped syringe and a drug called doxorubicin. His team had already researched the drug knowing that it could cause weakness of the heart muscle and make it harder for the

CHAPTER 38

heart to pump blood. He hoped the lethal dose would give him enough time to leave the IC unit before the heart monitors emitted their alarms.

As the elevator doors opened on the fifth floor, the intensive care unit appeared relatively calm compared to the rest of the hospital, each patient being in a separate room. Kevin Tan walked immediately over to the central nurses station and introduced himself.

'Hello, I'm Dr Chen. I've been drafted in from University Hospital Coventry due to the explosion last night at the Grand Hotel. I understand that many of you have been on duty by as much as eighteen hours or more. Admin asked that I check the patients on this floor and then return to Emergency.'

The red-headed nurse smiled up at him. 'Good! We could do with some help. It's a living nightmare right now. Just let me check your ID tag.'

Tan took off his tag and passed it to her. She checked it against her hospital intranet. 'Good. So, normally I would accompany you, but we are so short-staffed, I have to stay here. One note of caution, we have one patient under police guard. He will also need to check you out before you're admitted to see him.'

'Got it. I'll start at the far end and work my way back this way.' He went to walk away and then turned back. 'I hope all the other doctors are on pager standby should any patient alarms go off.'

'They are, but this isn't a normal situation. I understand it's chaos downstairs.'

Tan shook his head. 'I've never seen anything like this.'

He went to each ICU patient and although they were heavily sedated, he made a show of checking them and their charts.

He noticed that a Dr Varma was the doctor in charge of most of the patients.

When he looked through the glass door of Shen's room, he saw he was unconscious, his face covered with a ventilator mask. Heart, vital sign monitors and medicine pumps surrounded him.

The police officer standing directly outside Shen's room looked over at the nurse behind the central station. She gave the officer a thumbs up, but he didn't move.

'Who are you? I haven't seen you before?'

'No, you probably haven't since I've been brought in from University Hospital, Coventry to help out after the bombing last night. Dr Varma is currently in OR which is where I've just come from. I have to check on several of his patients while he's occupied there.'

'Let me see your ID.'

The officer studied it carefully. 'Okay, Dr Chen, you can go in.'

Tan walked to the bottom of the bed and checked Shen's medical chart. He confirmed he had a concussion and trauma to the head had fractured his skull. He was in an induced coma to reduce the swelling in his brain. Without waiting any further, with his back to the police officer, he filled the syringe with the doxorubicin and injected the full amount into Shen's arm. Shen remained still, continuing to breathe through the ventilator. Tan shoved the empty syringe inside his scrubs and left. He walked back to the central nurse station. 'Okay, everything's under control. I'm going back to emerge. I'll be back up again if admin wants me to.'

'Thanks, Dr Chen. Good luck down there.'

Tan nodded his head and walked calmly to the elevator. He

CHAPTER 38

returned to the locker room, changed, and left the hospital. He did not hear the medical alarm go off in the ICU indicating that Shen had suffered a fatal cardiac arrest.

Under grey rolling autumn clouds fanned by an easterly wind bringing in a low-pressure system, a black stick appeared above the surf of the Sea of Marmara. The stick appeared to grow taller and then the conical shape of a submarine conning tower broke through the surface of the lumpy water. Like a sinister black monster emerging from the deep, the Chinese nuclear submarine *Changzheng-5* surfaced, pushing a round bow wave ahead of it towards the port of Ambarli, Turkey.

Over the horizon, a Type 052 destroyer, *Harbin*, grew larger as it followed its silent, lurking companion towards the port. Hundreds of white-uniformed Chinese mariners lined the decks standing to rigid attention. Standing well under the awning out of the light rain at the port, President Zemin turned and shook hands with General Gulnaz on his Turkish state visit. He smiled warmly at his opposite number, keeping his thoughts to himself. *Napoleon Bonaparte had once said, 'China is a sleeping giant, let her sleep, for when she wakes, she will shake the world.'*

Had Napoleon been alive that day, he would have witnessed his prophecy of nearly two hundred years coming true.

THE END

Acknowledgments

Group of Eight (G8) | Facts, History, & Members | Britannica
https://2001-2009.state.gov/r/pa/ho/pubs/fs/85962.htm#yeltsin_visit
https://theconversation.com/chinese-irregular-migration-to-britain-has-a-tragic-history-how-routes-have-evolved-125839
https://www.dailymail.co.uk/news/article-7610213/How-people-smuggling-gangs-migrants-China-slaves-UK.html
https://www.scmp.com/news/china/policies-politics/article/1833273/chinas-qincheng-prison-tigers-cage
https://www.washingtonpost.com/archive/politics/1998/06/21/us-and-china-nearly-came-to-blows-in-96/
http://www.keremcosar.com/publications/Cosar-comment%20on%20Koymen-Boke.pdf
https//www.asiacentre.eu
https://www.statista.com/statistics/1056306/largest-export-commodities-of-turkey/
https://www.history.com/topics/middle-east/kemal-ataturk
https://ec.europa.eu/growth/sectors/raw-materials/areas-specific-interest/critical-raw-materials_en
https://www.rand.org/content/dam/rand/pubs/monograph_reports/MR1119/RAND_MR1119.pdf
https://www.britannica.com/event/Tiananmen-Square-incident
https://www.portofhalifax.ca/
https://www.britannica.com/place/Highclere-Castle
https://researchbriefings.files.parliament.uk/documents/

CBP-8988/CBP-8988.pdf
1996 APEC Economic Outlook
Hong Kong Returned to China - HISTORY
https://www.thegrandhotelbirmingham.co.uk/
https://www.anglicannews.org/news/1998/05/britain-50,000-people-protest-to-g8-about-debt-issue.aspx
https://www.realinstitutoelcano.org/
https://www.facebook.com/groups/bmtwww/posts/2365757870254020/ Courtesy of Les Robinson)

About the Author

Coming from a successful international career in the transportation and shipping industry, Richard has created a thrilling and sensational series of novels based on the business he knows best.

He is an avid writer that provides fast moving, riveting reading set against real-world events and political awareness. His series blends a combination of a family saga, mystery and crime set against a real-world backdrop.

For his stories to be convincing, he spends much of his time researching history and current affairs and then fuses it with his own business, travel experience and creativity. Interestingly, his wife thinks he has a criminal mind!

You can connect with me on:
- https://www.richarddross.com
- https://www.facebook.com/RichardDRoss.Author

Subscribe to my newsletter:
- https://richarddross.com/contact

Also by Richard D Ross

The Hybrid Enemy – A James Macrae Thriller Book 1/3

Facing seemingly insurmountable odds, James Macrae finds himself heading up his family's shipping business after his father suffers a sudden heart attack. Now he's not sure he can save the business or his family from disaster.

When a series of mysterious incidents occur at their international terminals, James learns these are acts of deliberate sabotage. With the clock ticking, James has to act quickly to save his business and family from calamity before it is too late.

His pursuit of his hidden enemy takes him across Europe and the Middle East only to discover the secret agenda of a rising superpower. A fast-paced rollercoaster of adversity, conspiracy and betrayal.

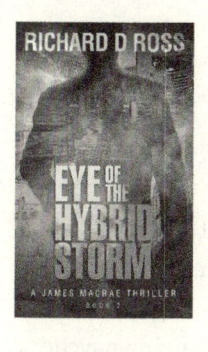

Eye Of The Hybrid Storm - A James Macrae Thriller Book 2/3

James Macrae has hardly had time to breathe after rescuing everything he holds dear in his life. Meanwhile his hidden enemy continues to plot and scheme against him. With vice like precision, the pressure squeezes James to breaking point. Trying to lead a normal life proves impossible as the odds of losing everything build up to bursting point with shocking results.

A fast-paced and enthralling story packed with tension, suspense and treachery.

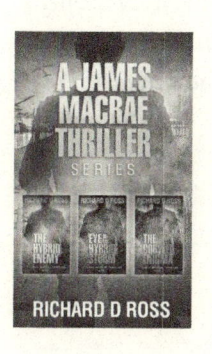

The James Macrae Thriller Series - Books 1-3
1. **The Hybrid Enemy**
    2. **Eye of the Hybrid Storm**
    3. **The Cobweb Enigma**

Coming Soon: The Cobalt Conspiracy

A standalone thriller novel

Book Cover Description

In the small Florida town of Baldwin, a tractor-trailer laden with fresh fruit and vegetables breaks down. For the owner-operator driver, it's the last straw. Not only is he broke, but he loses his friend and partner who's fed up with living paycheck to paycheck.

Stranded at a truck stop, he meets a mysterious person who appears to have an easy solution for his problems. But sometimes easy solutions are too good to be true. Sucked into a web of intrigue and crime, Marco Ferrero tries desperately to find out what he's got himself into. As the mystery deepens, powerful, ruthless people want him dead. In the race to find the truth it becomes a deadly contest of cat and mouse.

Made in the USA
Middletown, DE
18 November 2023